D1017052

What a Desi Girl Wants

What a Desi Girl Wants

SABINA KHAN

Scholastic Press
New York

Library of Congress Cataloging-in-Publication Data available

ISBN 978-1-338-74933-5

10 9 8 7 6 5 4 3 2 1 23 24 25 26 27

Printed in Italy 183
First edition, July 2023
Book design by Maeve Norton

To the readers whose love and joy for
my stories sustain me and fuel my words.
And always, to the four bright stars of
my heart: Jaanu, Sonya, Sanaa & Nikki.
I wouldn't be me without you.

CHAPTER ONE

I glare at my phone screen, willing the image on it to disappear or for the phone to spontaneously combust. Anything to erase what I'm looking at.

A few months ago I started following Aleena Obaid, an Indian social media influencer. She's also the daughter of Naz, the socialite my dad started dating earlier this year. Aleena's feed consists mostly of parties at opulent venues, incredible fashion, and perfectly styled photos—and my dad sometimes shows up in them too. I've gotten used to that. But now the caption of Aleena's latest post proclaims her desi royalty as soon-to-be stepdaughter of Nawab Reza Rabbani of Agra, India.

That's right—I have just found out through a social media post that my dad, whom I haven't spoken to recently or seen in almost a year, is engaged to marry Aleena's mother. I guess I should have answered when he called earlier.

Given how materialistic Aleena obviously is, her mother is probably some gold digger who's after my dad's royal title and wealth. Two things of which I know very little since I live with my mom in Newton, Kansas, a city known for . . . well, nothing much.

A loud clattering in the kitchen startles me. I smell something burning and quickly slide my phone into the back pocket of my jeans as Mom walks out, globs of something stuck in her hair and traces of her battle with dinner prep on her apron.

I raise my eyebrows. "I'll order pizza?"

She nods wordlessly on her way to the bathroom. I grab my phone and order a large mushroom, onion, and jalapeño pizza.

"Mehar, did you remember to bring in the mail?" Mom is back, all cleaned up.

I nod at the pile of unopened mail on the dining table, surrounded by papers, notebooks, packages, and everything else that gets dumped there.

"By the way," I add. ". . . Dad called earlier today."

"Yeah? What did he say?" Mom pages through the mail, adding a bunch of flyers to a growing stack of recycling.

"I didn't pick up." I avoid looking at her.

"Well, honey, you're going to have to talk to him sometime," she says. She walks over to the couch and settles in. I join her, tucking my legs under me and leaning against her shoulder.

"I don't know what to say." I mean, I didn't even before I found out that he was starting a whole new life without me. I know my mom is going to learn the news soon, but I can't bring myself to say it out loud.

She brushes back my hair and bends to kiss my forehead. "Just tell him what you told me. I know you want to patch things up, and he'll understand. He's your dad, and he loves you—"

Without thinking, I interrupt her. "If he loves me so much, how come he's not here, Mom? I mean, it's easy to call every now and then, but maybe he can try harder to actually be a part of my life, don't you think?"

I immediately regret my words. I can tell how much it hurts Mom every time I bring up the fact that my father decided to stay in India with his mother and sisters rather than live with us here. I wish I had more control over my tongue, because the last thing I want is to cause Mom any more pain. She's already had more than her share in her life. But I get so angry whenever I think about Dad and how he chose not to be in my life the way a father should. All I get are occasional visits, as if I don't matter.

"Look, Mom, I want to fix things with Dad, you know I do." I look into her eyes, trying to calm the anger that rises inside me whenever I think about my father. "But I'm also so mad at him. All the time. I don't know what to do."

Mom doesn't say anything, and I let out a deep sigh and snuggle even closer to her. I've mastered the art of not adulting, and I think I like it right here.

A little later, we've watched two recorded episodes of *The Voice* and devoured an entire pizza, and I have to peel myself off the couch. I have a late shift at the seniors' home in downtown Newton, where my best friend, Norah, and I work part-time.

November in Kansas is typically nicer, but today the skies are gray and cloudy. I peer through the windshield of my thirdhand truck, regretting that I ran out of the house without my raincoat or umbrella. Now I'm going to get soaked running through the parking lot and I'll have to borrow scrubs from one of the nurses to make it through my shift. They're always too big because I'm barely five foot two, and I look like I'm playing dress-up. It's hard enough to get the seniors to take me seriously. Especially old Mr. Watkins, who never wants to sit still during craft time and says he doesn't have to listen to anyone who barely reaches up to his waist. Short or not, I beat him at chess every time.

Norah and I always try to sign up for the same shifts. It makes the time go faster because after crafts and the occasional dance sessions, the residents are pretty tired and it's kind of hard for us to stay awake. Usually we work on school stuff, but today neither of us has much left to finish.

I pull out my phone, open the Instagram app to Aleena's post, and shove it under Norah's face.

"Is that Aleena? She always looks like a model."

"Sure, yeah. Anyway, she just posted this." Norah gives me a questioning look and I purse my lips. "My dad's getting remarried."

CHAPTER TWO

"Wait . . . what? To that Naz woman?" Norah has grabbed my phone and is reading the caption. "And what does she mean she's about to become desi royalty?"

I take a peek. "Oh yeah . . . that."

Norah gives me one of her Unbelievable™ looks. "You never told me you were royalty."

I roll my eyes at her. "I'm not. But my dad is . . . kind of. He's a nawab."

"A na-what? Explain, please."

"Nawab. It's kind of a royal title back in India from the olden days. After the British barged in, they basically took all the land from most of the nawabs, but some of them got to keep their titles. These days it's all really in name only, but it's still a big deal in Indian society."

"Wow." Norah looks a little stunned. "So, I'm sitting next to a bona fide Indian princess in the break room of Sunshine Manor right here in the heart of Kansas? That's pretty wild."

I shrug. "I'm pretty sure I was disowned years ago."

"Because your mom left and brought you back here?"

I nod. "I don't think we get to keep the title, especially after we basically rejected them."

Norah knows all about my mom and dad's history, about how my mom didn't want to live with my dad's family anymore because there were way too many rules and not enough personal freedom. At least that's what Mom always says about her life in India. She gave it her best shot at first, even stayed a few years, but in the end, she didn't want me to grow up with so many restrictions. She gave Dad a choice, and he chose his family over us. He chose to stay. So, she came back with me and built a new life for the two of us. And I like it just the way it is. Most of the time.

"I hate this," I say. "Aleena is all about the money and fancy cars and expensive clothes. I don't know her mom, but I'm pretty sure that they're only in it for his wealth."

"I thought you didn't care what your dad does?" Norah says. "At least that's what you've always said."

"I don't . . . I mean, sure, he can do what he wants. If he wants to marry Aleena's mother, then that's his choice. But it's not fair . . ." I trail off. It's not that I want my dad's money, but it doesn't seem right that she should be able to show up and use it either.

Norah pulls out a packet of red Twizzlers from her bag and opens it. She holds it out to me and I absentmindedly pull out a few strings and bite into one of them.

"She must be raking in big bucks for all the promo she's doing," Norah says, continuing to scroll through Aleena's feed. "It looks like she has a big following."

"Nah, there's no way she can make enough to afford that lifestyle. I bet my dad's paying for all of it."

"Well, you'll find out eventually," Norah says. "I mean, if your dad is marrying her mom, she's going to be your stepsister."

I glare at her. "You take that back, okay? She's going to be in my father's life, not mine!"

"I thought you said you were going to try to fix things with your dad."

I love Norah, but some days I regret telling her my deepest, darkest secrets, because she always manages to bring them up at the most inconvenient times.

"Sure, but this complicates things." I walk over to the coffee machine and fill a paper cup with the black sludge. "You want some?"

She shakes her head no. "So . . . do you think you'll go?"

"Where? To the wedding?" I give a hollow laugh. "No way, I don't want any part of it. Plus . . . I haven't exactly been invited yet."

If I'm being honest with myself, that part really stings. Almost as much as finding out on social media that my dad is getting married again. Even though I know it's probably my fault for avoiding his calls, the fact that he went ahead with it without telling us feels like he's officially giving up on Mom and me. Pfft. Communication is so overrated. Who needs it anyway?

• • •

I've jinxed myself. The invitation arrives a couple of days later, addressed to me. I'm surprised by my sudden curiosity as I open the envelope, carefully sliding out the card. It's gorgeous and delicate, with a cream lace inset and gold embossing. It screams old wealth. Mom always talks about that whenever she talks about the palace, her ex–in-laws, and Dad. They come from old generational wealth, the kind that's in their blood. Mom says that at first it was awesome not having to worry about money, being able to buy whatever she wanted. But then it started to feel excessive and wasteful and it filled her with guilt. She didn't have to step too far from the palace grounds to see that so many people lived in abject poverty, and there wasn't much she could do about it. Before she left, she did manage to connect with a couple of organizations that did important work on the ground in Agra, groups that helped the most vulnerable, and she kept in touch with them over the years to donate and help out even from right here in Kansas.

I stuff the wedding invitation back into my bag. I have no idea how Mom will react to the news. Sometimes I wonder whether she really has moved on. Every now and then I catch her lost in thought, her mind somewhere far away, and I know she's thinking about him, about her life before we moved back here. And I can't help thinking that maybe she regrets it; maybe just being my mom is not enough. I mean, I know I'm pretty amazing as far as daughters go, because no one else knows exactly how she likes her coffee or how she prefers to sit on the left side of the couch. And no one can make her laugh the way I do. Norah says I'm not as funny as I think I am, but what does she know? Mom always laughs at all my jokes and she wouldn't fake it. *Would she?*

But my avoidance only lasts so long. We're sitting down to dinner the next day when Mom's phone erupts in the Jonas Brothers' "I Believe." Someone needs a talk about ringtone choices. It's Dad calling on WhatsApp.

"Mehar, can you get that, please?" Mom walks away and pretends to look for something in the kitchen, but I know what's really going on. Lately she's been avoiding Dad's calls too. She thinks I haven't noticed, but I have. Does she know about Naz? Is Mom on Instagram?

The ringing is driving me up the wall and I figure I'll have to talk to Dad eventually, so now seems as good a time as any. Plus, the wedding invitation is burning a hole in my bag.

I take a deep breath and swipe up to accept the call just in time to see Dad's face disappear from the screen to be replaced by Dadi's. Or at least Dadi's nose.

I haven't had a video call with my grandmother for a while, and every time I see her and my dad together, I'm struck by how similar they look. They both have the classic aristocratic noses of their Mughal ancestors and the same intense, deep-set eyes. And they could both pass for white. I take more after Mom, with the darker brown skin and larger nose. Plus, I'm not tall and slender like Dad's side of the family, and neither is Mom. We're both rounder and also like to eat real food, unlike Dad, who swears off carbs and believes in sports. He's one of the top polo players in India and runs for fun. The only time I would run voluntarily is to chase after Ariana Grande or Harry Styles if they showed up anywhere near me.

"Hello, Mehar beta, how are you?" My grandmother speaks English fluently, but while Dad has sort of a British accent thanks to his English boarding school education, hers is purely North Indian. She rolls her *r*'s and has an almost musical cadence to her speech, which I find kind of cool. Dad, on the other hand, sounds very proper even when he's trying to be funny, which makes what he's saying seem way more hilarious than it actually is.

"I'm good, Dadi," I say to her nostrils. "How are you?"

"I am also fine, but I miss you so much." She moves the phone so I can now see the intricate web of veins on the inside of her ear. "Your dad says that you might be coming here for the wedding. Is that true? You must stay for a month at least. It would make me so happy to see you again before I die."

My eyes dart to Mom, partly out of panic and partly out of relief that now I don't have to be the one to break this news to her. But her face is completely neutral, which is somehow more unsettling than if she'd walked out of the room or something. And of course Dad is being so totally on-brand for using his mother to guilt me into going to India. And also, for Dadi to pretend like she's on death's door. She's been doing it for years. What am I supposed to say to that?

"I'll see, Dadi," I hedge. "I have a job lined up for winter break and I'll have to make sure that it's okay with them." Even as I'm saying the words, I kick myself mentally. What am I doing? I could have easily said no because I've already committed to a job. Now I've just prolonged the torture. What is wrong with me?

Dadi finally holds the phone in front of her face. "Why do you need to do a job, betiya?" she says. "You father is still alive, no? And it's important to visit your home, hai na? It's been too long."

"Okay, Dadi, I promise I'll try." It's the best way I can think of ending this conversation that's giving me all kinds of anxiety. I'm pretty sure I can easily find someone who will cover my shifts at the mall. I'm much less sure of whether I want to even try. A part of me can't help wondering if this might be my last chance to fix things between Dad and me. The other part is fine with leaving things the way they are—awkward but only when we actually talk, which is rare these days. But if I go there, I'll be putting myself smack in the middle of the mess. I don't know if I'm ready for that or if I'll ever be.

"Let me speak to your mother," Dadi says. "Is she there?"

I can see Mom out of the corner of my eye, shaking her head frantically and making murderous throat-slitting gestures with her hand. I shake my head. Mom can be so weird sometimes.

"Actually she had to step away for a bit," I lie smoothly from years and years of practice. "I'll tell her you called."

"Yes, please, and tell her to call me back one of these days." Dadi doesn't look like she believes me at all, but we've been playing this game for a long time.

Dad's face pops up on the screen.

"How is everything going, Mehar?" he says. "All good at school?"

"Yes, Dad. Everything's good. Listen . . . about the—"

"I've been trying to get ahold of you, Mehar," he interrupts. "Why haven't you been responding to any of my messages? I don't know if you saw yet, but—

"Yes, I did," I say quietly. "I saw it on Instagram."

"On Instagram?" He sighs loudly on the other side of the world. "I told her to wait," he mutters. "Look, I'm sorry you had to find out that way. I wanted to tell you about it myself, but you never answer your phone."

"Yeah, I'm sorry," I mumble. "Anyway . . . about the wedding, I don't—"

"You got the invitation card, right?" he says. "I'll arrange all of it. I'll fly you out first class, and you don't have to worry about a thing."

"Thank you, Dad, but—"

"And don't worry about this job of yours," he continues as if I haven't spoken at all. "I told you I would take care of college. Just do your best at school and make sure you get into the best one, okay, beta?"

There's no point in trying to get him to listen. Nothing ever changes with him.

"Okay, Dad, sure," I say resignedly, and we end the call.

I toss the phone on the couch and sit down with an exaggerated sigh.

"So, he's getting married again. And you got an invitation,"

Mom says. "When were you going to tell me about it?"

"Never?" I say sheepishly, grabbing my bag to pull out the card. I hand it to her wordlessly. She stares at the card and I wait for her to say something. I'm not sure what to do here. I showed Mom Aleena's Insta feed when I first started following her, so I'm sure on some level she may have suspected this was coming, but to see the actual card announcing the wedding has got to be hard. Then again, Mom's a pragmatist. She never expected Dad to stay single for this long, especially not with my grandmother probably hounding him to remarry and give her some real Indian grandchildren. The kind who wouldn't be strangers to her.

I watch Mom's carefully composed face. I wasn't sure how she'd react, but her expression doesn't reveal even an iota of sadness or regret.

"You should go," she says quietly.

"What?" I don't know what to think of her calm demeanor. In the past she's made it very clear to Dad that she would never want me to visit him in India, especially not by myself. Not that he's ever invited me before. At least not as far as I know. What changed?

"Your dad mentioned a while back that your grandmother isn't doing too well and it would be good to visit during the break. And then you might as well stay for the wedding."

So, it sounds like this change of heart is guilt-induced. I don't know how I feel about this.

"But I was going to work at Santa's Village at the mall, and then Norah and I were supposed to go to her parents' cabin. You know that." I can hear my voice getting whiny, which means I know Mom's going to try to convince me to be reasonable and see things from Dad's point of view. I *hate* being reasonable.

"I know, honey," Mom says. She reaches out to squeeze my shoulder. "But your grandmother is getting older. You may not have a whole lot of time left to spend with her."

I don't remember much about my grandmother from when we were together. I haven't been back since we moved, and I was only six at the time. My memories of her consist of a few special moments, like my fourth birthday, when she threw a huge party and invited every single one of our relatives. But that was mostly for her and for the grown-ups, because I don't remember having a lot of fun. There was a lot of cheek pinching and admonishing whenever I tried to get some of the other kids to play with me. There were many reminders of how proper young ladies didn't run around screaming, pretending to be pirates. I do have vivid memories of my mom getting into it with my grandmother, because no one gets to me without having to go through her first. I scrunch up my face. "I don't think she even likes me."

"Of course she does. She loves you. She's just old-school, so you have to be a little . . . you know, less yourself when you're around her. And this will give you a chance to reconnect with your father."

"But what about school? I can't just leave for a whole month. I'll miss two weeks."

"Mehar, you know you can catch up easily," Mom says. "Norah will keep you in the loop and you can do a little bit while you're away. You know they have computers and the internet there too, right?" she adds with a grin.

"You're hilarious." Sometimes I don't like it when she's right about stuff.

But I guess it's true that I might not have many more chances to see my grandmother, and if I don't go this time, I will probably regret it.

"It's going to be so weird being there," I say, thinking about how I'll have to see Aleena and her mom. My future stepmother. Eww.

"It'll be fine," Mom reassures me. Easy for her to say. She's not the one who's going to spend weeks with an airheaded social media influencer and her gold-digging mother.

"You don't know that." I feel like I'm going to start hyperventilating. When I woke up this morning, I thought this was going to be a normal boring day, and now it looks like I'm going to be spending my winter break thousands of miles away in my sort-of-estranged father's palace, watching him start a new life with his new family. How is this my life now?

CHAPTER THREE

"You're not going to believe this," I say to Norah as we walk to our favorite spot during lunch at school the next day. "My dad wants me to spend winter break with him in India so I can attend his wedding. And Mom thinks it's a great idea." I say the last part in a mocking imitation of my mother, with air quotes and everything.

Norah looks annoyingly excited at my announcement, and I hate her a little bit right now. "So, you're really going? Oh my god, JEALOUS!"

"Excuse me, I thought I was speaking to my best friend." I glare at her but she's not fazed. We've known each other too long and none of my looks have any of their desired effects on her anymore.

"You are, and I'm here to tell you to stop acting like a brat." She pins me with a stern look of her own. "Do you have any idea how many people would kill for an all-expenses-paid trip to India to spend winter break in a goddamn palace? *Please*, privilege much?" She rolls her eyes until it looks like they're going to pop right out of her head. I get the message.

"Have I ever told you that I hate this side of you?" I enter the room in front of her, making a beeline for our spot.

"Have I ever told you I don't care?" She plops her stuff on the table and sits down next to me.

I try to figure out what it is about Naz and Aleena that bothers me so much. It's not the wealth and status, because I don't even want my father's money. Although I frequently complain to Norah and Mom about my dad, sometimes I pretend to myself that the current state of our relationship doesn't bother me. But it's becoming increasingly clear that what I'm most afraid of is that Aleena will replace me. She seems to be a perfect fit for his fancy lifestyle, whereas every time Dad and I talk, it always ends up in an argument or, worse still, months of complete silence.

I figure if I'm going to India, maybe I'll finally have a chance to fix things between us.

• • •

At home later that evening, Mom has made my favorite Indian dish—and probably the only Indian food I ever eat—butter chicken. It has a mild and creamy sauce with tender pieces of chicken floating in it, and we have it with soft, buttery naan.

Mom and I are pretty basic people when it comes to food. I grew up on a steady diet of lasagna, chicken nuggets, and mac 'n' cheese. Cooking is not exactly one of Mom's many skills, and I'm happy to make the occasional grilled cheese or eggs for dinner when Mom's on a deadline for one of her freelance journalist jobs.

This has always been a bone of contention whenever Dad has visited in the past. When Dad visits, he never misses an opportunity to point out all the flaws in my upbringing. The way Mom rarely cooks Indian food, the complete absence of a religious education, and the freedom I have to go out as I please with whomever

I want are all things he doesn't approve of. Of course, he's never tried to understand that in the absence of an in-home chef and a full domestic staff, like the ones he has in India, it's pretty tough for the rest of us mere mortals to balance school, work, and everything else. Plus, Mom and I are more secular humanists, a term I've recently come across that describes us perfectly. Mom cares more about raising me to be a good human being than subscribing to any religious dogma, even though technically we're Muslim. Dad's family is a lot more traditional, so he kind of disapproves of our lifestyle.

And now I'll get to spend all of winter break being criticized not only by my dad but his entire family. Yippee!

"I should prep you for what to expect once you get to Agra," Mom says. "I think we should start with the family members."

I roll my eyes but don't say anything, concentrating instead on my dinner. I put a forkful of chicken in my mouth, dip a piece of naan in the sauce, and take a bite, savoring the delicate, creamy flavor. This might be one of the last times I get to enjoy food that doesn't burn my taste buds. From what I've heard, people in Agra love their food especially spicy. I wonder if they have Uber Eats in Agra. I might have to sneak in pizza and burgers at night unless I plan to starve.

"Okay, so first there's your dadi, obviously," Mom begins. "She's the big boss, and everyone from the staff to your dad is a little scared of her."

"I guess I'll stay out of her way, then," I grumble.

"She was always very fond of you," Mom says. "It's me she didn't like."

"Whatever." Is this talk supposed to get me excited about going? Maybe Mom secretly wants me to cash in the teen rebellion card and refuse to go.

"Be careful of Faiza Phuppi. She has a pretty sharp tongue and isn't afraid to use it."

"That's Dad's oldest sister?"

"Yes. But you know who I think you'll like a lot? Azra Aunty. She and I always got along really well." I know of Azra—she's the only one Mom's still kind of in touch with.

Mom's always been pretty straightforward with me about most things. More so than a lot of grown-ups are with kids. But she's never gone into too much detail when it comes to her relationship with Dad. I mean, I know there's a lot of animosity, given how much they fight every time he visits. But I've always wondered what happened to make her leave after seven years.

"Mom, since you think I'm old enough to go into the lion's den all by myself, I think I deserve to know everything."

She looks at me thoughtfully for a bit. "Okay, you're right. What do you want to know?"

"I've always wondered, you know . . . what made you finally decide to leave?"

"You know what happened." She starts to clear the table, a classic avoidance tactic if I've ever seen one. But if she really wants me to go to India, then I think I want to be prepared with all the information.

"I know what you told me about all the rules and restrictions. But you must have loved him enough at one time if you agreed to go and live in India in the first place."

She puts the dirty plates in the sink and comes back to the table. She starts to pick up the dish of butter chicken, then seems to change her mind and sits back down instead.

"I did," she says. "I loved him a lot." Her eyes get a faraway look.

"It must have been hard to leave your life here behind and move to India." I can barely deal with the thought of a month away from everything and everyone I know. I can't even begin to imagine how difficult it must have been to pack up her entire life and put everything into the hands of someone she loved. To trust him with her happiness and hope it all worked out in a strange country with people she didn't know and in-laws who weren't exactly thrilled to welcome her into the family. Even though my mom is Indian on her dad's side, her connection with India is nominal at best. She visited once when she was little, but my grandfather was very happy to live in the US and never thought of moving back.

"It was . . . but Reza's father died right after you were born, and your dad is the only son. He wanted to be there for his mom."

"Couldn't he have gone back and forth?"

"I think he wanted you to be surrounded by family and tradition," she says. "He knew you wouldn't have that here. You know what my parents are like."

My maternal grandparents are not exactly the kind who want to be a daily part of their grandchild's life. They're good for the occasional phone call or visit over the holidays, but they're more the long-distance kind even though they live right here in town. Most of the time they're on some cruise or other, so we're not super close. It's always been Mom and me. And that's been just fine.

"I kind of get that," I say. "I guess if you've grown up like that, you'd want that for your kids too." I'd be lying if I said that I've never wondered what it would have been like if we'd stayed. But then Dad would visit and there would be endless lectures on how I needed to learn more about my culture and call my grandmother more often and how the way I dressed was not appropriate. That's when I would feel grateful for the life Mom and I have built together, where I'm free to be me.

"At the time I thought it might be good for you, having cousins to grow up with and a real sense of extended family. And my work made it easy to be anywhere in the world so there was no reason not to try it out."

"So, what went wrong?"

"Well, you know how your dad is," she says. "Everything was always about the nawab title and family and what people would think. After a while it began to feel like I was little more than an afterthought and the only thing that mattered to him was his status. It got to be too much. I needed things to be real, not a life that was only for show."

I get that. I don't recall much about what he was like when I lived in India, but I remember expensive gifts in lieu of being present at birthdays later on or important things like kindergarten graduation and father-daughter dances. It was more performative than anything real. He would visit regularly, but it never coincided with anything that meant something to me or Mom. I got over it years ago, and I doubt that anything much has changed when it comes to my dad. He probably only wants me at the wedding because it would look bad for him if his own daughter, his only child, wasn't there for such an important occasion.

"When did you realize that you wanted to come back?" I'm trying to imagine her, younger and having to make such a difficult decision. It can't have been easy to break up her family and start her life from scratch after she came back with me.

"I was thinking about it long before I could admit it, even to myself." She looks sad now and I wish I'd kept my mouth shut.

The last thing I want is for her to relive those unpleasant memories.

"I'm sorry, Mom, I didn't mean to make you think about all that. Let's just drop it." I lean over to give her a quick peck on the cheek. My reluctance to make her relive the bad times wins out over my desire for all the details. Maybe I'll find out more during this trip. "Tell me more about the Dragon Lady," I add with a grin.

"Okay, but if you ever call her that out loud, I'll have to disown you." She tries to sound stern, but I can tell she's trying hard not to smile.

"Well, if the shoe fits . . ."

"Look, she's not so bad. I think I just wasn't the woman she expected her son to marry. She wanted someone who'd been raised in the same tradition, not an opinionated half Indian like me whose idea of a fancy outfit is a nice pair of jeans and a blouse instead of a sweatshirt."

"But Dad must have known what his family expected, right?"

"Honey, you might not believe me now, but trust me, the heart doesn't always listen to the head when you're in love." Her eyes get a little misty. "We were so in love back then," she says, almost to herself.

I don't want to pull her out of whatever happy memory she's in, so I sit there watching her for a bit. She shakes her head abruptly as if to rid herself of cobwebs and gives me a bright smile.

"You're going to be fine," she says. "You don't know when you'll get a chance to see your grandmother again once you start college, so this is a good opportunity. Plus, you've never been to an Indian wedding, and let me tell you, they're da bomb."

I hold up my hands in mock defense. "Okay, okay, I'll go, but only if you promise never to say da bomb again. Please."

I help her clear the table before going to my room to start reviewing for my upcoming finals. But one thought keeps nagging me: What if there is no salvaging my relationship with my father?

CHAPTER FOUR

The next few weeks go by in a blur. Between getting the recommended travel vaccines, shopping for luggage, and Mom buying supplies for every foreseeable emergency, I barely have time to panic about my upcoming trip. I'm checking two big suitcases, one for my stuff and the other for all the gifts Mom insists I must take. Besides the obligatory Toblerone bars and other assorted chocolates, Mom also splurged on expensive age-defying creams and designer handbags for my aunts and makeup for my cousins.

"Mom, do I seriously need to bring all of this?" I look at the spread on our living room carpet and then at the minuscule amount of space left in my second suitcase. "There's no way it's going to fit."

"If I've learned one thing from my dad, it's how to pack." Mom is determined. She squeezes, pushes, and shoves until everything miraculously finds a spot.

"Wow, this should be an Olympic event, Mom."

"Shut up and come sit here so I can close it." She grins at me and I join her on the hard top of one of the suitcases. "You have to bounce up and down a little to squish it all in." She reaches over to pull the zipper shut and I do the same on the other side.

"I'm so glad we didn't buy fancy crystal ware." I throw my arm around her and we sit on the suitcase just like that. It's starting to feel real, now that everything's packed and ready to go. Everything except me.

"It's going to be great," Mom says for the fiftieth time since Dad's wedding invitation came. It's cute that she's pretending I'm not going to be my typical bumbling self and make things weird.

• • •

"Remember what I said about not being your usual snarky self," Mom reminds me as we wait in line by the American Airlines counter. I want to make sure that my luggage gets checked through to Delhi, where Dad will meet me and drive us to Agra. I don't know how I feel about the fact that no international airline will fly directly to Agra. Of course, I know about the Taj Mahal and can't wait to visit, but other than that, all my research indicates that there isn't much else there. No wonder Aleena keeps running off to Mumbai or Delhi or Dubai, according to her Stories.

"I'm pretty sure we didn't have that conversation," I reply. I try to keep a straight face. "And anyway, I don't know what you mean by snarky."

"Ha ha, you're pretty funny." Mom digs a finger into my side. "I'm serious, though. Your dad is not as cool as I am. And your grandmother definitely is not."

"Wow, someone thinks highly of themself." I throw an arm around her shoulder and squeeze. "I'm going to miss you so much. How am I going to make fun of everyone if you're not there?"

"You'll be fine, honey." She pushes my bangs out of my eyes. "Do this for your dad. Trust me, you'll be glad you did."

The line starts moving again and soon it's time to say goodbye. After several rib-crushing hugs and reminders to call and be polite and fake smile at everything the relatives say, I'm finally sitting at my gate waiting to board. I check to make sure I have enough gummy bears, red Twizzlers, and M&M's to last the full twenty-seven hours of my trip. I have all the seasons of *Schitt's Creek* and *Kim's Convenience* downloaded on my phone, so I'm all set for entertainment. My sleep mask and noise-canceling headphones are in my backpack, and I shoot Norah one last text just as boarding for my flight is announced.

Goodbye. It was nice knowing you

OMG drama queen!!! You're going to spend winter break in a freaking palace

I'd rather spend it with you.

Mr. Watkins & I will have a glass of eggnog in your memory

You suck!!!

I'll miss you!

I already miss you

Once I've boarded and settled in the middle seat that I got stuck with, I regret declining Dad's offer of a seat in first class. I can't remember which point I was trying to prove when I said no thanks, because I'm pretty sure he pays for most of Aleena's flights and I cannot imagine her being wedged in like I currently am. I get ready to take a long nap, hoping that I don't drool on either of my neighbors while I sleep. As the plane takes off, I watch the familiar landscape become smaller and smaller until we're deep in the clouds, and I close my eyes, hoping that this trip won't suck too much. I'd barely slept last night, plagued by all sorts of worries. What if things are super weird with Dad? What if Dadi and Faiza Phuppi hate me? How am I going to get along with Naz and Aleena when I already don't like them? What if I get sick? What if I don't like the food? Luckily all the tossing and turning has left me extremely tired and I fall asleep almost as soon as the plane takes off.

• • •

About a day and two connections later I'm standing by the baggage carousels at Indira Gandhi International Airport in Delhi. I've been waiting for over an hour, and everyone's luggage except mine has arrived and been picked up. I run around to check the other carousels in case it has somehow ended up in the wrong one, but I don't see my two big suitcases anywhere. Mom thoughtfully tied neon-pink ribbons on the handles so they would be easy to spot in a sea of dark luggage. Unfortunately, that didn't help, since they didn't make it to their destination, and now the realization is slowly dawning on me that I might never see my favorite jeans and T-shirts again. And that I'll be showing up at my dad's palatial home empty-handed like some loser with no manners. What a great start to a trip I never wanted to take in the first place.

This place is buzzing with people, and a quick look around confirms that there's a lot of paparazzi, probably here because some Bollywood celebrity is arriving. Well, I sincerely hope that the airline hasn't lost their luggage as well.

I'm really glad that Mom made me put a nice kurta and

black leggings along with a pretty dupatta in my carry-on. At first, I protested because I don't usually wear stuff like that, but Mom said that my grandmother would freak if she saw me in my sweats and hoodie after all these years. And she said I'd better get used to dressing up a lot for the time I was here. People in the palace don't exactly run around in sweats and T-shirts.

As I wheel my carry-on toward the washrooms, I get the distinct feeling that I'm being watched. I turn to look back and sure enough, I see a few of the men with cameras looking in my direction. I shake my head—that makes absolutely no sense. I'm being silly and exhaustion is making me paranoid. I start walking toward the washrooms again, but now I swear I can hear them following me. I turn abruptly and a guy almost crashes into me with his giant camera lens. I completely freak out and sprint to the ladies' room, rushing into the first empty stall I find. Once safely behind locked doors, I wait for my breathing to slow down. Despite the cramped space, I somehow manage to change into an acceptable outfit without dropping anything in the toilet or on the sticky floor. I open the door slightly and peek out to see if anyone with a camera is there. The coast seems to be clear. Just a few other women, no one suspicious.

After freshening up at the sink, I slowly make my way out of the washrooms, hoping that the reporters decided I wasn't that interesting after all. I mean, I knew that Dad was sort of famous in Agra, but this is Delhi and I'm sure there are far more important people here than the estranged daughter of a nawab. I make my way to the baggage claims counter, only to realize I'm utterly mistaken. This time the reporters swarm me and suddenly microphones are being thrust in my face and I don't know which way to turn.

"Nawabzaadi, over here!"

"How does it feel to be back on Indian soil?"

"One photo, madam, please!"

Panic rises in my throat, and just when I feel like I can't breathe, someone puts an arm around my shoulder and steps in front of me.

"It's okay, I've got you," says a female voice. I'd recognize it anywhere because I've been obsessing about her ever since I found out my dad's getting remarried. It's Aleena. In the flesh. And she's every bit as gorgeous and composed as she looks online.

"Please, everyone," she says in a voice that demands adulation and attention. "The nawabzaadi has just arrived from America. Let's be sure to make a good impression, otherwise she may not come back for another twelve years."

The photographers laugh and the crowd parts magically, and I try to ignore her barb about me because she's helping me and I really want to get out of here.

"I'm so sorry about all this," Aleena says as soon as we're heading toward the main exit. "I don't know how they found out which flight you were arriving on."

I have a theory but I keep it to myself. I'm pretty sure she's the one who tipped them off so she could save the day and make herself look good. And I doubt if she'd ever miss a chance to get in front of the paparazzi.

"Thanks for helping me back there," I say instead.

"You'll get used to it," she says nonchalantly. "They follow us around all the time." She walks purposefully ahead of me while I'm dodging kids and suitcases, trying not to trip and make a spectacle of myself. Even though most of the paparazzi have fallen away, I'm pretty sure I still see a few of them watching us from a distance.

"I hadn't realized Dad was this popular." I guess there's way more that I don't know about Dad's life here than I'd previously thought.

"Your dad is amazing," Aleena says. "The press is obsessed with everything he does."

"Where is he?" I say. "I thought he was picking me up."

"He's outside, waiting for us. When he saw all the reporters, he thought it would be better if I came in to get you. He knows they love me." She throws me a smile over her shoulder.

Well, she's certainly not lacking in confidence, and I envy her ability to make people move out of her way as if she's using some sort of telekinesis.

We're almost at the entrance and the sliding doors open with a loud swoosh. A wave of hot, humid air slaps me in the face. Welcome to India, I guess. I scan the crowds, looking for Dad, and as my eyes finally settle on him, I let out a sigh of relief.

He's looking good, a little grayer than the last time I saw him a year ago. At six foot two, with an athlete's physique and sharp features, he always cuts an imposing figure, even in his jeans and casual shirt. The sunglasses and Princeton baseball cap he's wearing in an obvious attempt to remain incognito aren't exactly working. As I walk toward him, I can already see a group of young women eyeing him and trying to take selfies as surreptitiously as possible, while also noticeably swooning and giggling. There's more paparazzi here too, probably some of the same ones who were banished by Aleena inside, but Dad is completely oblivious to them. I guess it's not surprising given that he's had to deal with them for most of his life. But I'm beginning to get a clearer picture of what Mom must have felt like, being watched and followed constantly. It's creepy, to say the least. A smile breaks out on my face as Dad's eyes land on me and he waves excitedly, totally ignoring the commotion he's causing. I dodge a few brave souls who have edged pretty close to him and finally I'm standing right in front of him.

I hesitate at first, unbidden memories of the last time we were face-to-face flooding my brain. What if he hates me for what I said to him? But when I look into his eyes, all I can see is love glistening in them. I step into his open arms and all my doubts fade away. At least for now.

"Mehar beta, I'm so happy that you came." He slides my backpack off with one hand and gives it to the driver, who is right behind him. "It's good to have you here." We stay locked in an embrace for a minute before he loosens his grip on me and looks around. "You didn't bring any other luggage?"

"I had two huge suitcases. Mom sent so many gifts and now they're all lost somewhere." I lean into his hug again, inhaling the mild sandalwood scent of his aftershave, which always calmed me even as a little kid. My eyes well up and I don't know if it's the jet lag, but after weeks of fighting against the idea of coming here, I realize I've really missed him.

"Don't worry about your luggage," Aleena says from behind me. "I'll take care of it."

"This girl has contacts everywhere and she can do anything," Dad says, with unmistakable pride in his voice.

Can she make herself disappear? A knot instantly forms in my stomach. I've had a bad feeling about Aleena ever since she first posted a picture with my dad. And now, having met her in person, that feeling is only getting stronger. She's sidled up to Dad and has linked her arm in his so he's forced to break off our hug. She's up to something. I know it.

CHAPTER FIVE

"You should have flown first class," Dad says as we walk to the car. "I don't know why you insisted on flying economy."

I don't know how to explain my ambivalence about asking him for anything, so I stay quiet. Besides, I'm too busy plotting Aleena's demise. That girl needs to stay in her lane.

Someone jostles us and Dad immediately spreads his arms to create space for me. "We should hurry," he says, and takes my arm, navigating expertly through the dense crowd to the parking lot, with the driver walking briskly just ahead of us. I notice that we seem to have lost Aleena and look around to find her. She's still standing where we were a minute ago, posing for the paparazzi, waving and smiling. Of course. She wouldn't let a photo op like this go to waste.

We stop in front of a navy-blue-and-silver Rolls-Royce, and Dad opens the door for me while the driver deposits my bag in the trunk. The short walk from the terminal has already left my cotton kurta clinging to me, and my leggings feel like a second skin. I slide into the lush interior of the car and the driver puts the air-conditioning on full blast. I lean forward so the cool air is aimed directly at my face before it melts off from the heat. Dad settles in the back seat beside me.

"What about Aleena?" I say.

"Just give her a few minutes," Dad replies. "The press loves her and she cannot resist a camera."

I'm finding it difficult to accept that somehow my father has become so indulgent, when all he's ever been to me is a disciplinarian. Not that he never spoiled me, but mostly, especially in recent years, our communication has been in the form of lectures and criticism. Seeing him like this, so patient and indulging with Aleena, irks me more than I want to admit to myself.

The passenger door on Dad's side is opened and Aleena slides in beside Dad.

"So sorry," she says breathlessly. "Everyone wanted to take a picture. It was so hard to get away."

I'm sure it must have been such a struggle.

"Aleena, thanks for saving me from the paparazzi back there," I say, flashing her a brilliant smile. If Norah were here, she'd immediately know from my overly friendly tone and toothy smile that I was up to something. But luckily Norah is safely back in Newton, Kansas, and Aleena's just met me and is none the wiser.

"Oh please." Aleena waves dismissively. "It was nothing, I'm used to it."

A few minutes later we set off on our four-hour trip to Agra, driving through the busy main streets of Delhi. All these years I've pictured India only through the eyes of my parents. Their perspectives are wildly different, and growing up I always wondered which was the true India. For Mom it's always been a reminder of broken dreams and disappointment. But for Dad it will always be home, the best place on earth, despite things like horrible traffic and dense crowds. He focuses on the warmth of the people and the rich culture and the amazing food. I guess for most people, home will always be where their best memories were created. While Newton, Kansas, may not be the most exciting or diverse place, it's where I remember playing outside and making friends and living my best life. So, no matter where I end up going in my life, it will always be a special place for me.

And now I'm finally here, on my way to Agra, a city that was built on the banks of the Yamuna River, once the capital of the Mughal Empire, and home to one of the most recognizable monuments in the world, the Taj Mahal.

As we continue driving through Delhi, the main streets feel like they could be any other big city. But what I can glimpse of the side streets looks like a completely different world from Kansas. People hang from buses crammed to the brim, auto-rickshaws weave in and out of the utterly chaotic traffic, and, in the middle of it all, pedestrians calmly hold up their hands at oncoming traffic in order to cross the street. Miraculously, there is no calamitous incident as we drive along.

"Do you remember Delhi?" Dad asks. He pronounces it *Dilli*, in the Urdu way. "We used to come here quite a lot back when you were little."

"I don't," I say, stifling a yawn. "I'd like to come back for a quick visit while I'm here, though."

"I'm sure we can do that," he says. He turns to Aleena. "You come here at least once a week, right?"

"Oh, I'd love to bring you along," she says, leaning forward to look at me with a big smile. She has nice teeth, I'll give her that.

"That's so nice of you," I say. "But I wouldn't want to trouble you. I'm sure I can do a day trip on my own."

Aleena laughs and it sounds like bells, unlike my own laughter, which is loud and sounds more like a terrified goat.

"It's no trouble at all," she says. "And I don't think it's a good idea for you to come on your own."

"I go on trips alone all the time back home," I say, starting to feel a familiar vein throbbing in my temple. "I'll be fine."

"Mehar beta, this is India, not Kansas," Dad chimes in. "And you don't know your way around here, so I would be much more comfortable if Aleena is with you."

Of course he would be. I bet he'd be more comfortable if Aleena were his actual daughter instead of me. I blink back angry tears that are threatening to spill over and turn my gaze outside, where, unlike me, the people milling about know exactly where they belong.

"Oh, I almost forgot," Dad exclaims suddenly, startling me. He leans forward to reach for something in the front passenger seat.

"Do you still like these?" He holds out a little orange-colored carton.

My mood changes instantly. I take it from him with a laugh. "Oh my god, Dad, you remembered." I tear the wrapping off the straw and poke it through the little hole. The cold mango nectar is sweet and refreshing. "We've tried to find Maaza Mango juice in Kansas City so many times, but they never have anything good in the Indian stores there."

"You still like those?" Aleena asks with a smirk. "Over here only little kids drink that."

Who the hell asked her? I hope she won't share her stupid opinions about everything while I'm here, because if she does, there's going to be trouble.

"Of course I still like these," I say as cheerfully as I can manage without choking on my juice. "It reminds me of when I was a little kid and Dad would always make sure we had these in the fridge."

I relax back in my seat. The tumultuous Delhi traffic and colorful billboards keep my eyes wide open for some time, but eventually I drift off to sleep, oblivious to the sound of blaring car horns all around me.

• • •

When I open my eyes again, we're in front of the entrance to a hotel. The clock says it's noon, so I must have slept a good hour.

Dad hands me a plastic bottle. "Hello there, sleepyhead. We've stopped to get some food."

I'm still groggy, but a few sips of cold water revive me enough to realize that I'm starving. Aleena and Dad step out of the car and I follow them into the interior of the Imperial Hotel, New Delhi, which can only be described as utterly luxurious. As soon as the doors close behind us, we're ensconced in a cool haven, dotted with palm trees and beautiful white decor. An attendant is by our side instantly and we're escorted to a restaurant called the Spice Route.

I excuse myself to visit the restroom to freshen up. My hope to get a few minutes to myself is dashed because Aleena follows me, teetering precariously in her stilettos.

"Wait up," she chirps, and I'm tempted to increase my speed because I can walk way faster in my flats. But I take a deep breath and try to stay focused on the long game. I wait until she's caught up with me, and as I look around the lobby, I feel distinctly underdressed. Women in elegant saris walk by with their heels clacking loudly on the marble floors. Some are accompanied by men in expensive-looking suits, both Western and traditional, while some are in small groups, probably out for lunch with their friends. I wonder if Mom had these kinds of friends to hang out with when she lived here or if being the wife of a nawab made it impossible to have friends who weren't part of the very upper echelons of India's society.

Aleena stops abruptly as we pass a woman dressed in a silky flowing kameez and voluminous shalwar.

"Mona Aunty, how nice to see you," she gushes as the woman recognizes her and stops.

"Aleena, darling, I haven't seen you in ages." She turns her gaze to me and I swear she looks me up and down as if I'm from another planet.

"You'll never guess who this is," Aleena says, a little too excitedly.

Mona Aunty doesn't look like she cares.

"This is Mehar," Aleena says helpfully. "Mehar Rabbani."

Mona Aunty's mouth falls open in shock, but she recovers quickly enough.

"Reza's daughter?" she says incredulously, continuing to look at me as if I've sprouted horns or something.

I have never felt this uncomfortable.

"Yes, that's right," Aleena says. "She just flew in from America and we're driving her home."

Why does it feel like they're talking about a small child who hasn't learned how to speak yet?

"Assalamu alaikum," I say. "It's nice to meet you. So, how do you know my dad?"

Mona Aunty recovers from her momentary shock at my existence.

"Walaikum assalaam. Reza and I knew each other a long time ago," she says. "Before he met your mother."

Aha. She must be one of his old girlfriends, the ones who were devastated when he brought home a half-American wife and dashed all their dreams of marrying a nawab.

"Well, it's very nice to meet you," I say with all the politeness I can muster. "But I really have to pee, so please excuse." And with that I make a beeline for the washroom. Before I disappear through the door, I turn around to see if Mona Aunty has lifted her jaw off the floor yet. She hasn't, and now I'll probably be the talk of the town because what well-bred young woman talks about her bodily functions in such a crass manner. I do, that's who. There's a new nawabzaadi in town and her name is Mehar Rabbani.

Before leaving the washroom, I shoot a quick message to Mom on WhatsApp, letting her know I'm with Dad and that I'll call later. I don't see Aleena anywhere, so I make my way to the restaurant. I see her sitting beside Dad at a table by the window and I know instantly that she's tattled on me. What a brat. Now Dad's going to lecture me, and that's not how I wanted to start this trip. But to my surprise, he just smiles and waves me over.

He has ordered us fresh coconut water and some appetizers. Apparently, this is an award-winning restaurant, and I'm eager to taste all the good food. Our appies arrive, Kerala-style prawns stir-fried with slivers of coconut, curry leaves, and black tamarind. It's the best thing I've ever eaten. Aleena nibbles on one lone shrimp while I devour five of them. I'm hoping Dad will pick our entrées, but he insists that I select at least one dish. I choose Irachi stew, the one item on the entire menu that has no red chili next to it. It's mutton simmered with potatoes in coconut milk. I figure I should be safe.

They lied. Someone messed up and forgot to print a red chili beside it. Or five. If this is considered non-spicy here, then I'm pretty sure I'm going to stick to plain bread and butter for the rest of my trip. But despite the heat, it does have tremendous flavor, and since I have to drink copious amounts of coconut water between bites, I'm full pretty soon.

"Beta, you're going to have to get used to a little bit of spice," Dad says, most unhelpfully. "You're Indian, after all."

I nod wordlessly, too busy spooning extra raita on my plate, glad that the yogurt and cucumber salad is cooling my tongue.

"You'll have to get used to eating something other than hamburgers and pizza," Aleena says, grinning at Dad as if he's in on the joke.

She'll have to get used to getting slapped by me, but I choose not to say that out loud.

"Once you start to appreciate our flavors, you'll never go back to bland food again," Dad says. Is that a threat or a promise? I can't tell.

"Does that mean Dadi won't make me French fries like she used to?" I don't remember a lot about my early childhood here, but I do remember that my grandmother would go into the kitchen herself, something she rarely did, to fry up the potatoes just the way I liked them. She would sprinkle a little chaat masala on them to give them a slight kick of flavor, not heat, and that's always been my favorite way to eat fries. Back home, Mom always keeps a pack of chaat masala handy and Norah makes fun of me for carrying around a small container of it in my bag wherever we go.

"I'm pretty sure your dadi will do anything you ask," Dad says. "You have no idea how happy you've made her by coming here." He reaches across the table to squeeze my hand. "And me as well, beta."

I feel a lump in my throat again, but I quickly blink back the tears. I wish that we were alone, Dad and I, so I could tell him how I feel about the way things went down the last time he visited me in Kansas. That was a year ago when I was seeing Ryan, a boy Dad disliked instantly and who, of course, I was even more determined to continue seeing as soon as Dad told me he wasn't good enough, leading to our huge fight.

Dad's words echoed in my head the day I saw Ryan making out with another girl under the bleachers. If Norah hadn't dragged me there to catch him in the act I wouldn't have believed what everyone had been telling me about him for weeks. But in my mind, I kept replaying the huge fight Dad and I had before he flew back to India. I yelled at him to stay out of my life and the very last words I shouted at him still mortified me. I want so badly to apologize to him now and to tell him that he was right, Ryan was scum, and that I'm so sorry for everything I said. But I can't say any of that with Aleena here. I will never forget the look on his face when I told him that I'd rather not have a father at all than have someone like him in my life. He'd been crushed and at the time I was glad to have struck a nerve. But now . . . I would do anything to take back those hurtful words. Maybe that was why he chose to marry Naz, because Aleena was part of the package and she would fill the void I'd created.

"I have everything planned out for the next couple of weeks," he says now. "Unfortunately, I'll be in and out of town a bit until the wedding, so I wanted to make sure that you have a grand time while you're here."

My heart sinks and I try not to let my disappointment show. Why had I fooled myself into thinking that anything was going to be different? Dad has always been like this, too busy with work and his nawabi duties to spend a lot of time with me. And he thinks he always knows what's best for everyone.

He continues to talk, completely oblivious to anything I'm feeling. As usual.

"I've discussed this with Aleena," he says, turning to her with a smile. "And she's going to take you shopping with her so you can get clothes for the wedding."

"That's okay," I say weakly, suddenly very tired. "I can do my own shopping. I don't want to inconvenience anybody." Why did he even invite me if he didn't plan to be around most of the time?

"Don't be silly, Mehar," Aleena chimes in. "I love shopping and anyway . . . we're going to be sisters soon and it's going to be so much fun. I think we should do a total makeover." She's practically giddy with excitement. I can't help wondering if she ever had to take actual acting lessons or if she's just a natural at being fake.

"And please, beta, get anything you want," Dad says. "I want you to look like a princess, so I can finally show you off to everyone."

It's like I'm ten years old again and he and Aleena have already made all the plans for me. Fine. I promised Mom I'd try and that's what I'm going to do. Plus, I'm not about to start an argument with him when I've just arrived here. I mean, I do need new clothes for the wedding, and despite my opinion of Aleena, she does have impeccable taste and I'm far from caught up with all the latest styles here in India. So, I smile agreeably as I douse my burning mouth with more coconut water until it's time to leave.

CHAPTER SIX

Once we hit the Yamuna Expressway, traffic flows pretty fast. As we get farther and farther away from the Delhi city limits, passing Gurgaon and Noida, the landscape changes. The concrete skyline gives way to wider, more open horizons and smaller buildings. I start to doze off again as the landscape whizzes by, dotted by the occasional goats and cows walking by the side of the highway with their owners.

By the time I open my eyes again, we're driving down a long, winding road and I can see the palace in the distance. A multitude of memories flash in my mind as the gilded domes and arches come into view. The majestic sandstone structure with the massive steps leading up to the front triggers images of my six-year-old self running up and down on them with Mom chasing me until we collapsed in a heap of giggles.

And then another memory, this one of Dad standing at the top of the steps as Mom and I left in the car taking us to the airport. I remember sitting up in my seat, looking out the back window, waving at him, oblivious to the fact that I was never coming back. I'm wide-awake now, startled by the emotions coursing through me. There are people crowded around the massive gates that separate the palace from the outside world. As we get closer, I realize they're more paparazzi, hoping to get a shot of us. They disperse as the security guards approach to open the gates and the driver takes us past the steps to a smaller, private entrance on the other side of the palace. I see a cluster of people there, and as the car stops and I step out, I can see that they're holding bright garlands of marigold and trays of something, probably sweets. As I approach, I'm surprised by the way my heart clenches when my eyes land on my grandmother. It's one thing to see her face on a video call, but now, seeing her up close, I can vividly recall the feeling of her arms around me, squeezing me gently as she read bedtime stories to me. It's weird, this memory of something that seems so long ago but also just like it was yesterday.

My feet move toward her of their own volition and I watch in wonder as she practically shoves the others out of the way and comes toward me, arms outstretched and a huge smile on her face.

"Mehar, meri jaan," she cries, launching herself into my arms and almost knocking me over in the process. Thankfully Dad and Aleena are behind me to keep me upright. "You are here at last." She alternates between peppering my face with wet kisses and leaning back to look at me, cradling my face in her hands as tears stream down her cheeks. Her embrace is imprinted on my brain, because the warmth and strength of her arms feel familiar, as though the past twelve years have melted away. I squeeze her tight, unshed tears forming a lump in my throat. Then others step forward and I'm passed around like a new doll at Christmastime, showered with hugs and kisses and wonderment at how grown-up I am. I catch a glimpse of Dad as he steps around us and I can see tears glistening in his eyes too, just before they roll down his cheeks. I have never, ever seen Dad cry and I am not prepared for this. There's an unfamiliar ache in my heart at the sight of him so vulnerable, and my own eyes well up. Eventually all the hugging stops and we wipe our tears, each of us embarrassed at this display of emotion, except for Dadi. She's holding on to me as if she's afraid I might fly off, her viselike grip on my arm strangely comforting.

Behind my grandmother a lady appears, probably in her fifties. She must be Dad's older sister.

"Faiza Phuppi," I say, extricating myself from Dadi and moving to hug my aunt. I'm a little confused to see the woman's eyes widen and I notice Dad behind her, gently shaking his head and grimacing.

Just as I'm about to put my arms around her, I hear a voice behind me.

"I am your Faiza Phuppi."

I turn quickly, the blood already rushing to my face as I realize what I've done. I've mistaken the maid for my dad's older sister and the only thing I can do now is apologize profusely.

"I am so, so sorry," I say, putting my arms around her. She returns my embrace, but I can feel the frostiness emanating from her even though she makes a good show of affection.

"It is okay, beta. We are lucky that you remember us at all after so many years." And there it is, that passive-aggressiveness Mom warned me about. Although in this case I will let it go, since I did confuse her with one of the maids in front of the whole family and with most of the staff looking on.

"Achcha chalo, now let the poor girl step inside, na?" she says. She basically looks like a female version of Dad, only slightly shorter, but slender like everyone else in this family. She pinches my cheeks affectionately. "Such a chubby little cutie you are." She wiggles her hands so my face moves side to side.

Azra Aunty rescues me. "Mehar, you are a carbon copy of Bhabi," she says. "So beautiful." Mom's shown me old photos of the two of them together, so I recognize her immediately. She must take after my grandfather because she looks nothing like her siblings. She's shorter than them, her head just a few inches above mine and the lines of her face much softer than theirs.

She hooks her arm in mine and we walk in, the rest following close behind. There's a four-tier white marble fountain in the enormous foyer and the air is scented by the rose petals floating in the water that flows in each pedestal. Huge crystal chandeliers hang from the rainbow-hued vaulted ceiling, and as I crane my neck to admire the splendor and beauty of it all, I'm struck by this incredible moment. I'm standing in a freaking palace that belongs to my dad's family. My family. That's the part that gets me. This place used to be my home.

"How come we didn't use the main entrance?" I ask. I notice that Aleena has disappeared and I'm relieved because her presence feels like an intrusion on a very personal and emotional family reunion. She isn't family. Yet.

"We've turned most of the mahal into a hotel and museum," Dad replies. "It didn't make sense to keep the entire compound for just Ammi and me after Azra got married."

I've read that this is quite commonplace. India's royals, faced with financial realities, have turned their palatial homes, which they once occupied themselves, into luxury hotels for the booming tourist industry. It makes sense.

"There are a hundred and seventy-seven rooms in this place," Azra Aunty adds. "It seemed like such a waste."

"Azra, why don't you take Mehar to her room?" Dad suggests. "She's exhausted, it's been a long trip."

"Achcha betiya," Dadi says, clasping both my hands in hers. "You go and rest, but whenever you're ready, please come to my room, theek hai?"

"Ji Dadijaan, theek hai," I reply. I still understand Urdu a bit but I can barely speak it, and only with a heavy American accent. Mom grew up speaking English with her white mother who had never learned to speak Urdu. But Mom learned to speak it from her Indian father, and even though she's sort of fluent, she reverted to speaking English with me soon after we left India. The words feel strange on my tongue, at once foreign and familiar, like a long-lost friend I didn't realize I've missed intensely.

Azra Aunty shows me to my room, and when she opens the door, I can't believe my eyes. It's my childhood room and I recognize it right away because it looks like it's been kept exactly the same for all these years. The four-poster bed in the middle of the room with mosquito netting all around where Mom and Dadi would read me bedtime stories, the white desk with the chair in which I would spin around until I was dizzy, they're all here. As I walk into the room, it's as if I've been transported back to my childhood. There's even a wall covered in my art. I remember Dadi always gushing over my drawings, and my eyes tear up because now they've all been framed and hung up in neat little rows. There are at least five of me with Mom and Dad. I turn back to look at Azra Aunty and see that her eyes are misty too. She walks over to me and puts an arm around my shoulders.

"Ammi misses you a lot," she says. "And Reza Bhai thinks we don't know, but he comes here quite often and just sits at your desk for hours."

I don't know what to make of this revelation so I don't say anything.

"Let me know if you need anything," Azra Aunty says after I've been quiet for a while. "I'm going to put a few kurtas and churidars in your closet. If your suitcases don't get delivered in the next few days, don't worry. I'm sure you'll be doing plenty of shopping for the wedding, so you can buy some casual stuff as well."

"Thank you, Phuppi." I give her a hug and she kisses me on the cheek.

"I'm so happy that you're here." One last squeeze and she's gone.

I'm alone at last, here in my childhood room with all the memories swirling around in my head. I check the time and wonder if I should call Mom. It's still early in Kansas, but I desperately want to hear her voice. I start a video call and she answers right away.

"Mom, I'm sorry, did I wake you?"

"No, I couldn't sleep. It's too quiet without you here."

"Ha ha, remember that next time you complain about how loud I am."

"Okay, tell me everything," she says, and my eyes well up instantly.

More than anything in the world, I want to be curled up next to her right now.

"It's good, Mom," I say as the tears start to fall in earnest.

"Honey." Mom sits up and the light from her phone casts shadows on her face. She looks like she's been crying too. "Why're you crying? What's wrong?"

"Nothing . . . it's just, I didn't expect to feel . . . I don't know, everything."

"You're just overwhelmed, sweetie," she says. "It's a lot and you must be exhausted."

I give her a watery smile. "I know, you're probably right . . . but . . . you've been crying too," I say accusingly.

She starts to shake her head, but then smiles instead. "We're a couple of big babies, aren't we?"

"Mom, you're not going to believe this, but I thought one of the maids was Faiza Phuppi."

"No." Mom's trying to look shocked and not smile at the same time.

"Everyone was watching and now she totally hates me. She called me a chubby cutie."

Mom frowns. "Yes, that sounds totally like her. Just ignore anything she says. She's always been like that."

"I'm going to avoid her as much as I can."

"Good idea. And when you get back, you and I are finally going to do that spa weekend we've been talking about forever."

"Oh my god, that sounds like heaven." I start getting teary again and Mom blows me kisses.

"Get some rest, honey, and . . ." She grins at me. "Take a shower. I can smell you from all the way over here."

I grin back through my tears and blow her kisses too. "Love you, Mom."

"Love you too, beta."

I feel grounded now that I've talked to Mom. I realize that she cleverly avoided telling me why she was crying, but truthfully, I already know why. This can't be easy for her either. I sit at the desk for a little while longer, mostly because I'm too tired to move and also because I'm trying to figure out how I feel about everything.

Ever since Dad picked me up at the airport, I've had this heaviness in my heart, an ache I can't explain. But I'm starting to realize what it might be. Coming back here after so many years has brought back so many memories I thought were gone forever. I have a history with this place, with these people who are my family but from whom my connection has been severed for a long time. It's time to rebuild these relationships, because even though I was a little girl when I left, they are a part of who I am and it's a part of me I'm longing to rediscover. And I'm not going to let Naz or Aleena or Faiza Phuppi ruin this for me. Especially not if I want to figure stuff out with Dad. I can't help but be touched by how he remembered my favorite mango juice from when I was a kid. But then he also said he wouldn't be here much. So what am I supposed to make of that? How can I fix things if he's not here most of the time? Is there even anything left worth fixing or should I just be glad that we seem to be on speaking terms again? Maybe I should learn to accept that this is the best things are going to be between us. But I'm not sure if I'm ready to give up quite yet.

CHAPTER SEVEN

After the most refreshing shower of my life, I wrap myself in a towel and walk back into the room, the marble tile cool under my bare feet. In the walk-in closet I find the kurtas and churidars that Azra Aunty has left for me. I'm rooting through my bag for moisturizer when I hear a muffled sound. I look up, startled, clutching the bottle to my chest. There are three little girls and a little boy sitting in a neat row on my bed, watching me with great interest. I suppress a smile and narrow my eyes at them.

"Hello."

"You're our Mehar Baji," the little girl in a yellow floral dress states.

"I am?" I draw my eyebrows together, feigning confusion. "But who are you?"

"I'm Usha." She points at the girl beside her. "This is Asha."

"And I'm Nisha," the last little girl pipes up.

I turn to the boy. "And who are you?"

He puts his fingers in his mouth. "I'm Taimur," he mumbles.

"He's a baby," Nisha declares. She's probably all of four years old.

"And you must be fifteen, sixteen, and seventeen, right?" I ask, looking at the three girls.

They dissolve in a fit of giggles, rolling around on the bed.

"No, Mehar Baji," Usha says, barely able to speak through her laughter. "I'm six. Asha is five and Nisha is four."

"Girls, why are you bothering your baji? Didn't I ask you to play with Taimur?" Azra Aunty walks in, shaking her head. "Sorry, Mehar beta, these kids are always running off."

I smile at her. "No, it's fine. They're so cute."

"Talk to me again after you've been here for a few days." Azra wipes her forehead with her dupatta, clearly exhausted. I mean, who wouldn't be with four children, each barely a year apart from the next.

I feel awful that my luggage isn't here yet, because all the chocolates and other goodies I packed for the kids aren't here. But I remember that I still have an unopened bag of sour gummies in my bag and I take that out now, hiding it behind my back.

"Phuppi, are they allowed to have this?" They're already behind me trying to pry it out of my hands. "I'm so sorry, everything else I brought for them is in my suitcase."

"Mehar beta, please don't be so formal," she says, starting to protest as her kids successfully take possession of the candy and huddle in a corner to negotiate who will be in charge of it. She gives up and turns back to me. "Listen, don't worry. These four will drive you mad with their demands. So, no need to feel bad."

She pulls me down on the edge of the bed.

"Now, tell me, how is Gulnar Bhabi?"

It's sweet that she still thinks of Mom as her sister-in-law even though my parents have been divorced for years and my dad will be bringing home a new wife soon.

"She's good," I say. "She says you were always her favorite."

"I miss her." She tucks her legs under her and Taimur runs into her lap, ready for a nap. The candy war has tuckered him out.

"Mom says you two were really close." Even though I was never in touch with her after I left, Mom's talked about Azra Aunty enough to make me comfortable around her already.

"I wish we could have stayed close," she says. "But you know . . . it was hard on everyone after she left with you, especially your dad."

I don't know what to say, so I just play with the tiny tassels of her dupatta. I know it was hard for Mom too, being all alone and raising me by herself. I'll always believe that Dad should have chosen us. He could have found another way to be there for his mother and sisters, I'm sure of it. I make a mental note not to let them paint Mom as the villain of their story.

"Is Naz coming later?" I ask, more to change the topic than from any burning desire to meet the woman who will essentially be replacing Mom.

"She'll be here," Azra Aunty says. "She likes to make an entrance."

"I'm not looking forward to that." I let out a deep sigh. I know I'm going to have to put on a mask for this evening, when the rest of the family comes for the elaborate dinner I have no doubt Dadi has planned. Mom told me that my grandmother never needed an excuse to throw a dinner party or any kind of gathering. As the wife of the former nawab, she has always had a rich social life and people were more than willing to drop everything even at the last minute to attend the legendary functions at the palace. No wonder Aleena was so eager to have her mom marry into this family. It would cement her place in the upper echelons of not just Agra society but probably most of northern India.

"Well, get ready for some drama," Azra Aunty says. "Ammi is not a fan either."

Hmmm. Interesting. Very interesting.

"I follow Aleena on Instagram," I say. "Does she ever stop shopping? Anyway, what's the deal with those two?"

Azra Aunty makes a face. "I don't know what to tell you, beta. And I don't know if I should say anything negative about them since they're going to be part of our family in a few weeks."

"You can't tell me anything I haven't been thinking already, Phuppi."

"Well, I guess you're not a child anymore, so . . . Ammi and I don't like this at all."

"So why don't you say something to Dad?"

"Mehar, I love Reza Bhai more than anything," she says. "He's my big brother and I want him to be happy. As far as I'm concerned, no one will ever live up to your mom, but I know it's good for him to find someone new. Still . . . these two are something else."

"How do you mean?"

"Well, they seem to have Bhaiyya completely wrapped around their fingers. He can't deny even their most outrageous demands."

"He never had that problem with me or Mom," I say bitterly. I mean, there had always been a lot of gifts, but as I got older I realized that someone else must have been buying them for him to send to me. They were kind of generic, never things I really wanted, and it always felt as if he didn't even know what I was into at various times in my life or how I was too old for some of the dolls and stuff he sent. Basically, I always felt a lot like an afterthought.

Azra Aunty takes my hand and squeezes it but doesn't say anything. We sit in silence for a while until the girls are bored and demand that I go downstairs with them.

Azra Aunty shrugs. "I told you." She grins as I allow myself to be dragged out by the three little munchkins. It's a good thing I love kids.

Downstairs in the main dining room a veritable feast has been set up. The large dining table has seating for at least twenty people and is laden with dishes.

"Mehar beta." Dadi beckons from her chair at the head of the table and I rush to her side. She takes a lock of my damp curls in her hand and smiles. "Just like your mother," she murmurs. She leans back, still holding on to me with one hand. "You look so beautiful in this outfit, Mehar."

"Thank you, Dadijaan." I place a kiss on her cheek. "Azra Aunty got it for me."

"Come, beta," Faiza Phuppi says, taking my hand. She indicates the chair between Dadi and Dad, who're already seated. As the rest of the family file into the dining room and take their seats at the table, I look around at everyone and marvel at the fact that most of them bear some sort of resemblance to my father and grandmother. It would be easy for a complete stranger to see them together and instantly know that they are part of the same family. I wonder if a stranger would think that I was part of it too. I don't see myself in them, but I know that to some extent we share the same blood. They've all grown up in close proximity to one another and so even their body language and facial expressions are very similar. Once again, I'm reminded of how different I am and how separate from the rest of my relatives. It never bothered me much before, but now as I watch them sharing looks and interacting so effortlessly with one another, I can't help feeling a little envious of the ease and familiarity that is apparent in their interactions. And I can't help but compare this scenario with my normal dining routine. It's usually just Mom and me eating some hastily prepared meal while we talk about our day. I love that part of my day the most, because I can tell her anything and know that she'll understand. That's the kind of relationship we have, Mom and I, and I wouldn't trade it for anything. But this is special too, the whole family gathering at the table like this, kids having a hard time settling down, their parents trying to get them to eat, and siblings, cousins, aunts, and uncles talking over one another, joking, arguing, but all part of this large family. My family. I thought I'd met most of them when I arrived but clearly I've underestimated how many of them there are. It's not just my immediate family that are here. There are also Dad's many cousins with their spouses and children, as well as Dadi's sister and her children and their families. I'm never going to be able to remember who everyone is. It's a little overwhelming, but then Dad puts his arm around me and leans forward.

"Mehar, I've been dreaming of this moment for years." His eyes are misty and mine well up too. "Thank you for coming, beta. You've made me happier than you can imagine."

I'm too choked up to speak, so I just nod and give him a watery smile.

"Okay, enough with all the tears," Dadi says, wiping her own with the ends of her sari. "Mehar, welcome home. I pray that this is the first of many more visits."

Everyone else echoes her words and then we dig in. There's succulent leg of lamb smothered in a spiced almond sauce;

aromatic basmati rice dotted with raisins, pomegranate, seeds, and cashews; cumin-scented lentils; and an array of pickled mangoes, carrots, and lime. When I've eaten way more than I should have, dessert arrives. Shahi tukda, which Dad tells me translates directly to "royal piece," is kind of like bread pudding but fancier, with raisins and almonds garnishing the fried bread drenched in a sweet, creamy milk concoction.

"Dadi, I can't eat another bite," I say a little later when she tries to put another spoonful of the dessert on my plate. "I'm going to explode."

"Your dadi has been longing to feed you for years, Mehar. Better be prepared," Dad warns me, while smiling indulgently at his mother.

"Ammi, do you remember that mango murabba you used to make?" Azra Aunty says to Dadi. "Mehar used to sneak into the kitchen all the time and Bawarchi Saheb would give her some."

I remember the palace cook, a kind, gray-haired man who would always give me little treats, even when Mom and Dadi would say it would ruin my appetite.

"Is he still here?" I ask. "He was always so sweet to me."

"Mehar beta, he died a few years ago," Dadi says. "It was a sad day for us all after having him here for so many years. He knew I had a weakness for Mughlai parathay and he would make them especially for me whenever I wanted."

I feel a pang of sadness for a man I didn't really know beyond the fact that he was my source of treats as a child. I didn't spare him a single thought after I left and yet he played a significant role in my childhood, when life was uncomplicated.

My musings are interrupted when one of the doormen coughs discreetly for attention.

"Begum Naz and her daughter have arrived," he announces.

My stomach drops immediately. *Okay, Mehar, calm down. Just keep your cool.*

The clatter of high heels reverberates from the large hall all the way into the dining room, and then Naz appears in the doorway. Her peacock-blue-and-green sari drapes her slender body perfectly, long earrings dangle just above her collarbones, and a delicate gold chain adorns her neck. She moves her sunglasses to the top of her head, and even from a distance I can see the striking emerald green of her eyes. Her long black hair is devoid of any gray and cascades in perfect waves over her shoulders. She is absolutely stunning. She walks, no, glides toward us, making a beeline for me as her face breaks out in a brilliant smile.

My hands are clammy and I don't know what to do. It doesn't help that everyone seems to be staring at me as if they expect me to spontaneously combust or something at the sight of my future stepmother. It takes every ounce of willpower I possess to push back my chair and stand so that I can graciously greet this woman whom my father has chosen to marry. Oh my god, what's wrong with me? My lips won't move and my voice seems to be stuck in my throat. So basically, I'm just standing by my chair like an idiot with my mouth open and no sound coming out, looking like a fish that's been left out of water for too long.

And then Naz is standing right in front of me, putting out her arms to draw me into an embrace, and somehow, I manage to return her hug.

"Mehar, my dear, I am so very happy to finally meet you," she says.

Damn, even her voice sounds elegant, her accent surprisingly British.

Get a grip, Mehar.

"It's so nice to meet you too," I manage to squeak.

"Your dad has been talking about nothing else ever since you accepted our invitation." She turns to look at Dad and then back to me. "Look at him. I have never seen his face sparkling like this."

Dad turns a deep red, which is adorable. Naz is looking at me with a warm smile, as if she is genuinely happy that I'm here. I smile back instinctively and then kick myself mentally. Nope. Nope. Nope. This isn't how it's supposed to be. She's supposed to be awful, not lovely and sweet. It's definitely all an act. She's trying to convince Dad that she is this amazing person who's embracing his daughter from a previous marriage, but I'm not buying it.

"I wouldn't dream of missing this," I say, surprised that my voice sounds a lot steadier than I feel. "This was probably my last chance to visit before I start college."

Naz flashes me another brilliant smile and motions for me to sit back down while she goes to the empty seat on the other side of Dad. Aleena is at the table now as well. I must have been too busy staring at Naz to notice her come in. She's sitting beside Faiza Phuppi, chatting animatedly about something, most likely another shopping adventure. Now she turns her attention on me.

"So, Mehar, how are you holding up?" she says from across the table. "You must be pretty jet-lagged."

"It hasn't hit me quite yet," I say. "I'm sure I'll crash in a little bit."

Naz and Aleena help themselves to some food, and Faiza Phuppi passes me a plate of jilebis. They used to be my favorite when I was little, and clearly that hasn't changed because even though my stomach is about to explode, I can't resist taking a few bites of the sweet, sticky, crunchy swirls.

“Mehar beta, it’s so nice to have you here with us,” Faiza Phuppi says. “Have you heard anything about your luggage?”

“I’m sure it’ll be here soon,” I say. “At least I hope it will.”

“Yes, yes, but until then you will have to wear proper clothes here, not just T-shirts and jeans, hai na?” she says with a laugh, looking around the whole table.

I can feel my face starting to turn red and hold back the retort that’s on the tip of my tongue.

Azra Aunty pipes up from across the table. “Mehar, these kids are saying they won’t go to sleep until you tell them a story.”

I’ve never been so relieved before. “Of course,” I say quickly. The kids are already pulling my arm and I make my escape, lifting Taimur in my arms while the three girls scamper ahead of me up the stairs.

CHAPTER EIGHT

The next morning I've just stepped out of the shower and barely gotten dressed when there's a knock on the door. It's one of the maids bringing me a cup of hot coffee. Her face looks so familiar, but I can't place her.

"I'm Bilquis," she says in Urdu. "I used to take care of you when you were little."

I stare at her and start to recall. "You used to chase me around, trying to get me to eat."

She nods. "You were a very naughty child," she says with a smile. "But I was the only one who could sing you to sleep when your ammi and abbu were out for the evening." She puts the coffee on the bedside table. "Your mother used to like her coffee like this too, milky and sweet," she says, coming closer and placing her hands around my face. "So beautiful . . . just like Gulnar Bhabi." She dabs a finger under her kajaled eye and then touches it behind my ear. "Nazar na lag jaye meri betiya ko."

Mom does this to me on occasion when she wants to ward off the evil eye. I put my arms around Bilquis and squeeze her tight. I remember this embrace, the warmth of it and how it always made me feel better as a little girl. I remember now asking about her for months when Mom and I first left for the US. I was six, too young to understand the circumstances behind the move but old enough to remember the people who mattered to me. But as time went on, they were replaced by the new people in our lives and brand-new experiences. Mom and I didn't speak much about her time here, and whenever Dad visited, the arguments and fights between them became the dominant memories.

I feel guilty now, even though I know I probably shouldn't since I was just a child back then. But it feels wrong somehow, to forget the people who loved me so much once upon a time in my life. I continue to hold Bilquis as the memories wash over me. But then she leans back and smiles. "Your dadi is asking for you."

Bilquis shows me to Dadi's room and leaves to take care of her duties.

"Assalamu alaikum, Dadijaan." I enter the room and spot my grandmother sitting on a diwan by the window. It's still early, but the rays of the sun are streaming through the raw silk curtains already. A ceiling fan turns lazily, circulating jasmine-scented air through the room. I walk over to Dadi and bend to kiss her cheeks.

"Walaikum assalaam, betiya." She takes my hand and pulls me down gently next to her. "Did you sleep well?"

"Yes, Dadijaan, I did." I squeeze her hands, leaning into her.

"You'll ask for anything you need, yes?" she says. "This is your home, so don't be shy."

"When have I ever been shy, Dadi?" I reply with a grin.

"Yes, that's very true." She lifts my face to get a better look. "Masha Allah, I cannot believe how you've grown. Tell me, did you not miss me? How come you've never visited your old dadi before now?"

There it is. The awkwardness and guilt I've dreaded. What am I supposed to say? That my parents made decisions and choices that I had no say in? I remember being around ten when I walked in on Mom and Dad having a loud argument. Or at least the end of it. All I recall is Mom yelling at Dad's retreating back that she would never let him take me to India. She didn't know I'd heard them and something in my gut told me she didn't need to know. As I got older, her words would echo in my head and I figured Dad must have wanted sole custody of me and Mom would never allow anyone to take me away from her. It was one of the reasons I felt so protective toward her. I knew she had sacrificed a lot to give me the sort of freedom she knew I wouldn't have if I lived here.

"I'm here now, Dadi," I say softly, and just continue to hold her hand. We sit like this in silence for a while, each of us lost in our own thoughts. Then she lifts her head and leans toward me.

"I want to show you something, Mehar." I take her arm as she stands and leads me to a large teak almirah. She removes a bunch of keys from the waistband of her petticoat and unlocks it. I watch, totally intrigued, as she pulls out a dark blue velvet box.

"I had this made for your aqiqah," she says, opening the box to reveal a gold chain with an oval pendant. She hands it to me and I run my fingers over the pendant. It sort of looks like a question mark without the dot underneath.

"Was that the naming ceremony when I ate too many jilebis and got sick? Mom told me about that."

She nods with a little laugh, then points to the pendant. "It's the Urdu letter *meem*, for Mehar," she tells me.

"It's so pretty," I say, handing it back to her.

"No, beta, this is yours. Let me put it on you."

I turn around and she fastens the clasp behind my neck.

"Thank you, Dadi." I look at my reflection in the mirror on the almirah door. "It's beautiful."

"Your mom and I decided it wouldn't be safe to let you wear it when you were so little. So your mom kept it locked away. But after she left, I was going through some old things and found it. She left it behind."

Once again, I don't know how I'm supposed to react to this revelation. I'm debating whether to ask her outright, but as it turns out, I don't have to.

"Mehar, there are some things I need to tell you." She leads us back to the diwan. "I don't know how much your mother has said to you, or if she has said anything at all."

I'm not sure where this is going but I'm kind of relieved that she's brought it up. Maybe I'll finally find out more details about my parents' relationship back then.

"I'm afraid I did not treat your mother fairly when she first married your father." Dadi plays with the hem of her dupatta. "To be honest, your grandfather and I had already chosen a girl we had hoped would become our daughter-in-law."

Is this supposed to make me feel better? I'm not sure I like where this is going. Plus, this part I already know about. Is there an apology coming?

I've always known Mom and Dad's love story. They met and fell in love in college in the States. Dad was a couple of years older and came back to India briefly after college. They'd sort of broken up because Dad knew his family had certain expectations. But then he couldn't get Mom out of his mind, so he went back and they got married and started a life there. Soon after I was born, my grandfather died and Dad knew he had to come back to India and Mom agreed because it was the right thing to do. From what Mom said, Dadi never accepted her as part of the family. She did always tell me that my grandmother loved me with all her heart, but that wasn't enough to make her want to stay.

"Did you blame Mom for marrying Dad?" I blurt out. "Is that why you never accepted her?"

As soon as the words leave my mouth, I know I should have stayed silent. A look of pain comes over Dadi's face.

"I'm ashamed to say it, but I did."

I look at her in surprise. I thought she would be angry at my insolence.

"But why? Dad was an adult. He made his own decision." *Shut up, Mehar.*

"Beta, as parents we often forget that our children become adults and that they are allowed to make their own choices." She stares into the distance, her mind probably years in the past. "I thought I knew what was best for your father. But I was wrong."

I'm afraid to say what I'm thinking. If she'd realized this back then, my life could have been different. My parents could have been happy together. But despite the resentment that I feel bubbling up toward her now, I can't forget one important thing. Dad was the one who chose to let us go. I want to try to move past my anger, but I don't know how to. All I can do is hope that coming here was the right decision and that Dad will finally see me.

And I need to make sure that I see him as well. And maybe, just maybe, Dad can change too. I mean, if Dadi can admit she was wrong, why can't he?

"I've made mistakes, Mehar." Dadi leans back in her seat. She looks tired suddenly and I wonder if this whole conversation may have been a bit much. She seems lost in her thoughts. "I thought I was protecting my son," she says, almost to herself.

"From Mom? Why? She never asked him for anything." Except to be there for her and for me.

"In those days I thought your father was too naive to realize who truly cared for him and who was only with him because of his wealth." She looks at me and I can see tears shimmering in her eyes. "I should have known Gulnar was one of the good ones. She put up with a lot to make Reza happy. But I never gave her a chance."

I wish more than anything that Mom could hear Dadi now. It would mean a great deal to her, I think, even if it's been so many years. I think she would appreciate that Dadi finally understands what she tried to give up for Dad.

"Have you ever told her that?"

"We haven't spoken much since she left." She lets out a deep sigh. "I should have made an effort. But I let my pride get in the way."

"You can still talk to her, you know."

She smiles at me, but it's a sad smile. "Beta, there are some words that can never be taken back, no matter how much you want."

I shake my head slowly. "I don't believe that, Dadi. Mom and I have said things to each other before, in anger. But that doesn't change that we are family and that we love each other, no matter what."

Dadi is silent. A long time passes before she speaks again.

"That is where the problem lies, Mehar." She puts her hand on mine. "I don't think your mother ever thought of us as family."

"Did you ever think of her as yours?"

She looks at me in surprise and I wonder if I've gone too far.

But if there's anything I've learned from my conversations with Mom about family dynamics, it's that it takes two to play the game. And as far as I know, she tried. But you can only get so far if you're the only one putting in any effort. So, maybe Dadi needs to hear it. And if she doesn't like it, well then . . . too bad, so sad. I can live with that.

"I have to say, it's refreshing to be around someone who speaks their mind."

Now it's my turn to be surprised. This was not the reaction I expected. But speaking my mind is kind of my brand. It doesn't always work in my favor, but maybe this time it did.

"I don't think I'm capable of *not* speaking my mind." I help her to her feet and link my arm in hers as I walk her back to her bed. "At least not to the people who are important to me." But not if I'm scared that it might hurt them, like in Mom's case. Then I'm suddenly übercautious.

She leans in to kiss my cheek. "I am so happy that you came, Mehar. Really."

"I'm really happy that I came too."

CHAPTER NINE

The sunlight streaming through the windows wakes me and I carefully open first one eye and then the other, squinting against the glare. And then I sit up with a start, because someone is standing by my bed, staring down at me. She's tall, her brown skin a little darker than my own, and her hair in a long black braid that hangs over her right shoulder. She looks like she could be around my age, but I can't be sure because she has the same disapproving look on her face that Mom does whenever she walks into my messy room.

"I hope you had a good nap," she says. Her tone and expression tell me she couldn't care less about my nap.

I'm still only half-awake, but I sit up and try to look as dignified as I can with drool on my chin and my hair sticking out in all directions the way it usually does after a nap.

"We have a problem," she says, not waiting for me to reply. "I'm Sufiya, by the way. I'm your grandmother's assistant, but while you're here, I have been assigned to you."

Okay. That still doesn't explain why she's in my bedroom, but I guess things are different here. That's cool. I'm cool.

"Um . . . I don't think I need an assistant," I murmur.

"Your grandmother thinks you do," Sufiya says a little smugly. She waves a newspaper in my face. "You seem to have made quite an impression on the local press."

"What're you talking about?" I practically snatch the paper from her hands and peer at the section it's opened up to. I see myself dressed in sweats and a hoodie, looking decidedly un-nawabzaadi-like. The press must have taken this before I'd realized they were even there.

The headline screams *American Nawabzaadi in the Taj City.*

There's another picture of me standing beside Aleena. She looks flawless, of course, flashing a brilliant smile at the camera, while I look like someone who's just stepped off a roller coaster. Why is this my life?

"It's all over social media too," Sufiya says, holding up her phone. As if I need further proof of my humiliation.

Great. I've been in India for five minutes and already I've managed to insult my aunt and embarrass the nawabi family. This is so totally on-brand for me. I pull the thin blanket over my head and squeeze my eyes shut. Maybe this is all a bad dream and when I wake up, I'll be back in my room in Kansas.

"Excuse me, hello?" Sufiya does not sound amused.

I peek out from under my blanket and stare at her. She looks down her slender nose at me. Her lips are pursed and she does not look the slightest bit amused.

"You should get ready and come downstairs," she says. "Your father and grandmother are already there waiting for you. I've laid out some suitable clothes for you to wear."

"Thank you, but I think I can pick my own clothes."

"You would think so, but . . ."

How dare she?

"Fine, whatever," I say. "Can I have some privacy, please?" In other words, GET OUT OF MY ROOM.

Sufiya turns on her heel and leaves the room. What a peach. I'm sure I'm going to love having her around all the time.

After I've washed the sleep from my eyes, I get dressed in the outfit Sufiya has laid out for me on my bed. It's a pretty set, the churidar a deep blue with a lighter blue chiffon kameez that has the tiniest silver flowers embroidered all across the bodice. It's nice and simple, just how I like it, so I guess I should be grateful that Sufiya has good taste. If it had been Aleena, I'd probably be trying not to get dragged down by a heavy zari-embroidered dupatta just to leave my room in the middle of the day. As I drape the light, gauzy dupatta over my shoulders and look at myself in the mirror, I decide that my silver jhumka earrings will go perfectly with it. They were a gift from Mom for my fifteenth birthday and I don't get to wear them a lot. A little mascara and some rose-colored lip stain and I'm ready to dispel my newfound reputation as a slob. I'm desperately hoping that Dadi agrees and isn't furious with me about the unflattering photos.

I go down, and after a couple of wrong turns I find myself in the enormous, opulently furnished formal living room. It's more of a large hall than any living room I've ever been in. There are several seating areas with high-backed tufted-velvet sofas and armchairs, and large mahogany tables with intricately carved sides. Huge crystal chandeliers hang from the ceiling, illuminating the many paintings that adorn the walls.

Dad and my grandmother are seated at one end of the room and Sufiya is also there. I look around to see if Naz and Aleena are there, and to my great relief they're not. The last thing I want is to be lectured in front of them. I'm mentally preparing to be chastised and I've made a promise to myself to not let any of it get to me. I'm just going to let them say what they have to say and apologize even though no part of me is sorry for how I dress. I mean, what did they think I would wear while flying halfway across the world trapped in a metal can for twenty-seven hours?

I take a deep breath and open my mouth to give a preemptive apology, but before I have a chance to speak, Dadi takes my arm and pulls me gently down beside her.

"Mehar betiya, please don't worry about these photos in the paper," she says. "These press people have no sense of privacy at all. I am so sick and tired of them taking our pictures as if we are animals in the zoo."

For the first time in my life I am speechless from shock. This is not at all what I expected would happen.

"But, Ammi," Dad says. "She should have known there would be some press and dressed accordingly, hai na?"

My cheeks burn as I turn to glare at him.

"Mehar, you're going to have to be a little more careful how you present yourself while you're here," he says as if he doesn't see me shooting daggers at him with my eyes. "Maybe it's okay to dress like that in Kansas, but here you are representing the nawabi family. Please be more careful from now on."

"Reza, bas karo," Dadi says sternly. "Mehar is not used to this kind of attention and you should have taken better care about the press. Who told them about her arrival anyway?" She turns away and continues to mutter to herself angrily. "It must have been that Aleena with all her bakwas ideas, as usual. That girl will do anything for attention."

"Ammi, there's no need to drag poor Aleena into all this," Dad says. "She was doing everything she could to help."

"Hanh, hanh, I can see how she was helping herself," Dadi says, pointing to the photo in the paper. "I've told you over and over again, these types of people only know how to help themselves, that's all. But no, why should you listen to an old woman like me. You think you know everything." And with that she gets up and marches out of the room. Dad hesitates, but only for a moment before he walks out after her. Unbelievable. I can hear them arguing even after they've left the room, and I collapse onto the couch and rest my head against the back. I already have a throbbing headache.

I'm sitting there with my eyes closed when I feel someone taking a seat beside me on the couch. I open my eyes to see Azra Aunty smiling at me.

"Are you okay, Mehar?" she asks, gently stroking my arm. "I heard Bhaiyya and Ammi arguing." She points to the paper that is now lying faceup on the carpet. "I'm guessing it has something to do with that."

My eyes well up and I hate how easily I'm reduced to tears ever since I stepped foot in India.

"I should never have come, Aunty," I say. "I don't understand why Dad even invited me. I mean, clearly I'm nothing but a huge embarrassment to him."

"No, beta, don't say that." Azra Aunty puts an arm around my shoulder and pulls me in. We sit in silence like this, both of us leaning back against the couch. "I'll talk to him," she says after a while. "He's just under a lot of stress, with the wedding and taking care of all the business stuff."

I wonder if that's what everyone tells themselves to excuse his behavior. He's the man of the house so of course he must have too much on his mind to worry about silly things like feelings. Well, he seems to deal with all that perfectly fine when he's around Aleena.

"Is that what you all said to Mom when she wanted Dad to

pay attention to us?" I'm sort of surprised at myself for saying this out loud, but Azra Aunty makes me feel like I can be completely honest.

"I was pretty young when your parents split up," she says. "But you're right. I mean, that's how it is a lot of the time here. I used to hear your mom cry behind closed doors and she'd never tell me any details but I could put two and two together."

Obviously I don't remember all this, but now I can imagine how it must have been for Mom and the knot in my stomach tightens. I'm even more determined now to make Dad see that he can't treat me like this. Not if he wants to be a part of my life. I mean, Mom and I have been doing pretty great until now without him being there. The way I see it, this is going to be a last-ditch effort, mostly on my part I think, to see if there's anything worth salvaging. But if he doesn't step up, I'm done. He and Naz and Aleena can play house all they want, I don't care.

"I'm going to go and talk to Dad," I say, extricating myself from Azra Aunty's embrace. I walk back into the foyer and follow the murmur of voices until I find Dad and Dadi in the office wing. Sufiya is there too and there's a sudden hush as soon as I walk in. It's pretty obvious that they've been talking about me. It's fine. Whatever. I'm determined to smooth things over. I won't be blamed for not trying.

I clear my throat. "Dad, I'm sorry about the photos. I'll try to be more careful from now on."

Dad looks at me and I can't tell if he's still upset or not. Then he puts his arm on my shoulder. "It's all right, beta. Your dadi is right, I should have warned you."

"How did the press even find out?" Sufiya says.

My thoughts exactly, but I'm glad that I don't have to be the one to point that out.

I throw Sufiya a grateful smile. She doesn't return it. Okay, then.

Maybe Aleena should have done a little less preening and posing for the press and a little more damage control. But then again, I wouldn't be surprised if she was hoping for exactly what happened. An opportunity to look good herself while making me look like a loser.

"I'm sorry I embarrassed you," I mumble in Dad and Dadi's direction.

Dad shakes his head and starts to say something, but Dadi beats him to it.

"You could never embarrass me, my sweet child." She puts her arm around me and pulls me closer. "But now that this has happened, you have to be a little bit careful and remember that they're always watching, just waiting for an opportunity to take embarrassing pictures of us."

"I promise, Dadi, I'll be more careful."

Dad smiles at me. His annoyance seems to have dissipated. Yippee! #Blessed. "I'm sure this is all very strange for you," he says. "But I know you can handle it. Plus, Sufiya is here to help you, so you're in good hands."

Sufiya smiles shyly but doesn't say anything. So she does know how to smile back. Interesting.

She and Dadi start talking about one of Dadi's social work projects and I get up to wander around. I pull out my phone to send Norah a quick message.

Got here yesterday and I'm already in the papers.

I search and send her a link to an online picture of me in my glorious sweats and hoodie.

Little dots appear instantly and I do a quick calculation. It's four in the morning for her, but I'm not at all surprised that she's up.

Go Mehar! Making me proud as usual.

I smile at her response. I wish she were here with me because then this trip would be a real blast. I slide my phone back in my pocket and resume my tour of the living room. The paintings are mostly of people I don't know dressed in very fancy clothes, but the resemblance is undeniable. The set of their eyes and the hooks of their noses seem to have made it down to my grandmother and Dad. But not me. I can't see myself in them at all. But still, these are my ancestors, and I'm filled by a sense of pride and regret simultaneously, because I'm both a part of this family's history and yet somehow separate at the same time. I feel like I should know everything about them because their blood runs in my veins too, but they are complete strangers to me and that feels wrong.

"You come from a very illustrious family, Mehar." I hadn't noticed that Dad had come up to me and I turn to him now.

"Will you tell me about them?"

He nods and holds out an arm. He has this look in his eyes that I can't figure out. I hesitate for a moment before I put my arm through his. This elicits a smile from him, and we walk like this to the opposite side of the room to stand in front of a large painting that dominates the whole space.

"This is Nawab Wazir Khan, one of the first to come to India from Persia. He arrived here in 1724."

"Wow, that's, like, three hundred years ago."

"That's right, and our family history starts there," Dad says.

"It's so strange to think that we're related to him." I'm looking at a complete stranger from a time and place I can't even begin to fathom and yet I know for a fact that I am related to him.

"Are there paintings of his family? His wife and children?"

Dad shakes his head. "If there were, they're probably lost or destroyed in one of the battles."

"Which battles?"

He doesn't get a chance to answer because the doors to the room fly open and Aleena comes in, the aanchal of her sari floating behind her. She looks like a vision in the pink floral chiffon and I hate her but she is stunning. Dad puts an arm around each of us. "I'm so happy that you're both here."

Aleena immediately puts on a brilliant smile. "Yes, this is such a special moment," she chirps, pulling out her phone, while I resist the urge to gag.

"Smile," she orders us, and I start to protest while she clicks, like, a gazillion pics, blinding me with the flash. Of course, all of mine are ridiculous with my mouth open in various grimaces since I was trying to speak. Before I can say anything, she's already posted it.

My phone pings almost immediately and I open her post. The caption reads: *With my soon-to-be dad and sister, Mehar, fresh from Kansas, the heartland of America* and there are already hundreds of likes. I resist the urge to smack her because that wouldn't do any good. Half the world has already seen my under-eye bags and frizzy hair while she looks like she's just stepped out of a professional photo shoot. UGH. I HATE HER. Meanwhile Dad is admiring the pictures, acting like a proud papa. I feel like he's being intentionally obtuse and I hate it.

"Daddy, Mehar looks so tired in these photos, doesn't she?" Aleena says thoughtfully, looking at a particularly bad picture of me.

Dad turns to me, nodding. "Mehar beta, you should try to get more rest."

Oh my god, someone stop me before I murder them both.

"No, Dad, I'm fine." I lean forward to look at Aleena. "Aleena, could you maybe wait next time before you post pictures of me?"

Aleena immediately puts on a hurt and innocent expression.

"Oh, I'm so sorry, I didn't mean to upset you. It's fine, you don't look that bad at all."

Whatever. I close my eyes for a moment, hoping that she'll just disappear. But when I open them, she's still here. I guess I'll have to get used to this. At least she'll leave soon. Hopefully. I've never missed Norah and Mom more. This is all too much for me, the fakeness and the blatant show of wealth. It's just too weird.

"I think I'd like to explore the palace, if that's okay."

"Sufiya will take you around," Dad says, waving Sufiya over.

I don't need or want a babysitter. "Actually, I'd rather go myself. I want to get my bearings. It's been so long."

Dad shrugs. "Sure, knock yourself out." He pulls me in for a quick hug. "Just remember that Alamgir still lives with us," he adds with a wink before walking away.

Alamgir. I haven't thought about him for ages. He's the palace's resident jinn, a remnant of an earlier age when one of the nawab begums of the eighteenth century was supposedly possessed by a benevolent but mischievous jinn who decided to stay back in the palace after she passed away. My grandmother would tell us stories of this jinn to keep us in line, but I was never scared. I can't believe I've forgotten all about him. I set off to explore with a big smile on my face as I rediscover nooks and crannies in the palace, full of memories of playing hide-and-seek all those years ago.

CHAPTER TEN

I head off to the palace library, one of my favorite places in the world. Of all my cousins, I used to love it the most, filled with my grandfather's inherited collections of old, worn books, many of them original editions of works by Rabindranath Tagore and Sarojini Naidu. According to Dad, my great-grandfather had been an avid reader and loved all kinds of literature, from prominent Indian poets to the English writers of his time, and left a large, impressive collection to the family after he passed. Dad used to sit me on his lap and read me poems I didn't understand at the time, but the memory fills me with a warm glow as I make my way down the long, winding corridors, my feet somehow remembering exactly where to go. I place my hands on the huge double doors but they don't budge. I push again, figuring that maybe they're just old doors, but nothing happens. I don't remember them ever being locked when I was little, but clearly they are now. Guess I'll have to find someone with a key. I head back to look for Dadi, but the only people in the living room are a couple of the staff, busy replacing old flowers with fresh ones in the numerous vases and bowls. My stomach growls loudly enough to get their attention and they look up at me in alarm.

I smile at them and gesture vaguely to let them know I'm fine before making a beeline for the dining room. I'm hoping to find some food there, and I'm in luck because the large table is being set up for afternoon tea.

One of the women looks up at me. "Aap ke liye kuch lekar aayen?"

I have to think for a minute before I realize that she's asking if she can bring me something. I remember how there was always this delicious snack at teatime when I was little. It was a deep-fried round flatbread filled with a spicy lentil mixture and the palace cook would always have some ready just for me.

"Aaj kachra banaya hain?" I ask her, hoping she'll say that the cook did make some. My mouth is watering in anticipation. Her hand flies to her mouth and then she smiles shyly at me before disappearing down the hallway. I'm a little confused but quite proud of my Urdu prowess even after all these years. I guess I must have a natural flair for languages.

"You know you just asked her if they've made any garbage today, right?" an amused voice says from behind me. I turn to see Sufiya leaning against the doorframe, barely suppressed laughter making her lips twitch. Her eyes twinkle and I'm trying to remember what it was that I didn't like about her earlier. Oh yeah, she was being pretty bossy. But now she's clearly enjoying my terrible Urdu skills.

I try to give her a cold stare, but I can't help it. A smile breaks out on my lips.

"Are you serious? I was sure I was asking for those little deep-fried thingies . . . you know?"

"They're called kachoris," Sufiya says with a grin. "And yes,

I'm sure they made some. Your grandmother made sure that the cook prepared all your favorites."

"Oh good, I'm starving." I look around. "By the way, where is everybody?"

"They're all coming over this evening," Sufiya says. "But dinner isn't until nine p.m."

I'm going to have to get used to mealtimes here all over again. Afternoon tea is pretty elaborate, so it makes total sense that dinner isn't until much later.

The woman from earlier walks in with a large tray of food and I have to stop myself from pouncing on her. There is a large platter of kachoris with small bowls of various chutneys. A younger boy follows her, carrying another tray laden with bowls of cut-up mango, jilebis, and other assorted sweets as well as small clay bowls of sweet yogurt.

When they leave, I pull out a chair and sit, but Sufiya turns to go.

"Wait, you're going to leave me all alone here?" Suddenly I want her to stay, even if just to be polite.

She hesitates, then draws her eyebrows together. "I kind of got the impression that you wanted to be left alone."

Awkward. I guess she heard me talking to Dad earlier.

"No, please, don't make me eat alone. I'll stuff myself and then they'll have to carry me out of here. How're you going to explain that to my grandmother?"

She shrugs with a smile and I can't seem to look away. There's a softness in her face now that wasn't there before, and I wonder why she was acting so stern with me. Probably because she thought I was an entitled American brat who doesn't care what anyone else thinks. Well, she's half-right. I don't care what people think. Most of the time. Right now, though, all the food is calling to me and I focus my attention to the deliciousness of my favorite childhood snacks. There's tea and coffee and mango lassi. I grab a tall glass of lassi and savor the cool, sweet-and-tart flavor of the mango-and-yogurt drink as it slides down my throat. This has to be heaven.

"So, is it everything you remember?" Sufiya's voice breaks through my temporary food coma after I've inhaled about four kachoris, a small bowl of mango, three jilebis, and a full glass of mango lassi. Meanwhile Sufiya nibbles delicately at a few pieces of mango, watching me down half the food on the table.

"You have no idea," I say, leaning back in my chair. I'm eyeing the little clay bowls of sweet yogurt, but there's no way I can eat another morsel. "This is all so good."

"Your grandmother is going to be very happy to hear that," she says. "She's been worried that after living in America all these years you'll find Indian food too spicy."

I mean, I kind of do, but not in a bad way. It's just that my taste buds haven't had this much excitement in a while.

I push my chair back with a groan. "I need to get up now, otherwise I don't think I'll ever be able to move again."

She joins me as I wander around the perimeter of the large dining room. Thick curtains frame the large window and filter the bright sunlight. Several pieces of art hang on the wall, paintings of buildings, probably palaces of Mughal ancestors. But what I'm drawn to instantly are the portraits of men and women dressed in royal finery looking haughtily down at me. Just like the ones from earlier, I don't recognize any of them, but I imagine they must be older members of the nawab family tree. There is one in particular that I can't stop staring at. It's of a young woman, dressed in a burgundy sharara. The tunic skims over her hips to cover the top third of her widely flared pants. Her head is covered by an ornate dupatta and she's seated in a regal pose on a diwan. Her kajaled eyes are dark and intense and she looks vaguely familiar.

"That's your dadi, when she was sixteen or so," Sufiya says.

"She looks so much older than sixteen." It's hard to reconcile the Dadi I know with this young girl who looks as though she could rule the world if she wanted.

Sufiya smiles. "From what I hear, she was quite something back then." I can hear the adoration in her voice and it's obvious she thinks very highly of Dadi.

"She must have been," I say. "I was only six when I left, so I guess I missed out on a lot of her stories."

She nods. "I know. She misses you a lot. Especially lately."

I know there is something appropriate to say in this moment, but I can't think of anything. I don't want to lie and say I missed her too, because if I'm being perfectly honest, I think she eventually disappeared from my consciousness sometime after we left. Now that so many memories are coming back, I realize that I must have missed her a lot initially, but at that age I'm pretty sure I was fairly easily distracted as my life went on. But thinking about it makes me feel guilty every time.

"You said you're Dadi's assistant," I say, turning to her. "So, what exactly do you assist her with?"

"I help her with all her charitable works." She tucks back an errant strand of hair.

"She's on the boards of several organizations," she continues. "Then there's her social calendar."

"It sounds like she's a very busy lady." I should really get to know Dadi as much as I can while I'm here. In my mind she's always just been this judgy grandmother, but now I'm growing more and more intrigued by her.

"She's pretty amazing," Sufiya says. "There are so many other wealthy families that don't care about their communities at all. But your grandmother . . . she's something else."

Her eyes are shining, the light from the sun turning them into a warm brown. Once again, I find myself unable to look away.

"I hope I'm not keeping you from anything," I say. "I'm sure you have better things to do than babysit me."

"Not at all," she says. "Your grandmother asked me to make sure that you find your way around and have everything you need."

"That's very sweet of her, but really, I'll be fine."

"I'm surprised you haven't got lost yet," Sufiya says, only a hint of a smile playing on her lips. "And I'm here to make sure you don't. I can't let the Nawabzaadi of Agra disappear in this huge palace, now, can I?"

I grin at her. "It *is* ginormous, isn't it? But I'm surprised by how much I remember of this place. It's been so long, but it looks exactly the same as I remember."

"Would you like me to accompany you as you look around?" she asks. "Unless you'd rather be alone," she adds hastily.

"No, that would be great, actually," I say. I've decided that I do like her. A lot. First impressions are overrated. "Let's do it."

I walk back to the table and start cleaning up my dishes to take into the kitchen, but Sufiya gently takes my arm.

"No, no, just leave it. The kitchen staff will take care of it."

"It's fine, I can take my own dirty dishes to the kitchen."

"Please don't." She hands me a little brass bell. "Just ring this whenever you want anything and someone will come."

"Seriously? Who am I? The Queen of England?" I say jokingly.

"No, but you are the nawabzaadi of this family and it is not appropriate for you to go into the kitchen and definitely not to clear your own dishes."

I put down the plate and bowl reluctantly. "Are you sure?"

She nods. "It's not how things are done here," she explains. "There's a strict hierarchy that needs to be followed."

"That sounds pretty archaic." I know I'm in a nawab's palace, but sheesh . . . it's the twenty-first century.

"I agree, trust me, but those are the rules, and people here are quite particular about that sort of thing. Especially your grandmother."

"So I've heard." The words slip out and I see a cloud pass over her face instantly.

She stiffens a little and I make a mental note to be more careful of how I talk about Dadi in front of her.

"Well, I think it's time to go on a tour of the mahal," she says, marching out ahead of me. I have a bad feeling that I've put my foot in my mouth yet again. When will I learn?

CHAPTER ELEVEN

I follow her out of the dining room, leaving the dirty dishes on the table. Who would have thought that one day I would object to *not* having to clean up after myself? If only Mom could see me now.

"I was trying to get into the library earlier, but it was locked," I say. "You wouldn't happen to have a key, would you?"

"Yes, I do," she says. She pulls out a bunch of keys from her little purse, and when we get to the doors, she unlocks them and pushes them wide open. I walk in behind her and take it all in. The walls are lined with shelves packed tightly with books. One side of the room is all windows, the bright light streaming through them casting shadows on the floor. There's a large desk in one corner and beside it is a seating area with several armchairs and a sofa around a coffee table. Other smaller chairs and tiny round tables are scattered throughout the room.

"Your family has always been the biggest patrons of the arts here in Agra, and they have an extensive collection of books. A lot of first editions of Kazi Nazrul Islam's works as well as many

Western authors and playwrights." She sounds like a tour guide and I wonder how often she's shown others around the mahal like this.

"This is just as amazing as I remember it," I say, completely awestruck. "I think I'll move in here."

Her smile is back. "This would be my dream home. Just whatever's in here and I don't need anything else."

"Where do you live?" I ask, suddenly curious.

"About thirty minutes from here in Vijay Nagar Colony."

"What's it like there?"

"Nothing like this," she says with a small laugh.

"I mean, this is a bit extreme, if you ask me."

"I live with my parents and two younger siblings," she says, playing with her long braid. "I have thirteen-year-old twin sisters."

"Wow, you must never get bored." I've always wished I had a sister. Or even a brother. Just someone else to talk with about stuff that I can't say to Mom. Someone else who gets what it's like being me.

"They certainly keep us busy," she says. "But sometimes, it's nice to be all alone in a place like this. I come here whenever things get to be a bit much."

I can see that. It's so quiet and serene in here, one of the large windows overlooking the gardens. I can see the pond from here and the ducks gliding along the surface.

"You should see it during sunset," Sufiya says. "It's so beautiful."

"Yes, I remember," I say.

She doesn't say anything and I wonder what she's thinking.

"How long have you worked for Dadi?" I ask.

"Just a year." She sits down on one of the chairs by the window and I join her. "We met at an event I was volunteering for. She's on the organizing committee and when she heard that I was looking for a job she called me in for an interview." She plays with her long braid again as she talks, and I realize that she does that every time I ask her a question about herself. It's kind of cute.

"I'm glad it worked out."

"Me too," she says with a smile. "I'd hoped I could apply to college in the US, but I'm the eldest, so if I leave it's going to be really hard on my parents."

"I was supposed to work during this break and save up for college. But instead, I'm here and now I might never be able to afford the school I want to go to."

She throws me a strange look and it takes me a minute to realize how I must sound. She probably thinks I'm rolling in my dad's money.

"You probably don't know this, but my dad and I . . . we haven't exactly been on the best of terms recently."

I'm not sure why I'm being defensive to someone I just met who has no idea about me or my life.

"Actually, you'd be surprised about how much I know. Someone like me can be pretty invisible to some people." She gives a little laugh and leans back against a bookshelf.

"How do you mean?"

"Just that sometimes I hear things that I'm not meant to."

"So, what terrible things have you heard about me?" I'm only half joking. I'm sure over the years everyone in this family has had many opinions about me and Mom, and I can't imagine they were very nice ones.

"Nothing terrible . . . and let's just say I don't believe everything I hear." Her eyes linger on me for a moment before she looks away.

"So, what's your favorite part about working with my grandmother?" I have a sudden desire to get to know more about her. Or maybe I just want to know stuff about Dadi. I can't be sure which it is.

"Your dadi is seriously incredible," she says. "And I'm not saying that because I work for her."

"To be honest, I don't remember my grandmother that well. I feel like I should, but all my memories about her have to do with food." I grin at her. "I was a really picky eater when I was little."

"Is this your first time visiting since you left as a child?" She has an incredulous look on her face.

I nod.

"Anyway, she's amazing. She's done so much for the women in the rural communities, much more than all these politicians who make so many promises when they're campaigning, but then after they've been elected, they couldn't care less."

"You must learn a lot from working with her."

"So much. Most of all, I'm just so thankful that she's not one of those wealthy people who talk and complain about the state of our country but never actually do anything."

"I hope I can do something to help out while I'm here."

Am I a bad person because I feel a little bit resentful that Sufiya knows Dadi in a way I never have? I mean, all I know about her is that she was judgmental and basically drove my mother out of this family. But listening to Sufiya makes me realize I don't really know Dadi at all. Maybe she changed after Mom left with me. I know now that she regrets the way she treated Mom. Or has Mom's own resentment completely obliterated any good memories I have of Dadi?

"I'm sure your grandmother will be thrilled about that," Sufiya says. "You should ask her."

"You never answered my question, though," I remind her. "What's your favorite part?"

"I've always loved children," she says. "And Dadima started an educational initiative for rural children so that they can all have access to proper education." Sufiya's eyes shine as she speaks and I can tell how passionate she must be about this.

"You call her Dadima?"

She smiles. "I do. She's always treated me so kindly and I never got to know either of my grandmothers before they passed."

"I'm so sorry to hear that," I say. "About your grandmothers, I mean. Do you think you'll keep working for Dadi after you graduate?"

"Definitely, I've already spoken to her about it. She said she would make sure that I can still work here while I go to university."

"Here in Agra?"

"Yes, I'm hoping to get my degree in social work."

"That sounds amazing. It must be nice to have such a clear vision of what you want your future to look like."

"Well, I don't exactly have a lot of choices." Her eyes have lost a bit of the sparkle from earlier. "I mean, I have to think about my younger siblings. I can't do anything that will jeopardize their futures."

I get financial responsibility because Mom made sure I never got too comfortable with the fact that my father is wealthy. I've always been expected to contribute and doesn't ask Dad for money for anything other than basic stuff. I've never been able to buy the latest gadgets or drive a new car, like some of the other kids I know. I wouldn't be comfortable throwing money after stuff the way Aleena seems to. So, I get it to some extent. But Sufiya's situation seems to be way harder. For one thing, she's not just responsible for herself the way I am. She has to think about the rest of her family, and from the impression I get, her family is not wealthy. I wonder if she'll think I'm being facetious if I say I get it. So, I don't.

"That must be so hard."

"It is. But I'm lucky I have this job and an employer who values me."

"I'm sure Dadi must appreciate you a lot."

She smiles at me. "Are you ready to keep looking?"

We continue the tour down a wide hallway to another set of doors that opens to reveal the most opulently decorated room so far. It's currently unoccupied, but I can see why Dadi and Dad decided to turn a part of the palace into a hotel. There is a large four-poster bed in the middle of the room. I don't know what size is bigger than a California king, but this must be it. The bedding is luxurious, a burgundy, muted gold, and black motif repeated throughout the room. But the wooden swing at one end of the room has to be the most beautiful thing I've ever seen. It's made of two intricately carved pillars that sit on pedestals with peacocks carved into the bases. The pillars are connected by a shaft on which the swing hangs. The back of the swing has a line of cutout elephants, and small brass peacocks are perched on the arms. It's a stunning work of art, and before I can stop myself, I'm reclining on the soft bolster cushions with my eyes closed, swinging gently like some ancient queen. All I need is a bunch of grapes. It feels like time has bent backward over itself and transported me to those days when I had nothing to worry about other than which of my dress-up stash from Azra Aunty to wear.

"I think I'll go and catch up on a little work," Sufiya says, her voice breaking through the haze of my daydream. She starts walking slowly toward the door. "If you want, we can go back to the library tomorrow. There are some cool books I'd love to show you."

"It's a date," I call out to her retreating back.

She turns to give me a funny look but doesn't say anything as she walks out the door.

CHAPTER TWELVE

"I miss you so much," Mom says as soon as she answers my call. "Why did I think I'd be all right without you for this long?"

"It's been like three days, Mom." I blow her a kiss.

"How're you settling in? How's everything?"

"Honestly? Way better than I expected. Everyone's super nice and you were right. Azra Aunty's the best."

"She really is, isn't she?"

"And her kids are so adorable. Of course, they love me," I say with a grin.

"What about your grandmother?"

"She's been amazing. I was kind of scared that things would be awkward between us, but it's actually been great."

"That's so nice to hear, sweetie."

"Mom . . . we talked about a lot of stuff, and . . . she said she was sorry about the way she treated you back then."

Mom's smile fades away and I instantly regret bringing this up. My timing is the worst.

"What did she say exactly?" Mom says.

"Just that . . . she knows she wasn't fair to you and that she should have been kinder to you."

"Well . . . that's nice of her to say, I guess."

There's a bit of an awkward silence and I rack my brain to try to change the topic. Then I remember I never told her about the photos in the paper. That breaks the tension and soon we're talking normally again.

"How do you like the food?" Mom says. "Not too spicy, I hope."

"It kind of is, but I think I'm already getting used to it." I tell her about the kachori mix-up.

"That's too funny. Tell me, is that nice cook still there?"

"No, Dadi said he passed away a couple of years ago."

"Oh . . . he was always so nice to me. He made the best sweets, always made them a little bit less sugary for me."

"Bilquis still remembers how you liked your coffee," I say. "She told me the other day."

"Bilquis was the best," Mom says. "How did she like the face creams I sent for her?"

"My suitcases haven't come yet." I let out a deep sigh. "I'm never going to see any of my clothes again, am I?"

"If you're lucky, they might still show up."

We chat for a few minutes longer and then Mom has to go out, so we hang up after I promise to call again soon.

• • •

I decide to go and find Dadi. After what Sufiya told me about her, I'm hungry for details.

I find her resting in bed, propped up on some pillows. She seems to get tired quite easily, but I guess that might be part of getting old. At least she doesn't seem to be sick or anything, which is good.

"Come, beta," she says when she sees me dawdling at the door. "Idhar aake baitho." She pats the edge of the bed and I go sit next to her.

"Dadi, are you feeling all right?" I take her hand and pat it gently.

"How can I not be? You have brought such a light into my life, betiya." She leans back and looks up at me. "I'm going to miss you so much when you leave."

"But Dadi, I just got here," I say. "And I'm still here for a few more weeks."

"Then I will try to enjoy every moment with you." She squeezes my hand and studies my face. "So, what's on your mind, meri chanda? Are you upset about earlier? I told your father that he should not get angry at you about things like that."

"No, it's not that." I hesitate. I don't want to burden her with my problems, but she's the one who brought it up.

"What is it, Mehar?' she says softly. "You can tell me."

I take a deep breath. "I don't know if Dad said anything to you about the last time he visited me in Kansas."

Dadi doesn't say anything, so I continue. "We had this big fight and we never talked about it."

"I remember he was quite sad after he returned from that trip," Dadi says. "But he never mentioned anything and I didn't ask."

"I don't know how to bring it up and I don't even know if I should. It's hard for me to talk to him sometimes."

"That's not right, beta. It should not be like that between fathers and daughters."

"I never really had a say in it," I say. "Mom and Dad decided what my life should be like and I just had to accept it. I never got to choose what kind of relationship I would have with Dad."

"You have a choice now," she says. "You're grown up now and you can decide how you want things to be with your father."

"It's too late. Dad's getting a new family and I don't think I have any place in it."

Dadi takes my face in her hands. "Never say that again, Mehar. You are the only daughter of the nawab. You will always have a place in this family, even if a thousand others like Naz and Aleena come into your father's life."

"I won't force Dad to make space for me, Dadi. He chose not to be with us. I accepted that a long time ago."

"You don't have to force anything, Mehar. He's your father and he loves you more than anything."

"That's not what it felt like earlier," I say, the bitterness I've been trying to hide coming through now. "I think Dad just wanted me here for appearances more than anything. After all, there's going to be so much media coverage of the wedding; how would it look if his only daughter isn't here?"

"That's not true, beta," Dadi says. "Reza wants you here because you are his daughter and for that reason only. And yes, he can be very . . . how do you young people say it? . . . clueless sometimes, but his heart is in the right place."

I smile through my frustration because Dadi is totally right. Dad is pretty clueless when it comes to me. I guess I can be a little bit more patient and give him another chance. Or ten. "You know, he didn't want to be away from you," Dadi says. "He did it for me . . . for this family. Out of a sense of duty. And I realized too late that I should have pushed him out so that he could be with you and your mother. That's where he belonged. But I was afraid after your grandfather died. I was not strong enough to lead this family by myself. But I should have been."

She closes her eyes and lays her head on the pillow. I watch her as she breathes, her chest rising and falling under the aanchal of her sari.

"Why don't I let you get some rest," I say. "You look tired."

"Yes, beta. I'm very tired," she says. "But I'm so happy that we talked."

"Me too," I say. "And, Dadi, please don't worry about me and Dad. We'll figure things out. We always do."

"How can I not worry, betiya?" she says. "I am to blame for all this. And I don't know how to make it right."

"Please, Dadi. It's not your fault. Dad is a grown man. He makes his own decisions. Nobody forced him to do anything."

"Beta, familial obligations are powerful. Sometimes you do not have to ask. I never asked your father, but he felt it was his duty. Unfortunately, his sense of duty toward me was too strong. And I feel responsible because I am the one who raised him like that." She puts out her hand to touch my cheek. "And you, my betiya rani, are paying the price for that."

I sit with her until her breathing is even, and she's fast asleep before I leave her room.

CHAPTER THIRTEEN

I find Dad in the office wing. As a little girl, whenever I was looking for him, I'd find him at his desk in this wing, where the business side of running a palace takes place. As current nawab, his office is by far the largest. A beautiful sun-kissed space with imposing, heavy furniture in teak and mahogany. After my talk with Dadi I decided that she is right. I'm not a child anymore and I can choose to do something about my relationship with my father. I think the most important thing is to get some clarity on Dad's side of things. I need to know more about how things went down between my parents years ago, and I figure I might as well ask him before he takes off on one of his trips.

"Hey, Dad." I peek my head around his office door.

"Come in, come in, beta," he says, his face breaking into a huge smile. "How was your tour of the mahal?"

"Awesome. Sufiya should be a tour guide or something."

Dad waves me over to a seat by the window and joins me there.

"Wait until your grandmother shows you around. She lives for this," he says. "She loves to talk about our family's history."

"Talking about history . . ." I am nothing if not a genius in the art of the segue. "I was talking to Mom earlier and . . ."

Dad narrows his eyes. "What did you do, Mehar?"

"I was just telling her about something Dadi said about her and I think it made her sad."

"What did Ammi say?"

"Nothing bad," I say quickly. "Just that she's sorry for the way she treated Mom and that she never gave her a chance."

Dad doesn't say anything and seems to be mesmerized by his fingernails.

"Are you mad?" I ask when the silence becomes uncomfortable.

He looks up and, for a second, it's as if he's forgotten that I'm here.

"What . . . no, of course not, beta."

"I just feel like I only know Mom's side of things . . . you know . . . about why you guys split up."

He lets out a deep sigh and takes my hands in his. For a moment I marvel at how long it's been since Dad and I held hands. As a kid I'd always hang on to him whenever we went out somewhere as a family, probably because I didn't get to see him all the time. But that was a long time ago and I like how it feels now.

"Mehar, I want you to know something, and it's very important that you listen carefully."

Uh-oh. I sense a lecture coming. Maybe this isn't the best idea I've had.

"I need you to know that whatever happened between your mom and me . . . it was always between the two of us. You are the best thing we ever did. On that we never disagreed."

Now there's a lump in my throat and I swallow hard.

"Dad . . . I don't want to bring up anything that will make you sad, but I just . . . I think I deserve to know the full picture."

He looks at me and his eyes are glistening a little and this is just great. I've made both my parents almost cry today. I deserve a medal for being the worst daughter in the whole world.

"You're right," he says, to my surprise. "You should know the whole story."

I squeeze his hands but don't say anything.

"I always knew that it would be difficult for your mom to adjust to life here," he begins. "It's so different from the life she had growing up and she was the one who had to make the most sacrifices."

I listen with rapt attention, feeling as if I've been transported back to when my parents were young.

"The thing is, when I came back to India the first time without your mom, I knew instantly that I didn't want to live without her. So I went back and we started our life together."

This part I already know about. I also know about all the sacrifices Mom made when they both decided that they would move here with me.

"I was naive enough to think that our love would be enough to overcome everything. Your mom tried . . . I know she did. But no matter how hard she tried, there were some things she couldn't overcome. Like the fact that your grandmother never accepted her and that the rules were different here. Things have changed a lot since then."

"But then why didn't you come with us?" I blurt out. It's the one thing that's plagued me since I was a little girl. "Why didn't you choose us?"

Dad looks at me and I can see the regret in his eyes. "I wanted to, beta. So badly. But I had a duty. I'm the only son and that comes with a lot of responsibility."

"But didn't you have a duty toward Mom and me?"

He puts his hands on his head and then runs them through his hair.

"Of course I did, but . . . look, beta, it's complicated. Your mom and I spent a lot of time blaming one another for things that we shouldn't have. I was angry at her for a long time for deciding to break up our family and take you away from here."

"Well, I'm sure it wasn't exactly easy for her either," I say. "You weren't really there all those years when we first moved back. It was rough for her too."

"I know, sweetie." He sounds tired. "I did a lot of things I regret now. But I had to make a choice, and at the time I thought I was doing the right thing."

And that's it. The reason he chose to stay, the fact that he chose his mother, his duties as the only son, over us was his ego? Because he resented that Mom chose to leave a bad situation? It's not as if any of this is news to me, not really. But somehow hearing it from him directly has hit me a lot harder than I expected. But at least we're talking, and even if it's hard, it feels like a step in the right direction.

There's a knock on the door. I go to open it and find Bilquis standing there.

"Nawab Sahib, Naz Begum aapko bula rahi hain."

I turn to Dad, wondering how he'll react to being summoned by his future wife.

"Mehar, we still have a lot to talk about," he says, and I feel a tinge of happiness that he wants to keep talking. "We'll continue this later, okay?"

And my hopes are dashed again. Nothing I haven't felt before.

I shrug. "Sure, whatever."

"I promise, we'll talk more soon."

I watch his retreating back and wonder why I was stupid enough to think that anything was going to change. I suppress the urge to scream and run out of my father's office. By sheer instinct, my feet guide me to the library, and thankfully the doors are unlocked. I collapse on the seat by the window and take a few deep breaths. I feel utterly alone and my eyes fill with tears. I look out the window at the pond, its surface rippling gently from the breeze. Then I hear the door open and I quickly dab away the tears. It's Sufiya.

"I'm sorry, I didn't think anyone was in here," she says.

I don't reply because I don't want her to know that I've been crying. But she moves closer and I can see the concern on her face. She comes and sits by me, gently taking my hand in hers.

"Why are you crying?" she says.

I just shake my head, but my shoulders are heaving and she puts her arms around me, pulls me in, and just holds me. Now I start crying even harder and she strokes my hair gently until the tears subside.

I take in a deep, shaky breath and lean against the back of the sofa. I can't quite look her in the eyes because I'm embarrassed and a little confused by how good it felt to have her hold me.

"Thank you," I finally say. "I'm sorry . . . I got your blouse all wet."

She looks down at the damp patch on her light blue top. "It's going to be fine."

I'm not sure if she's talking about her blouse or what made me cry.

"I'm sorry," I say again.

"Do you want to talk about it?" she says. "I'm a great listener."

I look up at her, straight into her eyes. They're big and brown and I can see my face reflected in them.

"I was talking to my dad and . . . it's just that, when I came here I thought things would be different."

"It's been a while since you've seen your father, hasn't it?"

I nod. "A year. The last time he came to Kansas we had a huge fight."

"And you never made up with him?"

"I mostly avoided his calls. And when we did talk, it was short and polite, just stuff about school and grades." My eyes tear up again. "I guess I'd hoped that coming here would show him that I was sorry for what I said." I'm sobbing now and my voice has reached an unnatural pitch. "But then today I realized that none of it means anything to him. He just cares about this family, not us."

I'd honestly be surprised if Sufiya understood a word of what I just said, because with all the blubbering I'm pretty sure she can't. But she puts her arms around me again and lets me get it all out. She produces a handful of tissues from somewhere and after I'm all cried out, I blow my nose and give her a watery smile.

"I'm so sorry to dump all this on you."

She grabs another tissue and dabs my cheeks. "Please don't say that. I know how tough it can be with parents sometimes."

We sit like that for a little longer and as the sun begins to set, Sufiya leaves for home and I go to my room and get ready for bed. But I can't get her out of my mind, and as my eyes get heavy with sleep, all I can remember about this day is the feeling of her arms around me.

CHAPTER FOURTEEN

A few days later, I'm sitting on the giant swinging seat by the window in the drawing room when I hear yelling. I go to check out where it's coming from and find my way to the throne room, which I have heard of but haven't seen until now. I stop in my tracks at the sight of my seventy-five-year-old grandmother perched on the top rung of a very tall ladder shouting at the four decorators who are looking up at her in sheer fright. Sufiya is standing at the bottom of the ladder, her hands on her head.

I go to her and look up at Dadi. "What is she doing?" I ask Sufiya.

"The decorators weren't doing it right," she says, pointing to the elaborate swaths of silk and satin scattered across the stage for the wedding ceremony.

"Should she be up there?"

"Of course not," she says. "But *you* try to convince her to come down."

"Dadijaan," I call out. "Can you please come down?"

Dadi stops wrapping the long piece of fabric in her hand and looks down at us. "I'll come down as soon as I have shown these nincompoops how to do their job," she yells.

"Why don't you come down now and Sufiya and I will help you. Okay?"

Dadi looks at me, then lets out a deep sigh. "Okay, beta. I am feeling a little bit dizzy." She starts to come down, one rung at a time, and we collectively hold our breath until she's on solid ground.

"Okay, Dadijaan, please never do that again," I say, taking her by the arm and leading her to a chair.

"No one can ever do anything right these days," she says, a little out of breath. "When your grandfather was alive, there was a way things were done. Everything was taken care of properly. Now it seems nobody can do their job and your father is never around to look after things."

"I'll talk to him, Dadi," I say, stroking her arm gently. She looks a little pale and I turn to Sufiya. "Should we call someone?" I ask her.

"I'll call Dr. Kapoor," she says, pulling out her phone, but Dadi puts out a hand to stop her.

"No need for all that, beta," she says. "I only need someone to help me keep an eye on everything. Otherwise, nothing will get done on time."

"Don't worry, Dadima," Sufiya says. "Mehar and I will take care of everything, won't we?"

"Yes, of course, Dadijaan," I agree. "You just tell us what you want and we'll make sure it's done exactly like that. Let's go up to your room and get you into bed, and we can talk about everything there."

Dadi nods toward the door and I turn to see Bilquis standing there. "There's Bilquis," Dadi says. "She will take me. You two should stay here and make sure these people decorate the stage properly. Sufiya, where's my tablet?"

Sufiya runs to the stage and finds the tablet.

"This should give you an idea of what I want," Dadi says, swiping through several pictures before she finds the one she is looking for. "I'll trust that you both will get it right."

Bilquis and Dadi leave while we tell the decorators to take a break.

"That was fun," I say, staring up at the wooden beams around the stage. "Is she always like this?"

"Well, she does like things to be done a certain way," Sufiya says slowly. "But this is the first time I've seen her this agitated."

"Isn't it a little early to start decorating?" The wedding is still two weeks away.

"Oh no, this is totally normal," she says. "Have you seen the size of this place? It's going to take weeks to get it all done, plus Dadima is going to make them redo everything several times until she's satisfied."

"I guess she wants everything to be perfect for the wedding." It feels weird to say it out loud. Now that I'm here and seeing the preparations have started in earnest, it makes everything too real. I look around, taking in the massive space. Elaborately carved columns are spaced a few feet apart from each other along two sides of the room. In front of the columns on both sides are rows of high-backed chairs.

"This is where the Mughal emperors would hold their audiences," Sufiya says. "The viziers and other high-ranking officers would sit in those chairs and the people would stand in front of the emperor and state their requests or complaints."

"It's so hard to imagine that all this once belonged to actual Mughal kings," I say. "It's totally wild that there's so much history here. How did this palace end up being in the family?"

"The last Mughal king ruled until the British colonizers came in the sixteenth century," she replies. "They decided to appoint Murad Jehangir Rabbani as the nawab in this palace, and it's belonged to your family ever since."

"It must have been so different back then. Women were segregated, right?" I look around. "So, where's the zenana lookout?"

Sufiya points to a section above the main hall. There in a corner is an intricate lattice structure, a sort of divider where the women of the palace would sit in seclusion, watching the proceedings in complete privacy. I can't help but wonder what their lives must have been like, what stories they must have had to tell.

"There's a great collection of paintings from that time period in the library," Sufiya says. "Remind me to show it to you sometime."

"Yes, I'd love to see that," I say. "But now, let's figure out what we're going to do with all this."

We spend the next hour deciding exactly how to decorate the main stage, where Dad and Naz will sit on the two gilded thrones that occupy the platform. Sufiya has a great eye for design and soon we have come up with something that we're sure Dadi will approve of. We call the decorators back in and stick around to give them instructions.

"You're really good at this," I say to Sufiya when we take a break. Jameela from the kitchen staff has set up a little picnic for us in the gardens with freshly prepared pakodas and little lamb kebabs with a delicious date-and-tamarind chutney, along with ice-cold nimbu pani and bowls of cut-up mango. I lean back against a pillow on the thick blanket and sigh with contentment. I could get used to this. This space is less of a garden and more of a park, complete with a water fountain and beds and beds of roses. Tall date palms stand like sentinels around the perimeter and there's a little pond in one corner. I remember splashing in the pond when I was little and Mom holding me back so I didn't fall in.

"Do you remember a lot from when you lived here?" Sufiya asks as if reading my thoughts.

"I hadn't thought about it for such a long time, I was sure I'd forgotten," I reply. "But it's all starting to come back slowly. Like being here in this garden."

"It must be strange for you, no?"

"Kind of. I was so little when Mom and I left, I don't think I really ever thought of this as my home."

"Are you close to your mom?" She holds out the bowl of mango and I help myself to a few pieces.

"We're very close," I say. "We're kind of like best friends. What about you? Who're you closest to in your family?"

"My father," she says without hesitation. "Ammi always worries so much about me that she sometimes won't let me live my life. But Abbu's a dreamer like me and he always convinces Ammi to let me do what I want."

"It must be nice to have that sort of relationship with your father," I say. "Dad hasn't been there that much for me growing up." I'm surprised that I feel comfortable talking about this with someone I've only recently met. Maybe Sufiya has a superpower because I feel like I've known her a lot longer. She's just one of those people who can make you feel like that. I'm not usually the kind of person who overshares, but around her I seem to be. Maybe it's being in India and the fact that she's the only person I can relate to.

"Is it hard for you and your mom? Living by yourselves?"

"Not at all. My mom's always been independent and she's happiest when she can just live her life the way she wants."

"It's not easy doing that here," she says. She lies back all the way and looks up. The sun is close to setting, and the sky is a pretty pink in some spots and a burnt orange in others. I'm sure some of it is the effect of air pollution, but it's still pretty.

"What would you do if you could do anything you wanted?"

She looks at me, then quickly averts her gaze as if she's scared of what I might see in her eyes. She plucks a blade of grass and twirls it between her fingers. Then she lets out a huge sigh. "I can't even imagine that." She turns her head toward me. "You know, to be free like that, to do whatever I want."

"But if you could," I press on. "What would it be?"

She squints as she looks up at the sky. "I guess I would travel," she says. "See the world, meet all kinds of people."

"But you could do that, right? Someday?"

"I don't know. I have to think about my siblings, and once I'm finished with university my parents will want me to get married. Then I'll have to think about my husband and his family and what they need."

"But don't you get a say in your own life?" I don't know if I could do what she's describing.

"Of course I do," she says quickly. "I don't mean anyone would force me to do anything I don't want. But I can't just pretend there aren't people who are counting on me to make choices that will be good for them as well as for me. My parents have sacrificed so much to give me every opportunity. So, when it comes to making decisions for my future, I can't just leave them out. I have to do what's best for everyone."

"That's a lot of responsibility." I feel a little bit sad for her and I'm suddenly painfully aware of my own privilege. It's not as if I have it all figured out, but it's clear that I have way more freedom and many more choices than she does.

Suddenly I get this feeling that we're being watched. I narrow my eyes and try to peer through the sparser parts of the hedges, and sure enough, I can see the tip of a camera lens sticking out through the brush. I tug on Sufiya's sleeve.

"I think someone is taking pictures of us," I whisper.

She looks up in alarm. "What? Where?"

I point my chin to the spot in question.

Sufiya stands, smooths her kameez, and marches toward the fence with a determined look on her face. I follow her closely as she proceeds to yell angrily at the person with the camera, who promptly snaps a few photos of me while Sufiya adds some colorful language to her tirade. I can't help but grin. She is so cute all riled up, her face turning red with the effort of being rude. The guy totally deserves it and makes a hasty escape when Sufiya takes off her slipper and threatens to throw it at him.

She turns to me with her hands on her hips.

"Why are you grinning like that?" she demands, still breathing a little heavily.

"I'm sorry, but that was extremely entertaining to watch," I say, attempting to put on a serious face but failing miserably.

"These people are like vultures," she says. "You have to take them seriously."

"Oh yes, of course, very seriously," I say, my lips twitching from the effort of trying not to smile. I give up and burst out laughing. "Did you see the look on his face when you pulled off your slipper?"

She makes a valiant effort to stay serious but fails. "Yeah, that was funny. That guy is trouble, though. This isn't the first time we've crossed paths."

We sit together for a little while longer, watching the mynah birds fight over mangoes until Sufiya has to head home. I realize that I can hardly wait to see her again tomorrow. I try to ignore the fact that she and I have very different lives and the rules are different here. But that doesn't change the fact that I really, really like her.

I decide to stay out here and find my favorite spot at the edge of the pond, surrounded by beautifully fragrant gulmohar and jasmine trees, with mynah birds chirping all around me, and it's as if I'm the only person for miles and miles. The high walls and dense foliage insulate this part of the property from the outside world, except when they don't, like today. Just on the other side of the main building is a veritable circus. There are decorators, gardeners, an entire team of wedding planners, all preparing for one of the biggest weddings in Agra. The guest list has surpassed several thousand already and the flowers alone will probably cost a fortune. The house is bustling with designers who are busy putting together new outfits for all the members of our family. Aleena's been in an incredibly good mood the last couple of days, most probably because she's drowning in new clothes and jewelry. How anyone needs that many outfits is beyond me. Yesterday I overheard her telling someone that she has four outfit changes just for the wedding day. I can't help feeling sorry for the poor guy who'll end up footing the bill for her own wedding, if she finds anyone dumb enough to marry her.

CHAPTER FIFTEEN

I'm hanging out with my three little cousins. Azra Aunty is off with Rafiq Uncle and I wanted to spend time with the cuties because they're totally adorable. I desperately want to have kids one day and I'm enjoying every moment with these little ones. Since Sufiya has officially been assigned to me, she's hanging out with us too. Not that I'm complaining or anything. There's something that draws me to her, and I've been trying to figure out if it's all in my head or if it's real.

Currently I'm tied to one of the posters of my bed because the kids are pretending that I'm a pirate and Sufiya's the princess they're saving from my evil clutches.

"Aarrgh," I cry menacingly, and the girls run away screaming.

"You're so good with them." Sufiya smiles at me. She looks particularly cute today, in jeans and a T-shirt that has CHAIHOLIC printed across the front. Her hair is in two long braids, one hanging down over each shoulder.

"You look adorable." The words slip out and I panic. "Aarrgh." Oh my god, what's wrong with me? I can feel the blood rushing to my face and I'm desperately hoping that she blames my weirdness on jet lag, on being American, on anything but my ineptitude at flirting.

Luckily, I'm saved from further embarrassment by Dadi. She comes in, looks at me still tied to the bed, and shakes her head. The girls have probably forgotten that we were in the middle of a game and have disappeared.

"Sufiya, would you please untie my granddaughter. And then, Mehar, would you change and come downstairs? Naz and Aleena will be arriving any minute and your father wants you to be there to greet them."

She leaves and I turn to Sufiya with a grimace as she takes the chiffon shackles off my wrists. Her cardamon-scented breath tickles the tiny hairs on my forehead as she concentrates on the knot that seems to be reluctant to come undone. I feel a tiny shiver going up and down my spine at the feel of her fingers on my skin, and I hold myself perfectly still so that she can't tell the effect her proximity is having on me. *Get a grip, Mehar. Don't make things weird.*

She looks up at me with an apologetic smile and our eyes lock. Her lips quiver the tiniest bit and then she bends to undo the knot with her teeth. Her lips touch the tender skin on the inside of my wrist and I suck in a sharp breath. She's still trying to undo the knot and I'm still trying to hold it together. I'm very glad that I'm sitting and not standing because my knees are weak and my upper lip has beads of sweat on it.

"Oof, finally," she says, straightening herself with a triumphant smile. "I think I accidentally double-knotted it."

"Oh," I say, feeling completely idiotic. "Thank you. Well, I suppose I should go downstairs now. Do I really have to see them?"

"I don't think you have a choice," she says. "But I can help you pick out an outfit."

I look down at the ripped jeans and RBG T-shirt I'm currently wearing.

"Nah, I'm good. This is fine."

Sufiya's eyebrows go up slightly, but she doesn't say anything. I leave the room before I do or say anything stupid.

Dad is waiting for me by the private entrance, but I don't see Dadi anywhere. Not fair. She can avoid them, but I have to stand here in a receiving line for them? Whatever.

I see the look on Dad's face when he sees what I'm wearing and I can tell he's not pleased. Fortunately, he doesn't get a chance to say anything because a car is already pulling up. I take a deep breath, ignoring the gross feeling in the pit of my stomach, and plaster on a polite smile.

The doorman rushes to open the back door as soon as the car stops in front of us. Naz emerges, dressed in a long beige silk embroidered kurta with flowing pants and strappy high heels. She looks gorgeous, like the stars of the few Bollywood films I've watched.

Dad holds out his arms and they share a quick embrace.

"Assalamu alaikum, Aunty," I say. "It's very nice to see you again."

"Walaikum assalaam," she replies. "And please . . . you can call me Ammi or Mummy."

Over my dead body.

"Aleena calls your father Daddy," she adds, as if this is somehow a selling point. "It's so wonderful to see you again," she says. Speaking of Aleena, she finally emerges from the vehicle, phone in one hand, still in a conversation with someone.

"Aleena, darling, don't be rude," Naz calls out to her. "Come and say hello to your sister."

Barf. This would be a great time for an asteroid to fall from the sky. Unfortunately, no natural disaster comes to my rescue. Aleena finishes her call as she comes to the door. She's wearing a version of a kameez with a churidar, no doubt made especially for her by some famous designer. She looks like she's just stepped off a photo shoot and I immediately regret not changing into something nicer.

"Oh, hi, Mehar," she gushes as if she's overjoyed to see me. "Did you wake up early just for us. So sweet of you." She leans into Dad and I clench and unclench my fists a couple of times to avoid violence.

"I would never miss an opportunity to see you," I say, contorting my mouth into a smile. My face is hurting, but I have no choice.

"Well, why don't we all go in and enjoy the delicious lunch that's waiting for us," Dad says.

We all take our seats at the dining table. Jameela walks in with a jug of ice water and as she walks around the table filling everyone's glasses, I notice Aleena smiling and saying something to her in a soft tone. Jameela replies with a warm smile of her own. What's that all about? No one else seems to notice so I guess I'll just have to keep wondering. Dad and Naz sit at opposite ends of the table. I fold and unfold a napkin a few times before Naz pipes up.

"Mehar, tell us, how are you enjoying Agra so far?" She delicately pops a tiny piece of chicken in her mouth and puts down her fork and knife as if she's done with lunch.

"I haven't had a chance to see much of it yet. I've been helping Dadi with the wedding preparations."

"Yes, of course," she says. "I can't wait to see what you've done."

"And of course Aleena can help too," Dad says.

Oh joy. I glance over at Aleena, who's toying with a piece of cucumber on her plate.

"Actually, Sufiya's been helping and Dadi says she likes everything the way it is now, so there's really no need."

"Who is Sufiya?" Naz's eyes dart between me and Dad.

"She's Dadi's assistant," I reply.

"Oh, that mousy girl," Naz says dismissively. "But I'm sure we want this wedding to be most elegant, don't we, Reza?"

"I'm sure Mehar and—"

"Don't worry, Ammi," Aleena cuts off Dad mid-sentence. "I'll make sure everything is just how you like it."

I swear to god, if she does anything, I will punch her stupid face. And who does she think she is, being rude to Dad like that. Azra Aunty was right; Dad is letting them walk all over him. Well, not anymore.

"Actually," I say, "there are a lot of other things we could use your help on, since Dadi has already approved the decorations."

She doesn't reply, stabbing a tiny chunk of tomato with her fork instead.

"Well, I'm sure you two will figure it out," Dad says.

"Mehar, tell me a little bit about yourself. What are your plans for college?" Naz says.

I really don't want to talk about any of my plans with her. "Um, I haven't decided quite yet."

"Oh, I see," she says. "Well, do you have your top three figured out yet?"

I know she's trying to be polite, but I'm not in the mood.

"No, not yet." I haven't had a chance to eat more than a few bites since the interrogation started, so I focus on my food, hoping desperately that Naz will move on.

Thankfully Aleena monopolizes the conversation for the rest of the meal, regaling us with stories of all the cool parties she's been attending. It feels like hours later when I finally get a chance to escape and make my way to the library, which, thankfully, is no longer locked these days. Sufiya must have said something to Dadi. It turns out this is where I love to hang out, not just because it happens to be Sufiya's favorite room as well, although that is definitely a bonus. I'm not used to being around so many people all the time, so I like coming here to reflect and also to read. Today I pick up a book about Razia Sultana, the first and only female Muslim ruler of Delhi in the thirteenth century. I'm completely immersed in fascinating accounts of her rise to power and prowess in the battlefield, so I'm startled when Sufiya suddenly appears before me.

"Hey, I didn't hear you come in," I say, smiling up at her.

"I came to see how it all went earlier," she says, sitting down on the sofa next to me.

"Ugh, don't ask."

"That bad, huh?"

"It was horrible. I really can't stand them, especially Aleena. She's such a show-off. I had to bite my tongue so much the whole time. Please applaud me."

Sufiya claps slowly, grinning at me. "I'm very proud of you."

"Thank you. I deserve a medal."

"Actually, I have something to tell you."

"Okay," I say slowly.

"Your grandmother wants to throw you a welcome dinner."

"Like with the family?"

"Yes, but with your whole extended family," she says. "I'm not supposed to mention it, because she wants it to be a surprise. But I thought you'd want to know. It's going to be huge."

"Oh my god, I have nothing to wear."

"That's exactly why I told you."

"Will you help me pick something to wear?" I ask her. "Please?"

She smiles at me. "Of course, I'd love to. But just so you know, my taste might be a little . . . you know, pedestrian for this kind of party."

"Pfft, I don't care what a bunch of rich old people think about my outfit." I love the way she dresses and how she looks nice in whatever she's wearing.

"Still, you might want to get Aleena's stamp of approval," she says.

"Yeah right, like I give a rat's ass what she thinks. Of all people, hah."

"I'm just saying." She plays with the ends of her braid, and I remember the comment Naz made when she heard that Sufiya was helping with the decorations. I guess some people only judge others by how rich they are, and clearly Naz and Aleena are those people. Well, I'm not going to let them put Sufiya down or anything. At least not while I'm still here.

"Well, it's my outfit and my welcome party and I want you to help me pick out an outfit. So I hope you're ready to spend a lot of time with me because I suck at making decisions."

"It's really not a problem," she says.

"Thank you." I throw my arms around her. "You're a lifesaver."

"I like hanging out with you." She smiles shyly but makes no attempt to move away.

Something in the air changes. I pull back a little to look at her face and when our eyes meet, she doesn't look away. Instead she draws me even closer and I know something magical is about to happen, but then a flicker of movement by the window catches my eye and I let out a high-pitched scream.

"What the—"

Sufiya jumps away from me, her eyes wide with confusion as I point wordlessly to the open window. She looks toward where I'm pointing and lets out a loud groan. "Oh no, not again."

A monkey is peering at us through the window, its eyes darting back and forth. I run around the room flailing my arms as we figure out what to do. The monkey, seemingly stunned by my screams, has moved back a little bit and Sufiya goes to the window and quickly shuts it.

"Do you think it escaped from the zoo?"

Sufiya shakes her head. "These guys are a huge menace here. They've always been around, but lately it's been getting worse."

"He looks so adorable," I say. The monkey is back now, peering at us through the glass. "Maybe he's hungry. Can we give him some food?"

"Absolutely not," Sufiya says, grabbing her phone off the table. She speaks to someone in rapid-fire Urdu. "Someone will be here to take care of it."

"What do you mean, take care of it?" I say, utterly horrified. "They won't hurt it, will they?"

"No, no, of course not. They'll just take it and release it somewhere farther away from the city. They can be quite aggressive, especially when there are a lot of people around, and we can't exactly have the wedding guests be accosted by monkeys."

"No, you're right. That would be bad." Just my luck to have a potential first kiss be ruined by a monkey. I couldn't make this shit up even if I wanted to. The monkey has disappeared and we stand in awkward silence. Then the clatter of heels comes from down the hallway, the door opens, and Aleena waltzes in. This is just perfect.

"Oh, am I interrupting anything?" she says, her eyes darting from me to Sufiya.

"No, not really, we were just monkeying around," I say as casually as I can. Sufiya lets out a little snort and Aleena looks utterly confused. "Were you hoping to find a wedding magazine? I don't think there are any of those here."

She gives me a sharp look. "Well, people don't always come in here to read."

"So what're you doing here?" I say.

"I was looking for you," she says. "Just wanted to know if you still needed help with the preparations."

Oh great, she was actually listening to me at lunch?

"No we're good, actually, but thanks." I look over at Sufiya, who is trying unsuccessfully to blend into the bookshelves. "We don't need her help, do we?"

Sufiya shakes her head in response but doesn't say anything.

"Okay, then I guess I'm done here," Aleena says. She shoots Sufiya a cursory glance before turning and walking out the door.

"I think I should leave," Sufiya says as soon as Aleena is gone. My elation from moments ago dissipates.

I try not to let my disappointment show, but I wish Sufiya would stay so we could talk or something. I hate that the day is ending like this, but there's nothing I can say or do to stop her without making things incredibly awkward. And so I watch her leave and collapse on the seat by the window to figure out what my next move is going to be.

CHAPTER SIXTEEN

Dadi is too excited about the dinner party she's planning and spoils her own surprise. I think it's sweet of her to make such a fuss over me. She claims it's only family and close friends, but I'm fairly sure that will still amount to a pretty big party. I've tried to raise the point that I'll be meeting everyone at the wedding, but she insists she wants to do this so I can spend time with the people she's closest to. So, I've spent all morning in my room, trying to come up with an appropriate outfit, but it looks like a trip to the mall is inevitable. Sufiya couldn't be here to help since Dadi has her busy with work, so I'm on my own for now. At least my suitcases have finally been found and delivered. Seeing my old familiar clothes is making me all emotional for some reason. They remind me of my real life and also that I'm only here for three more weeks. That suddenly seems like too little time to get to know Sufiya the way I want to.

Several hours later, I'm coming down for lunch, and as usual at least a dozen voices filter out of the dining room. I'm almost by the door when I see her. Aleena. Ugh. I freeze and immediately flatten myself against the wall, hoping that no one has spotted me. No one's out here except for Bilquis and Jameela They throw me strange looks but are too busy getting lunch set up. Unfortunately for me, it seems that Asha, Usha, Nisha, and Taimur can smell me coming from a distance and they come running, screeching like baby dinosaurs. They drag me by my arms right into the dining room and I'm face-to-face with Aleena. She gives the kids a look of extreme annoyance before bestowing her judgment on me. She actually looks me up and down, scrunching her nose at my outfit. I'm in my usual ripped jeans and a plain black T-shirt, no makeup or jewelry, and judging by the expression on her face, I've clearly broken some sort of universal rule. I've been wearing this outfit all day and so far have only elicited a raised eyebrow from Dadi and a genuine offer from Bilquis to mend the holes in my jeans. And I'm pretty sure I heard one of the maids murmur that they thought Americans were rich.

"Hello," I say with as much coolness as I can muster. "How are you?"

Today she's stunning once again in a pair of unripped skinny dark jeans and a teal silk blouse. And she's wearing strappy heels inside the house. Rude! She has her back to Dadi, but I can clearly see the expression on my grandmother's face. We exchange a look and there's no need for words. Dadi hates her. I smile at her, but Aleena thinks the smile is meant for her and flashes her perfect white teeth at me.

"Have you heard the good news?" she says with barely concealed excitement. "It looks like we're going shopping."

"We are?" I look around in confusion and see Dad smiling beatifically at us. *Oh no. What have you done, Dad?*

"I thought you might like something special for your party," he says. "And who better to take you than our very own fashionista?"

I can think of at least a dozen other people I'd like to go with. Attila the Hun or Genghis Khan come to mind. Anyone but her.

"Actually, I've already asked Sufiya to help me pick something, so I'm good, but thank you," I say.

"Sufiya?" Aleena gives a little laugh. "I don't think she's the best person for this."

"What's that supposed to mean?" I narrow my eyes at her. "Do you think—"

"She just means that with her connections, it will be easier to get something custom-made, beta," Dad says hastily before I can finish my sentence. It's probably a good thing too, because I wasn't exactly going to say anything polite.

"I don't need anything custom-made, Dad," I say.

"But it would be nice, no?" he says. "After all, your dadi is going to all the trouble of having a party especially for you."

Well, there's not much more I can say now, is there? At least not without appearing ungrateful and spoiled. Maybe it won't be that bad. Maybe I should stop lying to myself.

• • •

It turns out that it was worse than I thought. I figured at most I'd have to spend a couple of hours at some mall in downtown Agra, where I would select a suitable gharara or shalwar suit. But no, since Aleena of course doesn't buy off the rack, why did I think she would even consider that other people might be totally fine with it? She suggested dragging us all the way to Delhi tomorrow so that one of her favorite designers could make an outfit just for me. But I quickly squashed that ludicrous plan. Instead we're looking at outfits online so that she can put her stamp of approval on my choices beforehand. Not that anyone asked for her opinion, but she insisted.

"Let's keep looking," she says, scrunching her perfect nose at the outfit I've just shown her on a local boutique's website. "We should check out all the options before we pick. There are going to be a lot of important people at this party."

"I thought Dadi said it'll just be family and friends."

"Yes, your grandmother's friends are very important people," Aleena says. "There are quite a few dignitaries and celebrities on the guest list."

"Oh . . . I had no idea." I should have known. From what Sufiya's told me about Dadi, it seems that she is very well-connected. But I thought that was mostly for her work, not that she would invite people from those circles to a dinner party for me. Maybe it's not such a bad thing that I'm stuck shopping with Aleena for this party. Sufiya and I would have liked the same outfits, I'm sure, but our taste is definitely too basic for the kind of guests who seem to have been invited for my welcome dinner. The last thing I want to do is embarrass Dad and Dadi in front of all their fancy friends.

• • •

"Do you feel like taking a walk?" I find Dadi in her office after Aleena has left in somewhat of a huff because I didn't like any of the outfits she picked out and she didn't even bother trying to hide her disdain for my choices. I'm glad it's Sufiya's day off so she didn't see us looking for outfits. I haven't had a chance to tell her yet that I've been bulldozed into letting Aleena pick something for me to wear.

Dadi's face lights up. "Yes, beta, that is an excellent idea. Let's go to the garden."

Dadi and I walk slowly toward the long hallway that leads

outside. The walls of the hallway are adorned with paintings of men and women dressed in elaborate attire and Dadi names them as we walk by.

I listen with rapt attention as she points out several of our ancestors with rich details, and I'm in awe of her ability to keep so many details in her head. But more importantly, I'm beginning to feel a sense of pride in my heritage, in my ancestors' constant pursuit of a better life and their colorful history. I realize that I come from a long line of warriors and rebels who fought for their country and tried to uplift its citizens.

We haven't even reached the end of the long hallway when Dadi starts to lean against me more heavily and I realize that it's time to cut this walk short and take her back to her room.

"I'm completely fine, Mehar," she insists when I try to convince her to go back.

"Dadijaan, I'm not going anywhere," I say. "We can continue this another time."

"I'll feel better once I have some fresh air," she says. She allows me to start walking her toward the door. "I just want to make sure that you know all about our family's history," she says. "If you don't know where you came from, how will you know where you're going?"

"I do want to know all of it, Dadi." I'm not even saying this just to appease her. I really want to know because for the first time in my life, I feel that I'm connected to something much bigger than just me and Mom and Dad. There are lifetimes' worth of stories I want to learn about, and tonight was just the beginning. I realize that somewhere between the day I received the wedding invitation and tonight, I've come to accept that I am a part of this illustrious family and that whatever happened between Mom and Dad is just a blip in the timeline.

We walk arm in arm to the French doors that lead to the outside. The heat is bearable even though my skin is sticky within minutes. We make our way to the pond, the date palms providing us shaded passage. I spot a couple of mynah birds on one of the many mango trees along the brick path that leads from the main house to the gardens. I swear if I sit here long enough, I might turn into a desi Snow White with all kinds of birds and other creatures sitting on my head. Much better than having to deal with Naz and Aleena all summer.

"Dadi, can I ask you something?"

"Can I stop you?"

Fair enough.

"How do you really feel about all this?"

"The wedding?"

I nod, stopping to look at the mynah birds that are directly above our heads now. They're beautiful, black with iridescent yellow-and-red plumage peeking out from underneath. Currently they're fighting over a single mango even though the tree is laden with them.

"There is no stopping it now, beta. All the preparations have started and everyone already knows. We have to make our peace with it."

CHAPTER SEVENTEEN

Everyone comes for dinner that night. Faiza Phuppi, her husband, Omar Phuppa, and Azra Aunty and her husband, Rafiq Uncle. Unfortunately for me, Naz and Aleena are there as well. I'm seated next to Naz and I wish I wasn't.

"Mehar beta, you must visit us at our home," she says. "We have an indoor pool and you can spend the day. My masseuse comes on Wednesdays and Saturdays and she gives the most divine massages."

"Thank you, Aunty, that's very nice of you." I smile at her.

"And Aleena was saying that she would love to introduce you to her friends, weren't you, beta?" She looks pointedly at Aleena and I can't help feeling sorry for the way Naz has just put her on the spot.

"Yes, of course. Actually my friend Tina is having a party next week," she says quickly. "It's totally casual . . . you should come."

"That's very nice of you, Aleena," I say, not knowing how to decline without being rude. Besides, it might be fun and she said it was going to be casual so I don't have to worry about what to wear. I can do casual.

I turn my attention back to the delectable coconut prawns and pulao on my plate. I've adjusted to the spice level of the food surprisingly quickly. For all my apprehension before the trip, I'm really enjoying myself. And I love that there's always someone to hang out with. Azra Aunty is frequently here with her kids, and sometimes other relatives drop in as is the norm here. The only thing that still bothers me is that Dad has not made much of an effort to spend time with me one-on-one. It's almost as if he makes sure that the few times he is around there's always someone else there. It's like he's actively avoiding being alone with me, and it hurts. A lot. But I'm going to try to stay positive. It's all I can do for now.

• • •

A few days later, Aleena and I are in the back seat of a vintage Rolls-Royce, which, according to her latest IG post, has historically been a favorite of India's maharajas. We are being chauffeured to Delhi, where we'll be attending a party thrown by Aleena's friend Tina. Compared with my rattly old truck back home in Newton, this is quite the cool ride. We make the four-hour drive into Delhi in a record three hours, even with Aleena stopping for roadside selfies a few times. Each time the caption reads *On the road with the foreign-returned Nawabzaadi of Agra* or *Me and my soon-to-be sis, Nawabzaadi Mehar Rabbani, on a road trip.*

The whole way there, I've been racking my brain, trying to figure her out. Something I hadn't realized before is that she's super polite to all the staff everywhere we go. But then whenever she talks to me or comments on social media posts, there's an undeniable snark and disdain in her tone. It's hard for me to tell who the real Aleena is, because she seems to switch quite effortlessly back and forth between the two. After watching her for some time now, seeing her flip-flop between being considerate and downright obnoxious, I'm finding it harder to pin down exactly who she is. She didn't have to bring me along to this party, and I was sure the other day at dinner she had just agreed to be polite. But sure enough, a couple of days later she messages me saying she's picking me up in two hours. A little more heads-up would have been nice since I had no idea what kind of a party this was. All she'd said was dress casual. So I met her at the entrance in my ripped jeans and a black top with short puffy sleeves and a lace back. I thought it was cute and casual, but when the car pulled up and I saw what she was wearing I almost turned around and went back in. But my ego wouldn't allow that so I slid into the back seat next to her and pretended that I wasn't bothered that she was wearing elegant flowy wide-legged pants and a beautiful silk blouse in a vibrant turquoise with long, dainty silver earrings and strappy stilettos. I looked like I was going out for burgers with my friends, while she looked like she was ready for dinner with a queen. I should have known she would try to show me up in front of her friends.

So here I am, alternating between stewing and being utterly confused by this annoying person who's about to become my sister. Why is this happening to me? The whole way to Delhi, I'm tempted to push her off every cliff we stop at for yet more selfies with a scenic backdrop. The only thing that stops me from losing my cool is venting to Norah in a series of furious texts that she won't see until several hours from now because of the ten-and-a-half-hour time difference.

It's early evening when we check into the Imperial, New Delhi. I'm not at all surprised by the familiarity with which she's greeted by the staff from the moment we enter. I'm surprised by how much it bothers me that Aleena is clearly much more suited to being the daughter of a nawab. She's completely at ease in this setting, whereas I've never even seen the inside of a luxurious five-star hotel room such as this one. She's obviously used to a life of opulence, and I'd be lying if I said I didn't feel a bit like a country bumpkin in the big city for the first time.

We freshen up and then it's time to go to the party. I'm expecting something lavish and over-the-top, so imagine my surprise when we pull up to a modest two-story house with several cars in the driveway. The front door is opened by a woman in a sari who ushers us in and leads us into the foyer. I look around and realize with a shock that this is definitely not what I was expecting.

"There you are." A young woman dressed in jeans and a black embroidered top greets us with a smile. "Aleena, looking fabulous as usual." She gives Aleena a hug and turns to me. "And you must be Mehar. I'm Tina."

"Thank you so much for letting me crash your party," I say, returning her warm hug.

"Of course, it's my pleasure. Aleena, you look so fancy, are you going somewhere else after this?"

Aleena looks a little flushed and for the first time since I've met her, I think she's embarrassed.

"So, how do you all know each other?" I ask.

"We used to go to the same school until four years ago," Tina said, leading us into the living room.

Everything here looks regular, like a normal house compared with the palace. It's pretty big and beautifully furnished, just not what I expected when Aleena said it was a friend's party. I expected a bunch of rich, fake people and a fancy mansion, but Tina seems really nice, as do the other people I meet through the course of the evening. I had hoped that seeing Aleena with her friends might help me figure her out but now I'm more perplexed than ever. Who is the real Aleena? And what kind of game is she playing with my father? What does he really know about her and Naz? I'm acutely aware of my own reluctance to talk to Dad about Aleena and Naz. I've been vacillating between wanting to fix things with him and telling him how I truly feel about his decision to marry Naz. Not that I've been doing a great job at hiding my disdain, but I think if Dad knew how much I actually hate this whole new family thing, it might just push him further away. And I don't think I'm quite ready to risk that yet. Especially not after tonight, seeing Aleena through a different lens.

We spend a few hours at the party before returning to our hotel room and I decide that it's time I gave her a chance.

"Hey, listen . . . thanks for taking me to your friend's party. I had a great time," I say. "I'm sure you'd rather be doing something else."

She looks at me for a long time before answering. "It's fine. I'm happy to do it." One side of her mouth curls up in a sort of smile. "After all, we're going to be sisters soon, right?"

"Right." I take a deep breath. Mom's always saying I need to stop being so quick to judge people. And Aleena is making an effort, so I should too. "So, since Dad and I sort of haven't been talking a lot before I came here, I feel like I barely know you."

"Why haven't you been talking to Daddy?" She looks up from slathering lotion on her legs. I can't stand that she calls him Daddy, but I push my irritation aside.

"He didn't like the guy I was dating."

"Oh." She continues to massage the lotion into her legs. "Well, I guess you're lucky, then."

"What do you mean?"

"At least he cares enough to worry."

I let out a deep sigh. She isn't going to make this easy.

"Yeah, I guess."

We don't say anything for a bit and it's starting to get uncomfortable.

"So what are your plans after high school?" I say. I hate that I sound like a total aunty, but I can't think of anything more riveting in this awkward moment.

"I plan to study fashion design," she says.

"That sounds perfect for you," I say with genuine enthusiasm. "Have you already applied to places?"

"I would love to go to France, but Ammi says I should go somewhere in the States."

"Have you ever been?" I ask, settling into bed.

"Yeah, I've been a couple of times," she says. "To LA and New York. I have family there."

"Is your dad there?" It's a shot in the dark, but I want to find out more.

But as soon as the words come out of my mouth, I wish they hadn't. A dark cloud has settled over her face and the openness from a second ago is completely gone.

"I'm sorry, I didn't mean—"

"It's fine, don't worry about it," she says quickly, turning away and fiddling with something on the nightstand.

I sit up to fluff my pillow. Maybe I should change the topic.

"So, how did your mom and my dad meet?"

Her eyes are closed and for a moment I think she's pretending to be asleep.

But then she turns to look at me. "Actually, I was the one who introduced them."

"Oh . . . I didn't know that. How did you know my dad?"

"We socialize in the same circles, so I've seen him at weddings and other functions, you know."

Not really.

"And so you decided to introduce your mother to him?"

"Yes, I figured they might have a lot in common."

It kind of makes sense. I mean, they do seem to travel in the same circles, and more than that, Dad looks so happy whenever Naz and Aleena are around. So, I guess I should be grateful that Aleena was responsible for that. Okay, maybe not grateful . . . I'm not that nice. And then there's that thing she said about me being lucky that I have a dad who cares enough to meddle. I hate to admit it, but now I feel like a bit of a jerk for being so suspicious of her without even giving her a chance. Maybe she just wanted to have a father figure in her life, and is that really such a terrible thing? I'm going to leave soon after the wedding and as it is, Dad and I aren't super close. We don't even live on the same continent. So if Aleena fills the huge daughter-shaped hole in his heart, who am I to deny him that joy?

I look over at her now, her face completely devoid of makeup, her hair pulled back from her face with an unassuming scrunchie, and she looks just like a regular girl. A girl I guess I could grow to like at some point, especially since she is going to be my sister soon. My stepsister. So, the question is, do I want to make an enemy out of her or try to build some kind of a relationship that will help me refrain from the desire to strangle her at least three times a day?

I turn over and go to sleep, determined to try harder with her.

CHAPTER EIGHTEEN

We have company and I've been summoned by Dadi. I find her in the drawing room, seated next to an elegant woman about Mom's age. Across from them is a young man who rises from his seat as soon as I enter.

"There you are, beta," Dadi says, her face breaking into a smile.

"Assalamu alaikum," I say to everyone in general.

"Mehar, this is Roshan Begum, a dear friend, and her son, Muzaffar," Dadi says. "He is here on summer vacation from Oxford University."

"It's very nice to meet you, Mehar," Roshan Begum says, patting the seat next to her. "Come and sit with me. Your dadi hasn't stopped talking about you."

I smile and go to sit next to her. "It's so nice to meet you too," I say.

"Tell me, Mehar, how are you liking Agra so far?" she says.

"I haven't actually had much of a chance to go around yet," I say. "Everything's been so busy with the wedding preparations."

"Well then, we must remedy that immediately," she says. "Muzaffar, beta, you must take Mehar and show her our beautiful city. She is our guest, after all."

Muzaffar has been minding his own business, smiling quietly this whole time, but now he nods. "Of course, it will be my pleasure," he says. "If Mehar is willing to have me as her tour guide, that is."

I hope I don't look as horrified as I feel right now. I have absolutely no desire to go gallivanting about town with a complete stranger. Plus, I can't be sure if he's just being polite or if he actually wants to show me around. But I don't want to insult Dadi's dear friend or seem ungracious. Aaaah!!

"That's very kind of you, but I wouldn't want to impose," I finally say, hoping they'll drop it.

Of course, I have no such luck, because Dadi pipes up. "Nonsense, beta. Roshan and Muzaffar are like family. No need for all this formality, hai na?" That last bit is addressed to Roshan Begum, who beams at Muzaffar and then at me.

Oh no. It never ends well when adults look at you the way these two are looking at us right now. There's no way for me to get out of this, so I guess I have a tour guide now.

Muzaffar is smiling now too. "Please, Mehar, I would be honored."

"Of course, that would be lovely," I say. How bad can it be? Maybe I'll come up with an excuse to get out of it later.

"And Sufiya will come with you as well," Dadi announces. "I will let her know."

Hmm, maybe I don't need to come up with an excuse after all.

The door opens and Aleena walks in. She teeters into the room on her five-inch heels and whatever fancy designer's outfit she has on, which looks absolutely fantastic on her, and stops right in front of Muzaffar, a slow smile spreading across her face.

"Hello, darling," she says, leaning into him for a hug. Apparently, the rest of us are completely invisible. Muzaffar returns her hug with obvious reluctance, but she seems blissfully unaware of this.

"Assalamu alaikum," she says to Roshan Begum and Dadi at the same time.

Begum Roshan mumbles a greeting and Dadi just moves her lips but doesn't make any actual sounds.

Aleena turns her eyes on me, acting surprised, as if I've just appeared out of thin air.

"Oh, you're here too," she says, an unexpected coolness in her tone. "It's nice to see you again."

Huh. I guess I'm the only one who thought of trying harder to have a better relationship. Why is she like this? Maybe she's embarrassed because she showed me a little bit of her real self? I haven't seen her since she took me to her friend's party. But after our conversation that night in the hotel, I thought things might be a little different between us. Maybe I'm being oversensitive. Or maybe she just hates me. Whatever. I'm done trying to be the mature one.

"Nice to see you too," I lie, kind of pissed off now. "Muzaffar was just offering to show me around Agra," I say, unable to hide my pettiness. Not that I'm really trying to.

"Oh?" Aleena's eyes dart from me to Muzaffar, who looks positively terrified. "When are you going? I suppose I can find time to join you."

Her self-confidence is mind-blowing. She must be super into this guy.

"No, no, Aleena," Dadi says before either one of us has a chance to respond. "You are so busy shopping for the wedding.

We couldn't possibly expect you to make time for this. They will be fine on their own, won't you?" She looks at Muzaffar and me for confirmation, and I don't know which one of us is nodding harder. Meanwhile Aleena is shooting daggers at me and simultaneously fake smiling at Muzaffar like her life depends on it. She's got mad social skills, I have to give her that.

"Well, okay, then, I won't feel so bad about not having any time to spend with poor Mehar at all," she says.

She did not just say that. Okay, lady. Game on.

"No, please don't feel bad," Dadi says. "We are all having the best time with Mehar. You just concentrate on all the shopping, my dear."

Aleena throws a murderous look in Dadi's direction before taking her leave. I'm not sure if it's wise to poke the bear, but I don't care. To be clear, the bear is Aleena. And by poking, I mean getting my flirt on with Muzaffar just to piss her off. This should be fun.

• • •

Sufiya and I are in the gardens again, watching the gorgeous sunset. The mynah birds are here too, and I swear it's the same couple that was fighting over a mango the last time. They seem to have a feud going or something.

"You have no idea that you've just made a mortal enemy out of Aleena, do you?" Sufiya says. Dadi's already told her about Muzaffar's offer to show me around Agra.

"Yeah, I think she was ready to murder me. Were she and Muzaffar ever a thing?"

"She certainly seems to think so." She puts a hand on my arm. "It was so nice knowing you," she adds with an evil grin.

"Shut up," I say, trying hard to ignore the warmth blooming where her fingers are touching my skin. "I didn't even ask him to do that. Dadi and his mom are up to something, I swear."

"His mother hates Aleena," Sufiya says. Much to my regret, she takes her hand off my arm. "Roshan Begum must have been overjoyed to meet you. She and Dadima are very close."

"I kind of got the feeling that they might be trying to set me up with that guy."

"Oh, they are. Absolutely." Sufiya seems to be enjoying this way too much.

"Now what am I supposed to do?" I'm starting to panic. This is not good at all.

"You don't have to do anything. At least you won't be alone with him. Dadima has asked me to chaperone the two of you."

"I know . . . but what if he thinks I'm interested? I don't want to encourage him. I mean, I just met him, but he seems like a nice guy. You should have seen his reaction when Aleena was throwing herself at him. It was like he couldn't get far away enough, but she stuck to him like a leech."

"Now imagine how much it would bug her to find out that you two are enjoying yourselves," Sufiya says.

I perk up immediately at that thought and Sufiya smiles.

"I knew that would make you happy." She grins at me. "See, I'm getting to know you pretty well, right?"

"Okay, fine, I'll go sightseeing with him, but you have to promise that you'll stick by me the whole time."

"I promise I'll be the pani to your puri."

"Huh?"

"You know . . . pani puri?" She raises her eyebrows.

"Ah . . . okay, I get it . . . good one. I hope you can visit me in Kansas one day soon. Then I'll take you sightseeing."

"Who's going to be our chaperone?" she says, her lips curling into a smile.

I don't say anything. Instead I just look into her eyes and wonder if she feels what I feel. I'm so afraid of scaring her off by saying too much and making things weird between us. I know things are very different here in Agra, in India, so I'm not sure how to let her know that I've been thinking about her day and night. I've been here for a week and a half, and I know that's not a long enough time to feel anything for anyone really. But I can't deny that I'm drawn to her in a way I haven't been to anyone since Ryan a year ago. It's not anything I can put my finger on, if anyone were to ask me what it is precisely that makes me feel this way. It's a combination of many things. Her softness—which masks her strength—the selflessness in her decisions, her devotion to my grandmother, and the way she always tries to make things easier for me and others. In such a short time I've come to respect the way she approaches situations that I myself would just barge into without much forethought. And then there's all the stuff we have in common, like our love for books and our disdain for people like Aleena. She wants to make the world a better place and she doesn't need a degree to do it. She just seems to do it effortlessly every day. And I love that about her. But I don't know if I can ever tell her any of this and that's killing me. I wish we could sit out here like this forever, but the mosquitoes and bats are out in full force and, regrettably, we have to make our way back inside.

Later that night I toss and turn in bed, trying to remind myself that I'm only here for a couple more weeks and the last thing I need is to complicate my life. But that night in my dreams, Sufiya and I are holding hands as we sit in the gardens of the Taj Mahal, admiring the epic monument to a love from centuries ago.

CHAPTER NINETEEN

We got an early start to the day so that we could see the Taj Mahal before it got flooded with tourists. Plus, apparently, the best time to watch it is at sunrise. It's barely light out when we arrive; the gates have just opened but there's already a line. Muzaffar asks me to hang back and steps into the line for Indian residents. There's a separate one for foreigners and the tickets are almost triple the cost, even though it's still ridiculously cheap in dollars.

"Why did he want us to wait here?" I ask Sufiya while we stand under a tree.

"They'll figure you out as a nonresident Indian in two seconds," she says. "Muzaffar could have arranged a private tour, but I think he wanted you to get the 'authentic experience,'" she adds, making air quotes.

"He seems nice enough," I say, watching as he steps up to the counter.

"He is. He comes to the mahal with his mother a lot. Dadima is very fond of him."

"I'm so glad you came today." I smile at her. "I don't think I could have lasted a whole day with just Muzaffar. It would have been so weird."

"Better me than Aleena, right?" she says with a grin. "It wouldn't be proper for the nawabzaadi to be seen in the company of a young man without a chaperone." She makes her voice deeper and puts on a ridiculous expression and I have an irrepressible urge to kiss her. I should get a medal for exercising this much self-control.

I wonder what Dadi would say if she knew that she's got the whole thing backward.

"Well, thank you for coming," I say. "I'm sure you have better things to do than chaperoning me, but I like hanging out with you. I don't know what I would have done these last couple of weeks if you weren't around."

Ugh. I sound like I'm talking to an aunty, not a girl I really like. Why do I have zero skills in the flirting department?

A slight blush creeps into Sufiya's cheeks and I immediately regret saying anything.

"I'm glad I came too," she says softly. "I told you I like hanging out with you."

I'm about to reply when I spot several men in the distance, their cameras pointed straight at us.

"Ugh . . . not again."

"What?" Sufiya looks at me, her eyebrows raised.

"It's those photographers again," I say. "There are three of them, right over there." I point in the direction I just saw them, but they seem to have disappeared. "Where'd they go? They were there a second ago."

"Over here, Nawabzaadi," someone calls out from behind me.

I jump a little and turn to see one of them approaching, slowly, with his camera held by his side.

"Madam, look over here, please," he said, waving his hand at me.

I don't get a chance to reply because Muzaffar is back with cold water bottles and some shoe covers. He immediately puts himself between us and the photographer.

"Sir, just one picture, please," the guy calls out.

Several others call out as well. Soon we're surrounded by at least six of them, with the crowd of onlookers growing bigger. A small wave of panic starts to rise in me, but then Sufiya grabs my hand and squeezes.

"It's okay, they just want a photo and then they'll leave us alone," she whispers.

"Madam . . . please, this way, idhar dekhiye," another man calls out. Then he points at Sufiya and motions for her to step aside. She pulls her hand out of mine slowly and steps away.

"Oh my god, that's so rude," I object, reaching out to pull her back to my side. But she shakes her head in warning and Muzaffar is calling my name and then all the voices start to blend and my head is spinning.

"Okay, thank you, everyone, please give us some room," Muzaffar says, his voice firm and authoritative, the way Aleena's was at the airport.

"What happened? Is it too hot for the nawabzaadi?" one of the men calls out in a jeering tone.

Another one joins him in derisive laughter. "She should go back to Amreeka," he says.

Muzaffar's jaw tightens and I can tell he's trying not to take the bait. I just want to get out of here. I don't care what these guys think about me. Besides, they were extremely rude to Sufiya.

Muzaffar and Sufiya guide me to a shady spot under a

gigantic tree, and after a few sips of the still-somewhat-cold water, I feel revived.

"I'm going to make sure that the press doesn't bother us anymore," Muzaffar says.

"It's fine," I say weakly, more embarrassed than anything else. "They have their pictures, so hopefully they're going to leave us alone now."

"Umm, no, they're not," Sufiya says. "They're relentless. Now that they've seen the two of you together, they won't let up until you've given them something juicy."

"What? No way." This is so annoying. Now I have to worry about being swarmed by reporters just because I'm here with Muzaffar?

"Aleena is going to be furious," Sufiya mumbles beside me. I look at her and she has this weird look of glee on her face. And just like that, something absolutely brilliant occurs to me.

I pull myself to my feet and lean against the tree for a second. Across the pathway, a little bit farther away from us, I can see that the number of men and women with cameras seems to have multiplied. Well, now I'm going to have to give them something to talk about, right?

I pull Muzaffar out from our little hiding place and march him straight into the center of the path so that the press have a clear view of us. Then I reach up with my hands to bring his face closer to mine and plant a big kiss right on his cheek. The expression on Muzaffar's face is a mix of utter confusion and shock. He seems to be rooted to the ground, but I'm ready to get away from the photographers, so I pull him as hard as I can and, with Sufiya following us, I start to walk to the main entrance.

Muzaffar is staring at me with his mouth slightly open.

"What was that all about?" he finally asks.

"Umm, I got them off our backs, didn't I? You're welcome."

He does not look impressed and neither does Sufiya. In fact, she looks like she might throw up.

"I don't think that was very smart, Mehar," she says, her tone extremely disapproving.

"Oh, come on, it was nothing," I say with a dismissive wave of my hands. "But can you imagine when Aleena sees these?" I cackle a little bit to myself.

"Yeah, that's not who I'm worried about," Muzaffar says.

"It'll be fine," I say. "You guys worry way too much. It's not like we made out or anything."

Sufiya and Muzaffar both turn beet red and I shake my head at them wordlessly as we walk on.

We put on our shoe covers and walk in through the massive arched gates. I've only seen pictures of the Taj Mahal and none of them even come close to doing it justice. There's a reason it's one of the New Seven Wonders of the World. The main building, the mausoleum, is made of ivory marble that reflects the hues of the sun. It is breathtaking and much larger than I expected. The central dome is majestic, there's no other word to describe it. It's surrounded by four smaller domes, and the symmetry and splendor are simply awe-inspiring. From the moment we entered the red sandstone gateway to the complex, I've been unable to speak coherently. There's something magical about this place, not just because of its history and the fact that it took almost twenty thousand men almost seventeen years to build it. It is truly the most magnificent structure I've ever seen.

I walk around the outside of the mausoleum for over an hour, admiring the Arabic calligraphy engraved on the marble facade, unable to stop marveling at the intricacy and perfection of the architecture. It's clear from the lack of noise, despite the great number of people, that I'm not the only one stunned into near silence. It's even quieter when we step inside to look at the octagonal marble chamber covered in carvings and semiprecious stones. The true sarcophagi lie beneath the tombs. I wander away from Muzaffar and inch slowly to where Sufiya is standing by an elaborately carved window. She hasn't noticed me sidling up to her and I watch the exquisiteness of her face in profile, the thick lashes framing her gorgeous eyes and her mouth relaxed with the hint of a smile, and I wonder if she's imagining us the way I do. I want so badly to reach out and hold her hand, lace my fingers through hers and just enjoy the beauty and atmosphere of this monument to love. Of course I don't do anything like that, and then she realizes I'm there and turns in my direction and I imagine that I can see in her eyes that she's thinking the same thing. But then I remind myself that it's all just wishful thinking on my part. A girl can dream, right?

Since there's no photography allowed inside, we go back out after a while to take a ton of pictures.

The love story behind the Taj Mahal is so heart-wrenching: the grieving emperor who wanted to dedicate a tomb worthy of his wife, whom he loved so dearly. It's all very moving, although it's a little bit weird because Muzaffar has decided to narrate everything, and I kind of wish he'd let me enjoy all this without talking into my ear the whole time. He seems to have gotten over his earlier embarrassment and, to be honest, I'm very relieved.

"So, how're you enjoying this historic monument to eternal love?" Sufiya asks, sidling up to me when Muzaffar finally excuses himself.

"Oh my god, please save me," I say dramatically, clutching her hands.

"What?" she says, looking wide-eyed at me. "You two make

such a cute couple. I can't wait to tell your grandmother. Or wait . . . I won't have to tell her because she'll see the pictures in the paper tomorrow. You're so dead."

"It's going to be fine," I say once again, but this time I start to feel a little nervous, thinking of Dadi's reaction. "But seriously, how do we lose him?"

"Umm, sorry, we don't," she says, turning down her mouth at the corners. "But . . . I do have an idea." She smiles mysteriously at me, saying nothing.

"Okay, so what is it?" I say impatiently. I can see Muzaffar approaching from a distance. "Hurry up and tell me. He's coming back."

"Meet me in the library later tomorrow evening," she says quickly, just as Muzaffar is upon us.

"So, what are we talking about?" he says cheerfully.

"I was just saying that you two must have come here a lot, right?" I say quickly.

"It doesn't matter how many times you've seen it," Muzaffar says. "It's still amazing every time."

"I feel like I'm seeing it for the first time again," Sufiya says. "Although it's been a few years since I've been here."

"I don't think I could ever get tired of seeing all this either."

"We can stay as long as you want," Muzaffar says.

"We should probably be heading out," I say, wiping the two beads of sweat that have formed on my forehead. "It's starting to get too hot."

"Of course, let's go and get some breakfast," he says, ushering us out through the gate to his car, where the chauffeur is waiting.

"Shall we go to the Taj Bano?" Sufiya suggests. "I think Mehar would really enjoy it."

"Yes, that's an excellent idea," Muzaffar says, turning to instruct the driver to take us there.

Soon we're sitting in the cool interior of the dining area of the Taj Hotel. I'm starving, so after we fill up our plates at the breakfast buffet we settle into our chairs and dig in. I'm starving but also dying to find out more about Aleena's father.

"Muzaffar, have you known Aleena for long?" I ask after I've devoured my omelet. Unfortunately, Muzaffar has just taken a bite of his dosa and it seems to have gone down the wrong way at my mention of Aleena because he's sputtering and coughing. I gently smack him on the back until he can speak again.

"I've known her for a while actually," he says, his eyes watering a little from his near-death experience. "We went to high school together in Ooty. But that was before her dad . . ."

"What happened to her dad?"

Muzaffar hesitates. "I don't know if I should be talking about her like this," he says. "After all, you two are going to be sisters soon."

I make a face and Muzaffar looks at me with concern.

"Are you okay?" he says.

"I'm fine. But could you tell me more about her dad?" I plead.

"Well, I guess it's okay—it's not really a secret." He takes a long sip of water. "He left when Aleena was thirteen. Aleena and I used to be friends, but then she left that semester and never came back. The next time I saw her was just a few months ago after your dad and her mom got engaged."

"Do you know why he left?"

"I don't know if you know this, but her mom is actually from a very prominent and wealthy family. But they didn't approve of Aleena's father when she married him, and everyone says he only married her for her money and took a lot of it when he left."

"Huh." That feeling I had in the hotel room that night comes back. I do not like this one bit. I don't want to get all mushy about her past and feel bad for her because after the way she acted last night when Muzaffar and his mom were over, I don't know what to make of her at all. But I do know that I want to find out as much as I can about her from Muzaffar. Just in case.

"So, you don't know what Aleena's been up to for all these years?"

He shrugs. "I wasn't in touch with her, but I heard things."

"What kind of things?"

"Just that she has a way of attaching herself to certain kinds of people."

"Yeah, I saw how she was trying to attach herself to you," I blurt out.

Muzaffar turns slightly red. "I'm not interested in her like that at all."

I grin at him. "I could tell."

"I was quite worried that she would accompany us today. I was so relieved when Dadima nipped that in the bud."

"Aww . . . you call my grandmother Dadima too. That's so sweet."

"Well, she's always been so loving to me," Muzaffar says. "I've known her all my life."

"She always speaks about you with a lot of affection," Sufiya says to Muzaffar with a smile.

"I've spent a lot of time at the mahal," he says. "It's like my second home."

I can't help it, but hearing them talk about Dadi like this fills me with regret that I haven't had any kind of relationship with her over the years. So, I decide to change the subject.

"I saw a billboard earlier about some kind of a show about

the Taj Mahal. Do you think we could watch that sometime?"

Muzaffar pulls out his phone. "I read your mind," he says with a smile, showing me three electronic tickets for the show later on today.

"I'm so excited." I'm starting to like Muzaffar a lot, and this outing is turning out to be way better than I anticipated.

We spend the rest of the day seeing the tomb of Itimad-ud-Daulah and wandering through the beautiful, lush gardens designed by Mumtaz Mahal herself. We get more food after we've seen all the structures and then it's time for the show. It's a stunning dance and light show with exceptional music, and it's the perfect way to end the day. I've even forgotten all about Aleena, but that joy is short-lived.

When we get home, she's lounging on the ornate sofa in yet another expensive-looking silk outfit. My earlier pangs of sympathy after hearing about her father dissipate instantly as she throws me a look of derision. She's clearly not happy that I've spent the day with Muzaffar. Oh well. Also, does she ever just chill in regular-people clothes? Or go home?

"Muzaffar, beta, you must stay and have some gajar ka halwa and tea," Dadi says.

"Of course; how can I refuse such a tantalizing offer?" Muzaffar replies.

Aleena peels herself languidly from the sofa and comes to sit next to Muzaffar. Anyone with eyes can tell from his body language that he isn't comfortable with her being so close. Anyone but her.

"I'm sorry I couldn't make it today," she says, pouting at Muzaffar. "I hope you still had fun."

I put my arms around Dadi. "We had so much fun," I say. "Muzaffar and Sufiya are great tour guides."

Dadi kisses my cheek. "I'm so happy that you enjoyed yourself."

I look directly at Aleena, calmly break off a piece of halwa, and pop it in my mouth, chewing it slowly, savoring its sweetness and the sour looks Aleena is throwing my way.

Dadi turns to Sufiya. "Thank you so much for accompanying Mehar. Please stay for some dessert if you like."

"Thank you, but I should be getting back," Sufiya replies. "It's already late and I have an early morning tomorrow."

"Ah yes, we have that meeting with the board of directors," Dadi says. "Please make sure the driver takes you home. I don't want you out there alone at this time."

I'm not thrilled that Sufiya can't stay, and an annoying voice in my head reminds me that she probably only came on her day off at my grandmother's request. Maybe I'm reading way too much into our interactions. She seems to enjoy hanging out, but I'm starting to think that to her, it might just be a part of her job. I could have sworn I felt something between us, though. I know it's only been two weeks, but then again . . . I can't be sure of anything really. And I only have two more weeks to figure things out. I mean, people act differently here and I just can't read them the way I do back home in Kansas. Maybe Sufiya's behavior is more about politeness and duty than any chemistry I might be imagining. I'm so confused and annoyed at myself for feeling this way.

I tap into my evil side and take this opportunity to sidle up to Muzaffar and sit very close to him, just to get under Aleena's skin. I can feel her eyes shooting daggers at me as I throw my head back and laugh at something Muzaffar said. He's not that funny and I'm not really listening, but seeing Aleena get all worked up is worth a few fake laughs.

"I had a great time today," Muzaffar says, offering me a bowl of rasmalai.

I take it from him with a smile. "Thank you, rasmalai is my favorite. And I had a great time too."

"We should do this again soon," Muzaffar says. "I'd love to show you around the city."

Aleena looks up from her phone and practically jumps over the sofa to stand next to us.

"Muzaffar, I was hoping you'd come with me to Arif's party next week," she says. "You know how it is when I show up alone." She turns to me. "Guys are constantly hitting on me if I don't have someone with me."

"That must be so hard," I say. "But Muzaffar has promised to show me around, so he's going to be pretty busy next week, right?" I turn to him and bat my eyelashes. But I think I may have gone overboard on the mascara this morning because my top and bottom eyelashes get stuck and I have to disentangle them with my fingers while Muzaffar and Aleena look on. Not my proudest moment.

"Yes, I'm so sorry, Aleena, but I already promised Mehar I'd hang out with her and she's only here for a couple more weeks."

Aleena gives him a dangerously sweet smile and walks away. I'm scared for Muzaffar but I'm enjoying myself too much at this point. This will teach Aleena to be snooty with me even though I was making an effort to be nice. At least in my head.

Hours later, Aleena and Muzaffar have left and I find myself tossing and turning in bed. My thoughts keep coming back to Sufiya and the possibility of her having any feelings for me. I know this is going to bother me until I get some clarity, so I decide to text her.

Hey you still up?

A few minutes go by and I'm starting to wonder if I made a mistake texting her at all. I'm convinced now that I've misread her friendliness completely. I mean, she was just following Dadi's request to entertain me while they were busy. I thought I felt a connection while we hung out helping with the wedding preparations, bonding over our mutual dislike of Aleena, and then all day today, but maybe for her that was all just part of her job. I feel a knot forming in my stomach as I close my eyes and try to go to sleep, mortified because now I'm sure I've made things totally weird between us. After what feels like hours, I finally hear a ding. I snatch my phone off the nightstand.

Sorry, my phone died. What's up?

I'm sorry, I shouldn't have bothered you so late at night.

The dots appear, indicating that she's typing a response. I've never hated the slow passage of time this much.

It's no bother.

I can't tell if she's just being polite or if she's glad I texted. I wish Norah were here. She'd know exactly what to do.

It's okay, it's late. I'll let you go to sleep now. Good night

Okay, then. Good night.

CHAPTER TWENTY

I'm not sure when I finally fell asleep, but I wake up feeling horrible. I have a crick in my neck and my arm is numb. I drag myself downstairs, and to my relief the dining room is empty. I don't have the bandwidth to deal with any other surprises Dad or Dadi might have in store.

I'm taking my last sip of coffee, trying not to move my neck and generally bemoaning my current state.

"Good morning."

I whip my head around at the sound of Sufiya's voice. "Owwww." My eyes tear up from the pain in my neck.

Sufiya hurries to my side, looking alarmed. "What happened? Are you okay?"

"I slept funny, that's all," I say while simultaneously rubbing my neck.

"Here, let me." Sufiya digs around in her purse and produces a tiny container. She takes off the lid and dips her finger in the contents. "Tiger balm," she announces, placing her hands gently on my neck. As she begins to massage it, I let out a groan because it feels incredible.

"Wow, you're very good at this," I say. My cheeks are burning as I suppress another groan because I'm pretty sure this whole scenario is quickly becoming extremely awkward. And the last thing I want is to make her uncomfortable.

"I do this for Dadima all the time," she says, really digging in.

Awesome. Now she thinks I'm just like my seventy-five-year-old grandmother.

"I think I'm good, thank you. It feels so much better now."

She stops and looks at me closely. "Are you sure?"

"Yes, thank you so much."

"I'm just going to wash my hands and then I'll be right back."

"No, that's okay," I say quickly. "I'm sure you have work to do."

She looks at me and I can tell she's confused by my abrupt tone. I didn't mean for the words to come out the way they did, but it's done now.

"I don't mind . . ." She starts to leave, then seems to change her mind. "Why did you text me last night?

"Oh, I'm sorry about that." I study my toes intently. "I shouldn't have bothered you."

"Please stop saying that," she says. "You're not bothering me."

I look up at her, debating whether I should speak my mind or just let this go. But then again, I've never been good at letting things go.

"I, um . . . I was just thinking that maybe you've only been hanging out with me because Dadi asked you to." There. I said it, and now I'm watching her expression closely to see if I'm right.

But she's smiling at me. That's a good sign. Or maybe she's going to tell me that she was only doing her job. For the love of god, say something.

"You're funny," she says, coming back toward me. "I *have* been hanging around because Dadima asked me to."

I knew it. My cheeks are on fire again because now she knows I've been thinking about her and she probably feels sorry for me.

"Well, I—"

"But that's not the *only* reason." She has this look in her eyes that I can't describe, but it makes me all warm inside. "So, do you want to do something fun?" she says.

"Always." I try to sound casual, but on the inside I'm a mess. Why is it so hard to figure her out?

"Okay, good, but you can't tell anyone, because technically it's not allowed."

A small bubble of excitement forms in the pit of my stomach.

"Umm, are you going to tell me what it is?"

"No, I don't think so." She bites her lower lip. "I think I'd prefer it to be a surprise."

"Oh . . . okay." I shrug. "I guess I'm going to have to trust you, then."

"You don't sound sure." She studies me for a minute. "We don't have to do it if you're not comfortable."

"No, no, it sounds great," I say quickly. Clearly my grandmother did not put her up to this, so there's hope for me.

"Okay, then meet me by the front entrance at seven p.m. tonight," she says.

"See you at seven."

Footsteps approach the library and the door opens. It's Bilquis.

"Nawab Saheb is asking for you," she says in Urdu.

I haven't spent a lot of alone time with Dad since our last heated conversation. He's been away a lot, and if it wasn't for Sufiya and Dadi, I would really be considering cutting my trip short since he isn't around that much anyway. As usual. Nothing new here. I wonder what he wants now.

I go to find him in his office and he's there seated behind his desk with Aleena perched on a corner of it looking disturbingly smug while simultaneously shooting daggers at me with her eyes. What fresh hell is this?

"Sit down, Mehar," Dad says. He sounds pissed, so I must have screwed up royally this time.

I pull out a heavy chair and Aleena sticks her phone in my face.

"This posted last night," she announces.

I look down at the screen. There I am in broad daylight with the Taj Mahal behind me, kissing Muzaffar on the cheek, surrounded by dozens of photographers and general gawkers. I've really done it this time.

"Can you explain this behavior, Mehar?" Dad's face is like stone, and I am all too familiar with this expression of his disappointment in me.

"It was just a joke, Dad," I say, trying my best to sound casual. Never show weakness to your enemy. The enemy in this case being Aleena, not Dad. The smug look of satisfaction on her face is enough to make me reckless, even knowing that this little stunt will cost Dad a lot of embarrassment.

"You think this is funny?" He stands and begins to pace. Again, familiar. "Do you have any idea what people will be saying? And what about Muzaffar and poor Roshan Begum?"

He shakes his head as if he doesn't know what to do with me. Just like when I was ten. And twelve. And seventeen. He's never known what to do with me. Or even really seen me. That can't be right, can it? That he's more concerned with what people will say than with what I'm feeling? And then there's Aleena, his perfect little soon-to-be daughter, sucking up to him like she's going to get a medal for her performance. I guess she is, in a way. My father. And a place in his family. That's her medal. I don't think I've hated anyone as much as I hate Aleena at this very moment.

"Dad, why is this such a big deal? Muzaffar's my friend. I was simply showing him how grateful I was that he took time out to take me around. I thought you all wanted us to like each other. So what's the problem?"

He stares at me, dumbfounded. "What's the problem, she says." Now he's muttering to himself. This is new. I must have hit a completely new level in frustrating him.

I take a deep breath and release it slowly. "Look, I'm sorry if I embarrassed you yet again," I say. "At least I'm consistent." And with that I turn around and leave the office. I've only gotten halfway down the hall when I hear rapid footsteps behind me. It's Dad. He grabs my arm to stop me.

"Mehar beta . . . please wait," he says. "I'm sorry."

"For what?" I'm surprised but not ready to let him off the hook.

"Look, I shouldn't have gotten so upset about that photo." He lets go of my arm, brings his hand to his temple and rubs it. "I need to stop caring about what people think . . . and worrying more about what you think."

Okay, now we're getting somewhere. I still don't say anything. Let him stew for a bit longer.

"I'm also sorry that I haven't been around much. There's been so much going on with work, it's been hard to make time."

"You don't seem to have any trouble making time for Aleena," I say, hating how my voice sounds so small. The truth is, I was not prepared for him to apologize. At all. It's never happened before.

"Beta, I invited you here because I wanted to . . . I don't know what I wanted." He sighs and runs his fingers through his hair.

"I'm still here for two more weeks," I remind him.

He smiles. "Yes, you are. And I promise I will make time for you."

I guess that's the best I'm going to get out of him. A promise. I think I'll take it. Baby steps. Dad moves in for a hug and from under his arm I see Aleena watching us from the office door. I can't tell what she's thinking, but I know that maybe I need to stop playing with Muzaffar. I wouldn't want to take my mind games with Aleena too far.

CHAPTER TWENTY-ONE

We're finally alone, Sufiya and I. Well, as alone as one can be here. The driver is taking us to Church Road Mall, which apparently has the best glass bangles in all of Agra. At least that's what Sufiya told Dadi. Is this the surprise? I'm confused. Why does buying bangles have to be so secretive? Not that I'm complaining because I'm happy to do anything as long as I get to do it with her.

But once we're there we ditch the driver, and Sufiya leads me back outside. There, she hails a rickshaw and asks the driver to take us to Dussehra Ghat, a pier on the banks of the Yamuna River.

"Are you going to tell me where we're going?" I say, one hand clutching Sufiya's sleeve so that I don't go flying off the rickshaw as it hits yet another pothole. I can barely contain my excitement.

She turns to me and smiles mysteriously. Then she slides an arm around my waist and my heartbeat quickens to an alarming level.

"Don't worry," she whispers, her warm breath tickling my face. "I won't let you fall."

I'm afraid to move because the tingling in my belly is agonizingly delicious.

Finally we arrive at Dussehra Ghat. There are only a few people around, three couples and a family with two little kids.

Sufiya leans in. "We're going to go on a river cruise. It'll take us behind the Taj Mahal." She's looking deep into my eyes and the sweetness in her smile is like warm syrup running through my veins.

"Why all the secrecy?" I ask.

"It's technically illegal to do this, but everyone does," she says.

"So, you're turning me into a criminal?" I grin at her, but on the inside I'm an unholy mess of nerves and excitement.

"I won't tell anyone if you don't," she says. "It'll be our little secret."

That last part she whispers in my ear, and it's a good thing we're still sitting on the back of the rickety rickshaw because I'm seconds away from melting into a puddle of desire and frustration. I have never in my entire life wanted to kiss someone so badly, and knowing that there's no way I can do that here is killing me.

We get off and start walking toward the water. Back in Kansas, I read up about the sanctity of the Yamuna River to the Hindu community. The river is worshipped as the goddess Yamuna, daughter of Surya, the sun god, and sister of Yama, the god of death. But during the Mughal rule, the riverbank seemed the most logical choice for the location and construction of the Taj Mahal. The river runs behind the structure and even as we approach the riverbank, I can see it in the distance, as well as its rippling reflection in the water. The moon casts a magical light over everything, and I hold my breath and stand absolutely still for a moment to soak it all in.

"Come on," Sufiya urges. "I see the guy over there."

The guy turns out to be an old fisherman who frequents this part of the river to make some money ferrying tourists so that they can enjoy the beautiful view without all the daytime crowds. I watch, fascinated, as Sufiya bargains for a reasonable price, which, I quickly calculate in my head, ends up being two dollars. We climb hastily onto the little boat and our journey begins. As we pull away from the shore, I lean over to dip my hand in the water, but Sufiya reaches out and grabs it before it touches the surface.

"I wouldn't do that," she warns. "See all that foam?" She points to the white crests on the little waves. "That's toxic stuff from all the pollution."

She's still holding on to my hand as the boatman begins to sing, and I don't pull away. It's a beautifully haunting melody. Even though I haven't the faintest clue about the meaning of the words, I'm still moved.

"It's an old folk song about Emperor Shah Jahan and his love for Mumtaz Mahal," Sufiya explains to me. "He's a pretty good singer, isn't he?"

"So good," I say, marveling at this moment where I'm on a moonlit boat ride along a sacred river admiring one of the wonders of the world, holding hands with a girl I'm really starting to like. This is not at all what I thought my trip to India would be like.

Eventually Sufiya's hand slips from mine and the song ends. The boat has stopped moving and I take in the view. The illuminated Taj Mahal, its reflection dancing in the water, and the lights of Mehtab Bagh, the beautiful garden behind the mausoleum, all create a magical scene unlike anything I've seen before.

We sit in silence, drinking in the epic view. After a while, the boatman begins to row us back to shore.

"What else do you like doing, besides surprising people with magical boat rides?" I say to Sufiya.

She laughs, and I find the courage to reach for her hand again. She doesn't pull it back and I feel ridiculously elated.

"Let's see . . . we play a lot of carrom at my house," she says. "My sister Rumana is pretty good and hates to lose, so it always gets really loud. But it's a lot of fun. You should come and play with us sometime."

"Rumana would love that. I've never played before, so I'll lose every game."

"Nah, it's easy," she says. "I'll teach you. There's actually a carrom board in the library. Your dad used to love playing, so they've always kept one in there."

It's weird to hear Sufiya say these things about my father as if he's a stranger I've only met recently. I guess it's not entirely untrue. I kind of am a stranger to my own family. Everyone here has this history with my dad and with Dadi. Soon Aleena will build a history with them too, and I'll go back to Kansas in a couple of weeks and it'll be like I was never here. Is that what I really want? Or do I want to be a part of this life even if it's from a distance?

I push these thoughts aside to focus on Sufiya.

"I'd love for you to teach me how to play," I say. "Mom says she used to be quite good, so maybe I can play with her when I get back. But I'll have to order a carrom board online first. We can't exactly walk into a store and buy one."

"Does your mom miss being able to buy Indian stuff?" Sufiya asks.

"I don't think so," I say. "Not really. She grew up in the US and my grandma is white. And my grandpa left India when he was very young, so he's more American than Indian, to be honest."

"That must be strange for you, no?" she says.

"How do you mean?"

"Just . . . having these two sides of you, Indian and American. Do you ever feel confused about where you belong?"

"I haven't actually thought about it in that way," I reply. "Mom and I have a pretty good life in Newton. Of course, it's nothing at all like this, but I have good friends and lots of freedom. All of that's really important to me and I wouldn't trade it for anything."

"Sometimes I wish I had more freedom to live the life I want." Sufiya looks away at the water and I think I see tears shimmering in her eyes. "I just wish I could be the real me with everyone at home."

"You mean like about what you want to do with your life?" I ask.

She looks at the water for a bit, lost in her own thoughts. "No, not just that. I mean, the real me, you know. Like this." She squeezes my hand and I finally get what she means and a wave of excitement surges through me.

"Do you think you could ever tell them?" I hold on tightly to her hand, afraid that this moment will slip away.

"I can't." She lets out a deep sigh. "They would try to understand. They want me to be happy. But it's not that easy. People would talk. And how can I do that to my sisters?"

I don't know what to say. It seems unfair that she should have to carry such a heavy burden, but I also get what she's saying. She obviously loves her family a lot and they love her back just as much. But it's still a very difficult situation for her. And I'm reminded once again of how different our worlds are. Not that it matters. If anything, after what she just shared with me, my feelings for her are growing stronger by the minute. And even though I can't deny the giddiness inside me knowing now that she feels the way I do, I can't stop a tiny bit of apprehension from seeping in. What am I getting myself into? I'm not at all sure about what this thing is with Sufiya or what I'm doing, but I do know that I want to be around her. And that has to be good enough for now.

CHAPTER TWENTY-TWO

Sufiya and I have been summoned by Dadi to pick out fabrics and saris for the wedding. I know that desi weddings are week-long affairs, if not longer, and we're going to need multiple outfits for all the events. This will be my first time attending an Indian wedding, so I'm still not sure what each event is, but I guess I'll find out soon enough.

"Have you thought about what you want to wear for the wedding?" Sufiya says as we make our way to the drawing room.

"Not really," I say.

"I think you should definitely wear a sari for one of the events." I feel closer to her after that night on the river and I can tell that she feels it too. It's in the way she stands just a little bit closer and leans in when she's around me.

"I've never worn one before," I say. "I wouldn't even know how to put it on."

"Don't worry, I can show you," she reassures me as we enter the drawing room. It has been taken over by luxurious fabrics, draped over every piece of furniture. Silks and satins shine in the light from the huge chandelier, which illuminates the sequin-and-pearl embroidery of the pieces. On one side is an array of saris in the most radiant jewel tones. Heavily gem-crusted dupattas are laid out on several sofas. And I can barely believe my eyes when I see Dad there too. There are several men and women already taking measurements for Azra Aunty, her kids, and Faiza Phuppi.

"Mehar beta, come here and look at these beautiful gharara sets," Dadi calls from a corner of the room. I rush to her side, a little overwhelmed by the gorgeousness of everything around me.

"Dadi, these are all so beautiful," I say. "I don't know how I'm going to choose."

"That's okay, betiya," she says. "Azra is here and Sufiya will help you as well." She smiles in Sufiya's direction and Sufiya blushes in the cutest way.

"I can help also," Dad pipes up. "I've been told I have a good eye for color," he adds with a smile.

I don't know what to say, but I can't stop smiling as I pick up a pale green pearl-and-gold-encrusted fabric and hold it up against me.

Dad nods approvingly. "That chartreuse color really suits you," he says, motioning for me to stand closer to the window.

He clearly has no clue what chartreuse actually looks like, but I love him for trying. I can see Dadi trying to pick her jaw off the floor since she's probably never ever seen him show any interest in women's clothing. It's hilarious and sweet all at the same time. We look through several choices and I finally settle on a delicate silk and organza gharara set in a soft pink, as well as the pale-green-and-gold lehenga set and a couple of saris. When the tailors are done taking my measurements, it's Sufiya's turn. She tries to decline Dadi's offer of new outfits for all the wedding functions, but Dadi will absolutely not hear of it.

"Sufiya, please," Dad says. "You have been a godsend the last few weeks. And Mehar is enjoying your company so much. You must choose something as a favor to us."

"Sufiya, please let me do this for you," Dadi says when Sufiya continues to protest. "You have been such a huge help with the wedding preparations on top of everything you already do. It would make me so happy if you accepted this small gift from me."

"Dadima . . . how can I say no to you." She hugs Dadi and then we spend the next hour picking out outfits for her.

Afterward, Sufiya and I take the saris to my room to try on. Everything else will be stitched and brought back for a final fitting, but Sufiya wants to teach me how to wrap the sari. Since my blouses still have to be stitched, she says I can roll up a T-shirt at the waist for now. Azra Aunty loans me one of her petticoats and we're all set.

"I think you should wear the lehenga for the wedding day and the sari for the walima," Sufiya says as I change.

"I actually don't know what most of the events are," I confess, a little embarrassed that I have to ask such a basic question. But then again, Mom and I don't have much opportunity to go to desi weddings back in Kansas, so it kind of never came up.

"Oh, okay, so the first will be a mehndi for Naz, which is basically a big henna party," Sufiya says. "There's going to be music and dancing, so it'll be lots of fun. Usually it's only women for that one."

"And then after that is the wedding, and the walima is a reception?"

"Exactly. Except sometimes people will add on a special musical night," Sufiya says.

I've changed into a T-shirt and petticoat. I come out of my dressing room and stand in front of the large mirror. Sufiya comes close and starts to roll up my T-shirt, securing it under the strap of my bra. Her touch is soft and warm and she smiles at my reflection in the mirror while I try to stay as calm as possible. Her fingers leave a trail of fire along my skin, and I have to concentrate hard to stay absolutely still so that I don't betray my feelings.

Even though she confided in me on our boat trip, I'm still a little bit uncertain about her feelings. I mean, she didn't exactly come out and say anything concrete. What if she wasn't talking about me when she said that thing about hiding her true self from her family? What if I'm reading too much into her words? I don't know if I'm brave enough to tell her how much my feelings for her have grown, how every minute I wait to see her again feels like an eternity, and how she comes to me in my dreams every single night. The last thing I want is to freak her out with all this and make things awkward between us. So I say nothing of the turmoil inside me.

She picks up the sari and begins to tuck a section into the top of my petticoat. Her fingers brush the skin on my stomach as she goes in and out of the band, all around, and it's excruciatingly delicious. The entire time, she's telling me about all the different styles of wrapping a sari by region and it's all I can do to stop my knees from buckling under me. She pleats a length of the sari, then takes the folds and tucks them deep into the band of the petticoat, right below my belly button. I bite my lips as our breaths mingle, her mouth tantalizingly close to mine. This is pure torture and I'm dying a slow death.

"Mehar?"

I break out of my fog and find her staring at me.

"Are you okay?" She's looking at me with that smile in her eyes that always gets me tingling.

"Yeah, are you?"

"Huh?" She looks confused, but I can't let her know how I'm feeling right now. I do know that if I don't do something about whatever this is soon, I'm going to explode.

"Sorry, this is a lot more complicated than I thought," I say quickly. "How do I make sure it doesn't all come apart? I mean, I don't think Dadi and Dad would appreciate me showing that much skin at the wedding."

"I'm going to be using a lot of safety pins," she says with a grin. "You should be more worried about stabbing yourself."

"Oh joy."

"It's going to be fine," she says. "I'll be there with you, so if there's an emergency, I'll take care of it."

I change back into my regular clothes, and soon after, Sufiya leaves to go home. As I fold and put away the saris, I can't help thinking that I'm in real trouble here. I'm getting way too attached to Sufiya and there's not a thing I can do about it. And the scariest part is that I'm not sure I want to.

CHAPTER TWENTY-THREE

We've been invited to dinner and a musical evening at Muzaffar's parents' mansion. Unfortunately, Naz and Aleena were invited as well, since apparently, they're already being considered part of the family. My entertainment for the evening has been watching Muzaffar dodge Aleena as she barely manages to disguise the fact that she's into him. Despite the numerous seating options, she has glued herself to his side and keeps inching closer and closer at every opportunity. As a result, he keeps sliding over in my direction and I'm worried that soon I'll run out of couch and fall off. I can tell from the horrified look on Dadi's face that she's mortified and keeps nudging Dad, who is blissfully unaware of the scene Aleena is creating as he and Muzaffar's dad chat animatedly about some polo match.

After an amazing dinner of various Mughlai dishes like murgh mussallam, pulao, lamb korma, and carrot halwa, the real entertainment is about to start. As the musicians, all nine of them, seat themselves on the stage, sitting cross-legged on a luxurious rug, Muzaffar leans his head close to mine and explains that they are going to sing qawwali, which originated from Sufi devotional singing.

"So, they're religious songs?" I ask.

"They can be," Muzaffar replies. "But sometimes they are about the beauty and anguish of love."

That sounds just about perfect for the mood I'm in these days.

The music begins and for the next little while I allow myself to be completely immersed in the hauntingly tragic melodies of the songs. Of course, I don't understand a single word because the poetic lyrics are too sophisticated for my rudimentary Urdu skills. During song breaks Muzaffar gives me the gist of the song that has finished. The evening feels special—the only thing that would improve it is if Aleena were anywhere else. I can tell that she's absolutely livid about Muzaffar showering me with attention, but she can't do anything about it without royally embarrassing herself. And I'm petty enough to enjoy it more than I should.

When the musicians take an extended break and chai and dessert are being served, Aleena joins me and Muzaffar on the diwan. Muzaffar jumps up immediately.

"I'm going to get some kheer," he announces. "Can I get you something for you?"

"No, thank you," Aleena says. "I couldn't eat another bite after that dinner."

"I'll take some gulab jamun," I say. "Actually, why don't I come and help you?" I jump up and follow him before Aleena has a chance to react. I have no desire to sit alone with her.

We go over to a large table covered with all kinds of desserts. There are the usual desi sweets like rasgullah, gulab jamun, jalebiyan, and kheer, but there's also gajar ka halwa, caramel custard, and shahi tukda. My mouth is watering just looking at it all and I try to hold back and only take a little bit of everything. I make a plate for Muzaffar too as he carries two cups of chai back to the living room with me. Aleena is still there, seething. She eyes my plate and then me disdainfully. Unfortunately for her, her withering looks are no competition for the lure of such scrumptious desserts and I dig in.

"My mom would love this," I say, savoring the creamy richness of the kheer.

"I'll make sure to ask Ammi to send a big box with you when you fly back," Muzaffar says. "She's always sending stuff for her Indian friends in the US."

"Oh no, I wouldn't want to trouble her," I say quickly.

"Are you kidding? Ammi's kheer is famous here in Agra and she would love to send some to your mom."

Roshan Aunty has wandered over to us and smiles. I really like her and her son. After spending the day with him at the Taj Mahal and then this evening, I can see why Dadi is so fond of them both.

"Mehar beta, did you eat well?" she says. "Muzaffar, I hope you're looking after her."

"Oh yes, poor Muzaffar has had to explain everything to Mehar," Aleena says. "I can't imagine living in America and missing out on such things. It must be so dull."

Roshan Aunty pins Aleena with a cold stare. "There are more important things in life than musical evenings," she says. "But, Mehar, I'm so happy that you are enjoying yourself. Now what's this I hear about sending mithai?"

"Ammi, we should send a packet of mithai with Mehar for her mother," Muzaffar says.

"That's an excellent idea, beta," Roshan Aunty says. "I will prepare an extra-special packet for her," she adds. "I'm so happy that you could join us, Mehar. And I can't remember the last time I saw your grandmother so happy." She leans in to kiss me on the cheek before going off to attend to her other guests.

"Aunty is so nice," I say, turning to Muzaffar. "I'm having such a great time. Thanks for explaining everything to me. I hope it didn't ruin the evening for you."

"Not at all . . . it was my pleasure," he says. "I'm so glad you came."

"Muzaffar, you're always such a gentleman," Aleena pipes up. "Hey, listen, a few friends are having a party tomorrow night. I'd love for you to come." She makes it a point not to look at me, and I can't say I mind at all.

"Aleena, you're being a little rude, aren't you," he says with an embarrassed laugh.

Aleena rolls her eyes a little before turning to me. "Of course, Mehar, you're welcome to come too. I didn't think you like that sort of thing."

"I actually have plans, but thank you for the invitation," I say. I don't even bother to fake smile. I'm so done with her. It's as if that conversation we had at the hotel in Delhi never happened.

I know I'm partly to blame for her churlish behavior. I haven't exactly been subtle about being super friendly to Muzaffar. The thing is, at first I was doing it mostly to piss her off, but now I genuinely like him and I'm not going to stop being nice to him simply because she has the hots for him. Plus, she's already been hogging Dad for most of my visit, so I feel like I deserve to get some attention too.

"Looks like it's just you and me then, darling," she says, hooking her arm into Muzaffar's and dragging him away. I feel truly sorry for him as he turns to throw me a look of utter desperation. Unfortunately, there's no saving him. He's on his own.

A couple of hours later we're in the car heading back home. Dadi is sitting up front with Dad, who's given the driver the night off. I'm sitting in the back with Naz and Aleena.

"How did you enjoy the evening, Mehar beta?" Naz asks.

"I had a great time." *It would have been a whole lot better if Aleena hadn't been there.*

"We are having the same qawwali group for our reception." Naz leans forward. "Reza, didn't I tell you they were the best in Agra?"

"Yes, my dear, you did," Dad says, smiling briefly in her direction before turning his eyes back to the road.

Dadi's eyes meet mine in the rearview mirror. She does this tightening thing with her lips, which by now I've learned is an expression for multiple things, chief among them extreme disdain, usually reserved for Aleena and occasionally for other people she's obligated to be polite to.

"Mehar, tell me, what are your plans after you return home?" Naz is like a dog with a bone, on an endless quest for bonding with me, unable to accept that it isn't going to happen.

"The usual," I say, watching the traffic go by outside at a dizzying pace even at this late hour. Right about now, I would love to switch places with any of the dozens of people hanging off the buses passing by.

"And what is that, dear?" She won't let up.

"School and work, mostly."

"Ugh, I can't imagine having to do that," Aleena says. "It must be so hard."

I wish I had something hard with me right now so I could hit her over the head with it. But I take a deep breath instead.

"What are your plans?" I ask her. "Do you know which university you're going to next year?"

"Actually, I'm not going next year," she says. "Dad said he's taking Ammi and me on a trip around the world."

All the air rushes out of my lungs at once, like I've been kicked in the stomach. I take in a sharp breath, waiting for Dad to say something, anything, like maybe they had only talked about it casually, or we'll see, like parents always do when they don't want to commit to something. But he's concentrating on the road as if no one said anything important. Meanwhile my world feels like it's shattering. All the times I begged Dad to take me to Disneyland, or anywhere really, just so I could also tell my friends that I went on vacation with him—all those memories come crashing down on me like a tsunami. Tears are lodged in the back of my throat, but I can't let them out. I can't give Aleena the satisfaction of knowing that my heart is breaking because my father, who never, ever took me anywhere in all these years, is planning to travel around the world with this girl who isn't even his real daughter but gets more of his love and affection and everything else than I ever dared to ask for.

I think I'm going to be sick. I take a deep breath, but it doesn't help. I need to get away from here before I either say something I'll regret or throw up.

We're pulling up to the entrance and I barely even wait for the car to come to a complete stop before I open the door and run out toward the grand staircase, taking the steps two at a time to get to my room.

I lock the door behind me and fling myself onto the bed, sobs shaking my shoulders as I cry into my pillow, letting out all my rage and frustration and heartache. I want so badly to talk to Mom right now, but she'll freak out if I call her when I'm like this. I wish more than anything that I'd listened to my gut and never come here.

There's a knock on my door. "Mehar, open the door."

It's Dad. I have no desire to talk to him, so I ignore him. But the knocks become louder and harder.

"Mehar, come on, please open the door. This is your father speaking."

It doesn't look like he's going to stop, so I finally open the door to hear what he has to say.

"Thank you," he says. "Mehar beta, can we please talk about this?"

"There's nothing to talk about."

"Aleena shouldn't have said that. I haven't promised her anything like that, but she seems to have gotten it into her head that we're going. She can be a little bit . . . pushy sometimes."

"Well, then maybe you should tell her that," I say coldly. "It doesn't have anything to do with me."

"Of course it does," Dad insists. "I know why you're upset, and you have every right to be."

I want this conversation to be over and I want him to go. But he seems intent on seeing this through.

"Look, Dad, it's fine," I say. "You have a new life and a new family and you want to do stuff together and I get it. It's not like you and I ever did a lot together anyway, so it's really no big deal."

"Is that what you think?" he asks. "That I have a new family so I don't care about you anymore?"

I shrug. Sure feels that way to me. "It doesn't matter what I think. You made your choice a long time ago and I'm here because you asked me to come, so let's just try to be civil until the wedding is over."

He stands, clearly agitated now. "Civil? I don't want to be just civil with my own daughter. I wanted you to come because you're important to me and I want you to be a part of my life."

"Since when, Dad?" I say. "Since when have you ever wanted me to be a part of your life?"

"What's that supposed to mean? I've always been there for you, you know that."

"Yes, you have. You've always paid for stuff. But you've always made it very clear that I'll never live up to your high standards. Well, now you'll have a brand-new daughter and I'm sure she's perfect and you'll finally have the family you really wanted."

"You and Mom were the family I always wanted," he says quietly. "But you two never wanted me."

I stare at him, utterly shocked. "Dad, what the hell are you talking about? Every single time you visited, all you could talk about was how Mom and I were doing everything wrong. All I ever remember is the two of you fighting."

"Mehar beta, you don't have any idea how hard I tried to keep us all together. But your mom wanted out."

"Of course, blame Mom for everything when she isn't here to defend herself."

He lets out a deep sigh. "I'm not blaming Mom for everything. I know I was far from the perfect husband back then. I took her for granted and focused too much on my other obligations when I should have focused on the two of you."

"You're right," I say. "You should have. You made your choice and now you're mad because I'm not overjoyed to be part of this new . . . whatever you're doing with Naz and Aleena. Well, I have news for you, Dad. I'm not overjoyed. I only came because Mom guilted me into it. But I wish I'd never come. I don't know why you asked me. There's no place in your life for me. There never was." My eyes sting again and I blink back the tears.

Dad comes over to me and puts his arms on my shoulders. "Do you really think that?" He takes a deep breath. "Mehar beta . . . please, you have to trust me when I say that nothing is further from the truth. I love you, you're my only child, and I want nothing more than for you to be in my life. Always."

I can feel a headache coming on. "I don't know how you expect me to believe that," I say. "Nothing I've ever done has been good enough for you. My grades, my friends, what I eat and wear . . . you've always had something negative to say about all of it."

"Beta, I have a right to comment on all those things. I'm your father and I want to protect you and make sure you're making good choices."

"Please, Dad . . . Mom protects me and Mom has taught me to make good choices." I have to laugh. This whole conversation has taken a ridiculous turn. "Just because you don't agree with my choices doesn't make them bad. Plus, you've never been around enough to have a say in any of it."

I'm surprised that Dad hasn't lost his cool yet. I'm deliberately provoking him, making him angry, because I'm angry. I've been mad at him for so long and what Aleena said sent me over the edge.

He's staring at me with this look I can't define. It's a mixture of sadness and surprise.

"Mehar . . . I don't know what to say," he says, his voice a little choked up. "You're all grown up now, so maybe you'll understand what I'm trying to tell you." He turns away from me and looks out the window. "When your mom took you and left, I was broken . . . for a long time. It took me a while to understand that I'd taken your mother for granted. I focused far too much on my familial obligations here rather than on you and your mom. That was my biggest mistake."

"You could have convinced her to come back," I say. "Or chosen to stay with us. You chose your life here." I'm not letting him off the hook or putting the blame on Mom.

"You think I didn't try to convince her?" he says, his eyes glistening.

Oh my god, is he crying?

"You never even invited me here before," I say. "I know you guys had a custody agreement. But still, if you really wanted, you could have fought for me."

"I did fight for you, Mehar," he says quietly. "But your mom . . . she was so afraid that I would keep you here for good that she threatened to sue for sole custody."

"What? No. Mom would never do that." Mom has always encouraged me to be on better terms with Dad and Dadi. She was the one who convinced me to come here. Why would she do that if she didn't want me to be close to them?

"I couldn't believe she did either at first," Dad says, sinking into an armchair in the corner of the room. "I was so angry and so scared that I would lose you for good. And I guess she was too. I think as you got older she was worried that I'd convince you to come here and stay permanently or something. She made me promise never to invite you here. But now that you're eighteen, I don't care what she says. You can make your own decisions."

I don't know what to say. I know Mom and Dad have never had the best relationship. But somehow it's never occurred to me that she would actually stand in the way of a good relationship with my father and, even worse, let me believe that he didn't care.

The door opens with a creak and Jameela pokes her head in.

"Naz Begum aapko yaad kar rahi hain," she says to Dad.

Surprise, surprise. Naz can't survive a few minutes without my father and now he's going to walk out like he always does.

Dad throws me a look before turning to Jameela.

"Unko bolo hum kal baat karenge."

Is he actually blowing her off? I don't think this will go over well with Naz, but still. He's actually choosing to continue this conversation. Will wonders never cease?

He comes closer and pulls me down on the edge of my bed. I can tell he's struggling with whatever it is he's trying to say and yet I'm enjoying his discomfort.

"Mehar, I know that it's going to be hard for us to get back to the kind of relationship we had when you were little," he says. He raises his eyes to look at me. "But I really want to try. You're my only child and I can't bear the thought that I might lose you forever."

Okay, someone's being a little dramatic.

"You're not going to lose me," I mumble. "Though I guess it does feel like you're replacing me."

He takes my hand in his and holds it tight. "That would be like replacing my own heart. I could never do that."

My eyes well up immediately and I lean closer until I'm resting my head on his chest. My anger from seconds ago dissipates. It feels good to sit like this.

"Are you sure?" I ask. "Aleena seems to fit so much better with all of you."

"Please don't think that, beta. I know this is all very different from what you're used to. But it's also a part of who you are, just a different side. And as far as Aleena is concerned, you need to understand something."

I lift my head off his chest. "What?"

"She's had a rough time ever since her father left them. She just needs some guidance and a father figure. She's not a bad person, but definitely a little misguided."

"You really think so?"

"I do," he says. "She's also insecure about her place with me and her mother right now, and I don't want her to feel neglected."

"Okay, fine, I'll try to be nicer," I say with a reluctant smile. "But she started it."

He smiles and pinches my cheek. "Meri pyari betiya," he says before planting a kiss on my forehead. He hasn't called me that in years. His darling daughter.

I wrap my arms around him and squeeze.

CHAPTER TWENTY-FOUR

"Mom, can I ask you something?"

"Sure, honey, what is it?"

Mom and I haven't been talking as much lately as when I first got here. The last couple of times we tried we missed each other because of the time difference and so it's been almost five days since we've spoken. And a lot has happened in those few days. After my conversation with Dad, I decide that it's time to have a real talk with Mom, even though I wish I didn't have to because I know it's going to be tough. Ever since I can remember, I could talk to Mom about anything except when it came to Dad. Every time I brought him up it always felt like I was hurting her, so I dropped it. But not today. I've been thinking about what Dad said. I know it wasn't easy for him to tell me what Mom did. He knows how close Mom and I are and it was clear he didn't want to damage our relationship. But I need some clarity.

"Why didn't you ever tell me that Dad used to invite me to stay here for the summer? He said he asked you so many times but you always said no."

There. I said it, and now the words are out there.

"Well . . . it's complicated . . . I think I was trying to protect you."

"Protect me from what?"

"From . . . you know how your dad is. He doesn't always have his priorities straight and I wanted to make sure that you were well taken care of. Especially if I wasn't around."

"Everyone here talks about how much they missed me. Even Dad. And he said he only stopped asking because you threatened to sue him for sole custody if he kept insisting. Did you really say that?"

"I don't know what to tell you, Mehar." Mom sounds tired, and she has this look in her eyes that I don't recognize. "I tried to do the best that I could and I'm sorry if you think that I stood in the way of you and your father. But you're there now so you should make the most of it." Her eyes have a suspicious shine to them and I'm pretty sure that she's going to cry. "Look, I really have to go now, but we'll talk again soon, okay?"

She ends the call and I realize I never got a real answer. I fall back on my bed with a sigh. Maybe it's for the best—it would've been kind of hard to have a proper fight when we're thousands of miles away from each other.

• • •

Last night I finally went to sleep after my disastrous call with Mom. I'd stayed up for a long time going over everything in my head. All those years I always assumed Dad had sort of written us off, but now that he's told me what he went through after Mom took me and left, I find myself reassessing a lot of my feelings toward Dad. I wonder if Mom felt that she might have lost me to Dad if I'd come to visit him here as a kid and that breaks my heart. I hate to think that this is something she would even consider . . . that I might somehow start loving her less if I spent time away from her. And it made me think of how scared she must have been when she took me and left, never knowing if it was the right decision. I can't help thinking about what Dad must have gone through as well, losing his wife and daughter like that. For all the anger I've felt toward him for years, I'm only now beginning to realize that there are two injured parties in this case and I think I've been massively unfair to him. Once again, I'm plagued with doubt. What if it's too late to fix things?

I mope in my room all day, refusing Dadi's repeated requests to come down for breakfast and then lunch. I have no desire to be around anyone. Bilquis finally brought me a tray, but everything on it is cold now and I'm starving, so I decide to go down. Hopefully no one is around.

I don't know what excuse Dad made to Naz and Aleena for my behavior last night, and I don't really care. I take a quick peek around the living room, but no one's there. I find the usual elaborate tea laid out on the table, and from the looks of it no one has touched any of the food yet. What a waste. Jameela appears and asks me to eat before everything gets cold. There are potato patties with date-and-tamarind chutney, spiced chickpeas, samosas, and cut-up mangoes. I help myself to a bit of everything and take the cup of coffee Jameela has made me and head on over to the library. The sun is low on the horizon and casts a warm glow on the shimmering surface of the pond. From my seat by the window, I can look over the entire garden, with its many date palms, mango trees, and jasmine shrubs. Being here soothes me. I wonder if Mom had a favorite place in the mahal, if she too sat here wondering about her life and the choices she made. I try to imagine her during the unhappy times, feeling the way I do now, looking for some quiet and solitude, a place to nurse the wounds in her heart. Did she sit here among all these books and watch the beautiful sunset while tears rolled down her face? Did she feel as alone as I do right now? I let out a deep sigh and take another sip of my coffee.

Yesterday was a weird day. Just when I thought that there was no hope for me and Dad, he shows me this other side of him that I haven't seen since I was a little girl. It's such a strange thing, how one act of kindness and understanding, a single moment of connection, can make such a difference. Last night when I ran out of the car, I was thinking about changing my flight and going home. But now I feel like I belong here just as much as I do back in Newton, Kansas. I love how I feel when I'm around Dadi and Azra Aunty and my cousins. And then of course there's Sufiya with her shy smile, her soft brown eyes, and her assuredness that draws me to her like no one else has done before. How will I ever go back and leave her behind?

The door opens and she walks in, as if I've somehow manifested her with the longing in my heart. She's wearing a flowy off-white shalwar kameez with white sequins embroidered on the bodice and looks positively ethereal. There's a string of jasmine braided into her hair and I smile as she walks toward me.

"I heard about yesterday," she says, settling next to me on the sofa. "Wanna talk about it?" She takes my hand and cups it in her own. My eyes immediately fill with hot tears.

"Only tell me if you want," she adds quickly. "I don't mean to pry."

"You're not prying," I say. "I don't have anyone else to talk to."

I tell her everything about the fight with Dad and then how things turned around and what happened with Mom. She listens without interrupting and when I'm finished, I put my head on her shoulder and it feels right and there's an electricity between us as we sit in the warm glow of the setting sun. I look up at her and see something in her eyes that I can't define even as her face comes closer to mine, until our lips touch in a mix of tenderness and uncertainty. Her hand brushes back wisps of hair from my forehead and I pull her closer, adjusting my body so that we fit perfectly, like two pieces of a puzzle. But then we hear footsteps approaching and we jump apart, both of us quickly smoothing our hair and sitting up straight on the sofa, and just in time, because the door opens and Azra Aunty walks in, followed by Usha, Asha, Nisha, and Taimur, who come at Sufiya and me like tiny rockets and launch themselves into our arms. "They wouldn't stop asking for you," Azra Aunty says. "I had to look all over the mahal, but I should've known this is where you'd be. This is where I always ended up finding Gulnar Bhabi too."

The last thing I want right now is to think about Mom. I'd like at least one moment to freak out about the fact that Sufiya and I just kissed, thank you very much. I guess that's too much to ask, and clearly the munchkins don't care because they're pulling me and Sufiya to our feet so that we can chase them down the hallways of the mahal.

The kids eventually tire themselves out and then Dadi wants Sufiya for something and she leaves and we haven't gotten a single moment alone with each other. I head back to my room and after I eat the sandwich Jameela brings me for dinner. I lie in bed, watching the ceiling fan rotate lazily, and Sufiya's face swims in front of my eyes. I wonder if she's thinking about me too. I pick up my phone to message her and then I wait. Several minutes later there's still no reply. A heaviness begins to settle in my heart. Maybe I shouldn't have kissed her. What if I've ruined everything?

I toss and turn at night, going over and over that moment in my mind. Who made the first move? Was it me or her? I shiver a little as I remember the way our lips met, the knowledge that someone could come bursting through the door at any minute, adding an extra thrill to the moment. But what if she thinks it was a big mistake?

As I drift off to sleep, I can't help wondering whether Sufiya was relieved that the kids and Azra Aunty came in when they did.

• • •

The next night, Muzaffar and I are out for dinner at a rooftop café called Tease Me. He came by to see if I wanted to go to his favorite place with him and Dadi practically pushed me out the door. The decor is amazing, but the evening is slightly chilly and I regret not grabbing a cardigan. But Muzaffar is very sweet and insists that I wear his light jacket because he can see the goose bumps on my arms. Despite the cool vibe of this place and the fact that I really enjoy Muzaffar's company, I can't help obsessively checking my phone every few seconds to see if there's a message from Sufiya. She hasn't responded to any of my texts, which kept getting more and more frantic over the course of the day, so I'm convinced that I have made a colossal mess of things with her.

"Expecting a call from someone?" Muzaffar says, peering at me over his menu.

"What? No . . . I'm so sorry, I'm being rude." I flash him my most charming smile and put my phone away.

"No worries, I'm glad you were able to join me," he says.

"Looks like you're a regular," I say, smiling as a server brings us mango juice in tall frosted glasses. I can tell from the way the staff greeted Muzaffar that he's a big deal here.

"It's not so much me as my family's name," he admits with a shrug. "I get the royal treatment wherever I go."

"You don't sound particularly thrilled about it." I take a sip of my mango juice and savor the rich sweet taste as it slides down my throat.

"To be honest, sometimes I feel like a bit of an impostor." He looks away into the distance and for the first time I take the time to really study him. He looks a lot like his mother, deep-set eyes, dark and intense, but with a softness shining in them. His thick hair is brushed back but a few wayward strands keep getting away. He smooths them back with his hand and notices me staring.

"How do you mean?" I say hurriedly. "Why would you feel like an impostor?"

"It's just . . . I haven't really earned any of the privileges I enjoy, you know?"

I do understand what he means. Being born into a wealthy family with a title that goes back generations must be wonderful, but I'm sure it comes with its own set of issues. At least for some people. Others, like Aleena, who sort of manipulated her way into one, probably never waste a moment worrying about whether they're entitled to what they're taking. Strange how Aleena always has a way of barging into my thoughts. Ugh.

"Well, I'm sure you have plans to do your own thing, don't you?" I say.

His eyes light up and he smiles at me. For the next thirty minutes he regales me with the details of his big dream. He wants to make documentaries about superhero fandoms around the globe and how they overlap. I can tell from the look on his face as he tells me that he is so into this. I'm sure it won't be hard for him to get started, because he'll never have to worry about things like rent or bills. Must be nice. But he's a good guy and at least he's trying to follow his dreams.

We finally get around to ordering and the choices are mind-boggling.

We start with herbed fish skewers and peri-peri fries, then order malai kofta and stuffed mushroom tikka along with lachha paratha and garlic naan. Everything is delicious and I love that he's as obsessed with fries as I am. I'm truly enjoying myself and almost forget to ask about Aleena. After what Muzaffar shared last time and what Dad mentioned about her having a rough time, I want some more details. I mean, if Dad wants me to give her a chance, then I'd at least like to have all the facts. So when the hibiscus-and-rose iced teas arrive, I casually bring her up and he's happy to oblige.

"You said her dad ran off with her mom's money, right? So how can she afford all the stuff she buys?"

"I assume she gets paid by sponsors for promoting their products," he says. "I mean, I don't know for sure, but she's always been very resourceful. She's had to be."

"I guess."

"You know she had a rough time after her father ran out on them," he says.

"That's the second time in two days I'm hearing that," I say. "What exactly happened?"

"I think she blamed herself for his leaving. She was only thirteen and I think it really messed her up."

I try to imagine what she might have been like a few years ago, but try as I might, all I can see is the way she is now. But I do feel bad for what she must have felt, the guilt of being responsible for a parent leaving. I know a little bit about that myself. When I was about nine or ten years old, I remember that during one of Dad's visits he got mad at me about something I'd done and Mom got mad at him for yelling at me, and after he left I would stay up nights wondering if he'd ever come back and blaming myself for making him leave. But he always came back. Aleena must have stayed up nights wondering about that too and her father never came back. And then I remember the look on her face that night at the hotel in Delhi when she pointed out that at least my dad cared enough to want to interfere with my life.

"Earth to Mehar." Muzaffar's gentle voice pulls me out of my thoughts.

"Sorry . . . I was just thinking."

"I like to do that from time to time." He grins at me. "May I ask what had you scrunching up your nose like that?"

"What . . . I was not scrunching my nose," I say, flashing my eyes at him.

"Oh yes you were . . . see, like this." He wrinkles his nose and puts his hand on his chin. "That's what you looked like."

I throw a fry at him. Some chili sauce splatters on the pristine tablecloth and I immediately grab my napkin and start to dab at it.

Muzaffar shakes his head. "I can't take you anywhere." He gently pulls the napkin from my hand and puts it on the table. "You're worried because Reza Uncle is marrying Naz Aunty, right?"

"Kind of. I don't want him to make a huge mistake."

"I get that. It's hard to trust people if they're showing different faces to the world."

"Exactly. Did you see her video from the other day? The one that says there's a new nawabzaadi in town? And she was filming all the preparations inside the mahal. I mean, did she even check with Dadi if that's okay? And she acts all chirpy and bubbly online, but then when she talks to me she's all snarky. Except when Dad's around. Ugh, I hate fake people."

"She used to be really nice and a lot of fun, you know," Muzaffar says. "But what her dad did to them . . . it changed her. And I can't blame her for that."

I think I'm going to have to make a real effort to try to get to know Aleena. It seems like Dad and Muzaffar both see a side of her I haven't yet, so maybe it's time I try to see it too.

"Did I tell you that I'm going to be in the US next month?" he says.

"Really? Where are you going?"

"New York and California for a couple of weddings. My parents can't go, so I'm representing the family."

"You have to visit us in Kansas," I say. "It'll be great to see you there. I can take you to my favorite place to eat and hang out. It's not fancy like this, but the food's good and you'll love my best friend, Norah."

He raises his iced tea and we clink glasses. "It's a date," he says with a boyish grin.

He pays for dinner after throwing me a horrified look when I pull out my credit card. On the drive home, he plays Harry Styles's latest album and we sing along, both of us terribly off-key. This has been the best evening and it's kept my mind off the fact that I still haven't heard from Sufiya, and for that I am grateful.

CHAPTER TWENTY-FIVE

It's the day of my welcome party and I haven't heard back from Sufiya yet. Despite my almost stalker-level number of messages, there's been nothing but radio silence. I wish she would reply. If we could talk about it, we could figure it out together.

I feel a little tingly just thinking about it, but more than that, I'm terrified of what's happening. After the whole debacle with Ryan, I haven't allowed myself to get close to anyone romantically.

Ryan was cheating on me for most of the time we were going out. And of course, I was the last to find out. I'd been blind to all the whispers and hushed laughter in the hallways at school because everyone else seemed to know. If it wasn't for Norah taking me to the spot behind the baseball field so I could catch Ryan in the act, I probably would not have believed it. Dad had known right away that Ryan couldn't be trusted. Maybe it was him being overprotective, or maybe he saw something in Ryan I was too blind to see, but he tried to warn me. And when that didn't work, he tried to forbid me to see him anymore. But all that did was make me even more determined. My cheeks burn with shame when I remember what I said to Dad. I told him he wasn't even a real dad because if he were, he would choose us and stay with us. How I told him I'd rather have no dad at all than have one like him. That's when all the yelling and arguing stopped. Until he called to invite me here.

So now this new thing with Sufiya feels exciting but also very scary. It's like my heart wants to be open to something that may end up being special, but at the same time I want to protect myself. I'm only here for a few weeks, and our lives and realities are too different. But wouldn't it be nice to let myself feel something after all this time?

• • •

Sufiya finally shows up in the afternoon, and my heart skips a beat when she walks in. I'm afraid of what I might see in her eyes but I'm relieved that at least she's here now. I guess she couldn't ignore Dadi as easily as she did me. Dadi had insisted that she come to the dinner as well, so here we are, getting ready, pretending that everything is normal and that nothing happened in the library the other day.

"Why didn't you call me back?" I say in hushed tones so no one hears.

"I'm sorry," she whispers. "I panicked and I needed some time to figure things out."

Well, I was not expecting that. I thought she'd make up some sort of excuse, but the fact that she's being completely honest with me makes me like her even more. I smile at her and I hope she knows what I'm thinking. And then finally everyone leaves the room and we're alone, surrounded by clothes and makeup and accessories.

We get dressed in silence and then I pick up a pack of glass bangles that match my lehenga. I start slipping them on my left hand, a few at a time, but I can't get them past the bony part at the base of my palm. To my surprise, Sufiya grabs a bottle of lotion and wordlessly starts rubbing it all over my hand, going gently in circles until my hand is slippery. Then she takes four of the bangles and begins to slide them over my wrist.

"Does it hurt?" she whispers, and her breath on my face makes tiny little shivers all over me.

I shake my head, unable to speak as she pushes a little harder until the bangles slip over my bone and onto my wrist. Then she picks up the remaining bangles and does it all over again. I don't know which is more torturous, her touch on my hand or the fact that I can't pull her to me and kiss her beautiful mouth, which is tantalizingly close to mine. Finally I have all my bangles on and I take her hands and massage the excess lotion into her skin. Our eyes are locked and we're both totally caught up in the moment and we move even closer to each other and I'm almost a hundred percent sure we're going to kiss again, but then Sufiya pulls back. It's the subtlest movement but it's enough to make my stomach drop.

"We should go downstairs," she says. "The guests are arriving and Dadima wants you to be ready to come down the staircase once everyone is here."

She holds my gaze and her eyes beseech me to understand. I do. And I don't. Why does this have to be so hard? She gives my hands one last squeeze and then we're walking out of the room and she disappears around the corner.

I would rather have greeted the guests at the door with Dadi and Dad, but apparently that's not a grand enough reveal for the nawabzaadi of the Rabbani house. So, when everyone is here, I teeter across the marble tiles and down the staircase, precariously balanced on six-inch heels. My only goal is to not trip over my flowing skirt and face-plant in front of all the one hundred and twenty guests assembled in the large hall that has been opened and decorated for tonight's bash. I make it all the way down without mishap, somehow managing to smile the whole time. I let out a sigh of relief when Dadi takes my arm at the bottom of the staircase. She walks me into the party hall as everyone makes way for us to pass through.

"Assalamu alaikum, my dear friends and family," she says, surprisingly good at projecting her voice to such a large crowd. "We're honored that you could join us today in welcoming my granddaughter Mehar, who has returned from the US after many years."

Everyone claps and comes to greet me, and soon I'm swallowed up in circles of close friends and family members, none of whom I remember.

"How is your mother, dear?" an older woman asks me. Faiza Phuppi has introduced her as my great-aunt Shahnaz Begum. "I was saddened to hear that she decided not to come back."

"It is very difficult for someone to adjust if they have not been raised here," Faiza Phuppi states. "Her mother is an American, after all."

"Well, she had her reasons," I say, already irritated with this conversation. Shahnaz Begum raises an eyebrow and Faiza Phuppi shoots me a warning glance. I guess I've lasted a whole five minutes before saying the wrong thing.

Luckily Azra Aunty rescues me. "There you are, Mehar," she says, slightly out of breath. "I want to introduce you to so many people." She drags me away and pulls me into a corner. "Listen, I know today might be a bit much, so whenever you start to feel overwhelmed, come find me," she says under her breath. "And I'll try to stay close as much as I can."

"Thank you." I squeeze her hand gently. "Hopefully I won't get in too much trouble tonight."

"You'll be great," she says, and then disappears around the corner to chase one of her kids.

I turn around and see Aleena and Naz directly in my line of vision. Despite my sort of change of heart about Aleena over the last couple of days, I'm still not ready to deal with these two right now. I consider diving to the floor and hiding under one of the massive tables laden with food, but Aleena has already spotted me with her eagle eyes and is making a beeline for me. Great. I quickly plaster a fake smile on my face as she approaches with Naz at her heels.

"There you are," Aleena says, surveying my outfit. "Not bad, even if I do say so myself."

My mouth falls open at her audacity, but she acts as if nothing is amiss.

Naz nods approvingly. "You look very nice, beta," she says. "Aleena told me you were having trouble choosing something suitable. I'm glad she was there to help."

"It's not her fault, Ammi," Aleena says. "She spends most of her time in jeans and T-shirts, so it was hard choosing such a fancy outfit."

"Well, that's what sisters are for, aren't they?" Naz smiles sweetly at us before turning around and moving toward her next unsuspecting target.

Meanwhile I'm standing in front of Aleena, trying to hold on to my last shred of self-control because what I really want is to slap that smug smile off her face.

Dad joins us, smiling proudly at me. "Mehar beta, you look stunning," he raves enthusiastically.

"Thank you, Dad." I walk into his outstretched arms.

"Aww, you guys are so cute," Aleena says. "Let me take a picture."

And with that she peels Dad's right arm off me, puts it around her own shoulder, and poses. Why did I think tonight would be about me?

"I'm so happy to see my best girls together like this," Dad says, and I almost gag. "Aleena, thank you for helping Mehar choose an outfit. As usual your choice is top-notch."

"Of course, Daddy, it was my pleasure," she chirps. "After all, what are sisters for, right, Mehar?"

I promised Dad I'd try to be nice, so I do.

"Yes, you're absolutely right," I say, and put a tentative arm on her shoulder and pat her awkwardly. But to my surprise she pulls me in for a hug. A real hug.

"You look very nice, you know?" she says softly. "I'm glad you listened to me."

Okay. That lasted a whole second.

I look over Aleena's shoulder. "Oh, I think Azra Aunty is waving to me," I say as convincingly as I can and make my escape. I disappear into the crowd, and I'm trying to figure out which direction to head in when I bump into Muzaffar.

"Oh, I'm so sorry," I say quickly.

"Mehar . . . wow. You look amazing." Muzaffar's mouth hangs open and I'm a little insulted. Do I usually look that terrible?

"Thank you," I say, my cheeks getting a little bit warm under his scrutiny. "You look very nice yourself." He's wearing a sherwani, midnight blue with tiny cream crisscross patterns, and a cream-colored churidar. Around his neck is a beautifully embroidered cream silk scarf.

"Thank you," he says with a shy smile. "Why do I get the

feeling that you're trying to run away from your own party?"

I look over my shoulder before replying. "I need to get out of here for a bit."

"I know the perfect spot," Muzaffar says, taking me by the elbow and leading me out toward the hallway. I almost laugh out loud when we end up standing in front of the library doors.

I grin at him. "This has been my hiding place since day one."

"It's been my favorite room in the palace for as long as I can remember." Muzaffar opens the double doors and steps aside to let me in. "When I was little, I'd get so bored while the grown-ups talked, I'd come in here to read my comic books."

I try to imagine him as a little boy without his mustache, but it's impossible.

"My favorite used to be Hulk, but now it's definitely Ms. Marvel," I say.

His eyes widen. "No way, mine are Hulk and Black Panther." Suddenly he rushes to one of the bookshelves in the far end of the room. I follow him, wondering what has gotten him so excited.

"I stashed a few volumes here when I was a kid so I wouldn't have to keep bringing them with me," he says, running his fingers over the spines of several books until it seems like he found the one he was looking for. He removes it from its spot and reaches into the space behind. Then he pulls out a large rolled-up bundle secured with a thick ribbon. "They're still here," he says loudly, holding them out triumphantly. It's kind of adorable.

"Ssshh . . . do you want Aleena to find us here?" I ask.

"Sorry, oh god no." He pulls me down next to him on the sofa by the window and unties the ribbon, then spreads all the comic books in the space between us. There are several issues of Hulk from 2014 and I smile as I think of little ten-year-old Muzaffar hiding in here with his comic book.

I pick up Hulk #9 from December 2014 and thumb through the pages.

"I remember this one," I say. "I think I was in fourth grade when I read it the first time."

"So, you were around eight or nine?" he asks. "I was the same age when I started reading these. And I've been obsessed ever since."

"Me too." It's great to have someone to share my nerdy superhero obsession with.

"Can you imagine if you'd grown up here and we knew each other as kids?"

"That would've been cool," I say. I'm really starting to like him. Back home, none of my friends are into comic books, so it's kind of been my own thing. It's nice to share it with someone else.

"I wonder if we'd be friends," he says.

"I'm sure we would. I mean, our families are close, so we'd end up hanging out a lot."

"Can I tell you something?" He suddenly looks shy. "I think Ammi and Dadima are secretly trying to set us up."

"It's not much of a secret, is it?" I roll my eyes. "It's so hilarious to me that they think we wouldn't catch on."

"Yes . . . hilarious." He has a weird look on his face.

"Aleena isn't too happy about that," I say. "I'm sure she's caught on too. They've been trying so hard to make it all seem super casual."

"I told you we used to be kind of close as kids, right?"

"Yeah, I know."

"I never really saw her in that way, you know. But I don't know how to tell her without hurting her feelings."

I shrug. "She'll figure it out eventually." I pick up a worn issue of Valkyrie. "I dressed up as Valkyrie for Halloween when I was nine. I was showing off to my friends and jumped off a swing and broke my wrist. I was so sad that I had to miss all the trick-or-treating."

"You must have looked so cute," he says.

"I did," I say with a flip of my hair. It's a clear night and the moonlight is streaming through the window. I'm actually having a better time in here than out there with all the snooty guests. I lean back with a sigh of contentment. Muzaffar is staring at me. Something about the look on his face sets off alarm bells in my head. Oh no. I freeze. I think he wants to kiss me. Shit. This is not what I was expecting at all. He's so nice and I don't want to hurt his feelings. But I also don't want him to kiss me. Aaaahhh. I have to do something. Wait, what if I'm imagining all of it? Maybe he's just happy to share his love of superheroes with someone, like I am. Calm down, Mehar. He's a nerd, exactly like you. Nope, he's moving in and I'm frozen. Several things happen at once, in slow motion. Muzaffar is still moving closer and starting to close his eyes as the door opens, and I whip my head around just in time to see Sufiya's shocked face before she turns on her heel and runs out. Fuck. Of course, now my arms decide they can work again and I push Muzaffar away, dashing to the door to run after Sufiya. But as soon as I open the door, I find Dadi walking by. She stops when she sees me.

"Mehar, where have you been? I've been looking all over for you." She doesn't wait for an answer, grabbing me by the arm and marching me back into the fray. "Everyone is asking for you," Dadi continues. "You can't leave your guests like this. It's rude."

I throw a desperate look down the hallway, but Sufiya isn't

there anymore. I manage to see Muzaffar coming out of the library before we turn the corner. Aleena is leaning against a wall talking to someone and raises her eyebrow in amusement as she watches me being herded back to the party.

I'm absolutely miserable for the rest of the night. My cheeks hurt from all the fake smiling, and if one more person makes a snide remark about Mom or being too American, I am going to completely lose it. I can't feel my feet anymore in their pointy-heeled and strappy prisons. I keep tripping over my lehenga and I wonder if Aleena purposely asked them to keep it extra long. I'm sure she would love nothing more than to see me totally embarrass myself. Well, I'm not going to give her the satisfaction.

"Where's your little sidekick today?" Aleena asks lazily, adjusting her dupatta in the hallway mirror as I'm walking back from the restroom. She's like a fungus that keeps cropping up everywhere I turn. "Didn't make the cut, huh?"

"What the hell's your problem?" I turn to her, my eyes blazing. "Why do you always have to be so horrible?"

"Well, well, someone's a little cranky," she drawls, and I want so badly to smack her across the face. But there's a roomful of guests and I can't do this to Dadi. Or Dad, even though maybe he needs to know what he's getting into. So instead, I take a deep breath.

"You know what? Stay out of my way until I'm gone, and I'll stay out of yours." And with that I turn around and head back to my guests. This evening has officially placed top of my list of Worst Nights Ever.

CHAPTER TWENTY-SIX

It's been three days since the party, and I haven't seen or talked to Sufiya yet. She called in sick the morning after my welcome dinner and once again isn't answering my calls or replying to the eleven million texts I sent her. I'm one hundred percent sure that I've ruined everything before it even started, which seems to be right on-brand for me.

Dad mentioned something about a surprise trip today and I'm kind of glad because I could use the distraction *and* the alone time with him. We have a lot to talk about.

"There you are," Dad says when I come down. He grins at me. "I thought you might have fallen into the pond again."

"Ha ha, very funny." I fell into the pond once when I was little because I'd dropped my doll in the water and was trying to reach it. Clearly Dad thinks it's hilarious to tease me about something that happened fourteen years ago.

"You ready to go?" He takes my backpack and slings it over his shoulder.

"Where exactly are we going and am I dressed for it?"

Dad surveys my kurta and jeans and nods his approval. "You're perfect."

An hour later, we're still driving, and I see signs for Mathura.

"I see we're not in Agra anymore. Where are we going?"

"Just wait and see," Dad says mysteriously. "I promise you won't be disappointed."

We're approaching a complex, and as soon as I see the large sign, my heart skips a beat. We're at the Wildlife SOS Elephant Conservation and Care Centre. I haven't thought about that day for years. Mom and Dad brought me here for my sixth birthday, and soon after Mom and I left for the States. I turn to Dad, smiling from ear to ear.

"I can't believe you remembered." I throw my arms around him and he hugs me back.

"There's more, but I'll tell you after we go in." He kisses the top of my head and I swear I've never felt closer to him. The start of my trip was rocky, but I feel as if Dad and I are finally in a good place. I'm beginning to recall how I cried when he brought me here as a kid. The center rescues elephants that have led horrible lives of servitude and abuse, catering to tourists and circus owners. I was heartbroken when the staff relayed the story of each elephant to us. I remember sobbing for days about how awful it must have been for those helpless, majestic animals.

Now we're greeted by Suresh, a member of the staff here. From the quick conversation Dad has with him, it seems like he knows Dad well.

"The Nawab Saheb is one of our biggest donors," Suresh tells me. "Without his generous contributions, we would have been in dire straits."

I look at Dad in surprise.

"You don't have to be so shocked, Mehar," he says. "You and I, we're not all that different. You know I love animals as much as you do."

He's absolutely right. I can't help wondering when I stopped seeing him. Really seeing him, not as my dad through Mom's eyes, but as a person, as the father he's always been. There for me, even when he wasn't. It's little things, like this, that are actually the biggest things.

"Dad, this is the best surprise ever." I link my arm through his as we follow along with Suresh. He introduces us to each of the elephants and tells us a little bit about their story.

There's Zara, a twenty-one-year-old who arrived here a few years ago. She used to be a begging elephant, forced to perform tricks for tourists in exchange for money. Now she enjoys splashing around in water and eating watermelons. My eyes tear up as Suresh hands me a large chunk of watermelon to give to her. She takes it ever so gently out of my hands with her trunk. As I gaze into her beautiful eyes, I curse every single person who would harm such an innocent animal. Kalpana is a forty-five-year-old with scars on her face and trunk from years of abuse at the hands of her owner. She's eating sweet potatoes as we walk by. Suresh tells us about the many things still needed to adequately care for these elephants. I make a mental note to talk to Mom about this. As a freelance journalist, perhaps she can write something that will increase awareness of this center. Once I get back, I'm sure I can try to raise some funds for this worthy cause, especially since I'm seeing it firsthand.

After about an hour or so, we take our leave. Sometime later, we stop at a roadside stall for some chai and dessert. Soon, a little boy from the stall hands us each a steaming cup of chai and places a heap of jilebis on top of several layers of newspaper on the rickety table between us. I'm pretty sure I'll need to get a tetanus booster from sitting on the ancient bench, but it's kind of fun to not be at a fancy restaurant for a change. The open air is nice and fresh, unlike the polluted air I've been breathing in the city since I arrived. We're sitting under the shade of a large tree and the sun is close to setting and casts an orange glow on everything.

This visit to the sanctuary has been eye-opening in more than one way, and even though I'm leaving with a heavy heart, I'm determined that I'll come back as long as I'm here. Maybe next time Sufiya might like to come too. That is, if she ever speaks to me again. I can't believe how messed up everything is between us now. At least things with Dad are better, which is good because I can only stand to destroy one relationship at a time. It feels like I have a real talent for that.

"You still do that scrunchy thing with your nose." Dad's voice pulls me out of my thoughts.

"What scrunchy thing?"

"You know, when you're worried about stuff. You used to do that even when you were little."

I bring my finger to my nose to make sure it's completely unscrunched. Why is everyone so obsessed with my nose? First Muzaffar and now Dad.

"So?" Dad asks. "What's on your mind?"

I let out a deep sigh. "Nothing much."

"C'mon, Mehar. You used to tell me stuff."

I did. I remember telling him when kids in the playground at school used to bully me as a kid. I'd tell him about this boy who would always roll my pencil off my desk and then got me in trouble when I yelled at him. But that was when things were simpler. My life has gotten so much more complicated since second grade.

"Anyone special in your life these days?"

I look up at him in surprise.

"It's okay, beta. I know you didn't mean all that stuff you said."

I lean into him. My eyes tearing up. "I'm so sorry, Dad."

"I'm sorry too. I shouldn't have pushed so hard."

"Well, you were right. He was a cheating jerk."

"I'm sorry." He pulls me closer. "I didn't want to be right."

We sit in silence for a bit, and somehow, it's more soothing than any words we could say to each other.

"You didn't answer my question," he reminds me. "Is there anyone special?"

I hesitate. I don't know if coming out to Dad when things have just gotten good between us is the right decision. I mean, I kind of think he'll be okay with it, but what if he's not? Mom was totally fine when I told her, but now, here with Dad like this, it doesn't feel like it's the right time. Maybe I'll tell him when he visits me back home. For now I'll keep this thing with Sufiya private. Plus, I don't know if there even is anything with her. I don't know if she'll ever talk to me again, let alone anything more.

So I lie to my father. "Not really."

"You know you can tell me anything, right?" he says.

"I know."

I finish the rest of the jilebis while Dad watches me indulgently, and then it's time to head back to the palace.

Soon after we get back, I'm soaking in a bath Bilquis has prepared for me, complete with rose petals to soften and scent my skin. A Multani mitti mask is drying on my face and I decide to call Mom and make her jealous. We haven't actually talked since she hung up on me that night. But then the other day I was really missing her and so I sent her this cute puppy video. And then she send a different one to me, and since then we've been communicating mostly via memes and videos of adorable animal babies doing even more adorable stuff. Somehow that's been easier than actually talking because I'm still mad at her, but I don't think I want to hash all this out from a distance. There's going to be plenty of time to do that after I get back home.

"Mehar beta, how is everything?"

"I'm good, Mom. I miss you," I say, getting a little choked up. There's so much we both need to work through and I know we will eventually. But for right now . . . "Mom, look . . . Bilquis put rose petals in my bath. How fancy am I?" I strike a royal pose and she smiles at my silliness.

"Are you having a good time?"

"Yes, Dad took me to the elephant sanctuary today. It was so cool." I leave out the part about how Dad and I have really been connecting this past week or so.

"I remember you loved that place," she says. "It's nice of your dad to take you."

I tell her all about Sufiya and as we talk, I realize how much I miss being able to confide in her. I feel absolutely no hesitation in telling her about my feelings for Sufiya. It's strange to realize that no matter how mad we are at each other, she's the only one I can say this stuff to. Well, except for Norah, of course. I can always talk to her. After my bath, I snuggle into my pajamas and get ready for bed. But thoughts of Sufiya are never far from my mind, and as I fall asleep I rack my brain to figure out a way to make things right with her.

CHAPTER TWENTY-SEVEN

The wedding's only ten days away now, and the next morning Sufiya is here, running around and barking orders at the wedding planner's team. I haven't seen her like this before and she almost knocks me over when she comes barreling down the staircase, holding various pieces of gauzy fabric in both arms.

"Sufiya, can we talk? Please?" I say, reaching out to grab some fabric pieces that are trying to escape the bundle in her arms.

She snatches them back from me and keeps walking without even looking at me.

"Sufiya, c'mon, please." I grab her hand and pull her to the side. "Just talk to me."

Some of the workers have stopped what they're doing and are watching us with interest. Jameela passes by with a basket full of flowers and throws a curious glance our way.

"Please stop," Sufiya says coldly. "Are you trying to get me fired?" She pulls her hand out of my grasp and walks away.

I feel like someone has thrown a bucket of cold water on my face. Why would she say something like that? But then I look around. Some of the workers are smirking a little as they watch me slowly walk away. Is it that obvious that there's something going on between me and Sufiya? I guess the way I grabbed her hand and pulled her aside would look strange to someone and they might wonder why the nawab's daughter was being so familiar with a member of the staff. I didn't give it a second thought, but I can see why Sufiya is even madder at me now. If anyone, she'll be the one to get in trouble, not me. Even if we haven't done anything wrong, the appearance of impropriety is a big deal here.

So, I wait for a better opportunity, because impropriety or not, I'm not about to give up. At first, I stick around as she makes sure that everything is perfectly aligned and measured for the tents in the garden, the stage in the main hall, and the garlands and other decorations that will go up. Finally, at the right moment, when no one is paying attention to us, I pull her into the library.

"Seriously? This is where you want to talk?" she says, avoiding my eyes.

"I've been trying to talk to you for days."

"I didn't want to talk to you," she says. "I thought that was clear when I didn't reply."

"So, you're not even going to let me explain?"

"I understand what I saw perfectly," she says. "No explanation necessary."

"Wow . . . you . . . so you've just made up your mind and that's it?"

"What else is there to say?" She finally looks at me and I see the tears poised to fall from her eyes. My anger dissipates immediately.

"What you saw . . . that was Muzaffar getting the wrong

impression. Believe me, we were talking about comic books and he said he used to come here all the time as a kid and then suddenly he was trying to kiss me."

"But you let him," she says softly.

"No! I didn't. It happened literally just as you walked in. And then you ran off, otherwise you would have seen me pushing him away."

"You didn't even come after me."

"Trust me, I did, but then Dadi was right there and she dragged me back to the party."

She doesn't say anything, but the tears roll down her cheeks and I reach out to wipe them with my fingers. She pulls away, shaking her head.

"It was a mistake. I should never have—"

"What do you mean, a mistake?"

"I mean that you're the daughter of the nawab and I'm just someone who works for him." She starts to walk away, but I grab her gently by the hand and pull her back.

"Why would you even say such a thing?" I say. "I'm not like that. I don't care if you work here or if you're a princess. I just really like being around you."

Her gaze softens a little. "I like being around you too. But I forgot myself. And that's on me." She turns to leave and this time I don't stop her.

I fall onto the sofa by the window, incredibly tired all of a sudden. I don't know how I'm supposed to feel. I never meant to hurt Sufiya and I never expected Muzaffar to try to kiss me. I didn't realize that sharing a mutual fondness for superhero comics was the logical prelude to a kiss. Although if I'm being perfectly honest with myself, I have to admit that I might have led him on a little bit. In my eagerness to get under Aleena's skin, I probably gave him some mixed signals. And it's not as if he can read my mind; plus, we hit it off early on, so can I blame him for misreading the situation? Not my finest moment. Muzaffar hasn't shown his face here since that day and I don't blame him. He must be mortified. But I care most about Sufiya and what she said. My life in Newton is so far removed from all this, but I have to accept that for Sufiya and everyone else here, my identity, my roots, aren't just my own. They belong to something bigger, older, and Sufiya doesn't think she has a place in it. According to the family she probably doesn't, but I don't buy into any of that. I'm drawn to her and want us to be closer. Even if it's scary as hell. But how can I make her accept that too?

I hear footsteps scurrying in the hallway and then someone calling out my name. I quickly go out into the hall. One of the maids tells me that Dadi is asking for me. She's waiting in the main living room.

"Mehar beta, the tailors are here for the fitting," she says when I walk in. "I have asked them to make a few extra outfits as well, so please pick whichever ones you like. You will need at least five or six in total."

"I thought I'd already picked one for each event. Why the extra ones?"

"I'm planning to have a small tea party for some people who weren't able to attend your dinner," Dadi said. "And I've decided that I want to have new family portraits taken while you're here. So you'll need the extra outfits for that too. Plus, you didn't pick anything for the mehndi. You'll want something in a warm yellow for that," she says.

She pulls me in for a hug. "I know you probably won't have much occasion to wear a lot of these clothes once you go back.

But they will be a little reminder of your time here." She tightens her embrace before leaning back to look at me. I'm surprised to see tears in her eyes.

"Dadi, what's the matter? Please don't cry."

"I'm so afraid that this might be your last visit," she says.

"No . . . Dadi, please don't say that."

She pats my back. "It's okay, betiya. I'm very happy that you are here now. It is more than I dared to hope." She wipes her tears and we get back to the fitting. I model the outfits for her and she gushes over how beautiful they look on me. I feel like a princess and I know I will cherish these moments when I'm back in Kansas. For the time being, they are a great distraction from the whole mess I've made with Sufiya.

• • •

Something wakes me and I sit up in bed, my hair stuck on my face and the sun streaming brightly through the curtains. I grab my phone off the nightstand and see that there's a text from Sufiya. My heart speeds up a little as I open the message.

Can we talk?

It's from late last night. I must have fallen asleep during my own pity party and missed it. Crap. Now she probably thinks I'm ignoring her.

I'm sorry. I fell asleep. Just saw this.

Then I wait, I check to see if the little dots appear. Nothing. Great. I get out of bed to brush my teeth and then nearly trip over my own feet as I dash to grab my phone when it pings again. I sit on the edge of the bed and click on the notification.

Meet at the library at noon?

Yes! See you then!

I look at the time and let out a little squeal. It's 11:45. I have fifteen minutes to get dressed and try to look cute enough that Sufiya will stop being mad at me. I remember her saying that she liked my RBG T-shirt, so I look for it in the walk-in closet. I find it crumpled up behind my backpack and immediately regret not listening to Mom when she nagged me for years to pick up after myself. I lay it on the bedspread and smooth it out with my hands. It doesn't look too bad. I pick it up to take a whiff. Okay, maybe not. I look at the time. It's almost noon. I run around in a panic and decide to use some jasmine body spray on my shirt. There, that'll have to do. As I run downstairs, I realize that I could have chosen anything from the abundance of clothing that's in my closet but I guess now I'm stuck in this slightly ripe T-shirt and I have to hope that Sufiya doesn't run away from the smell before we have a chance to make up.

She's not there when I enter the library and I breathe a sigh of relief. Despite the air-conditioning, I'm already sweating from running through this massive place to get here. I'm flapping my arms to air out my pits when the door opens and she comes in. I can tell right away that she's been crying and I feel awful. Her eyes are puffy and her nose is a little red. I resist the urge to run to her and gather her in my arms. Instead, I walk toward her at a regular pace and keep my arms at my sides.

"I was so happy to see your text this morning," I say. "I'm sorry I didn't see it sooner."

"I thought you were angry with me when you didn't reply last night."

"Look, Sufiya, can we start over?" I say. "I think there's been a huge misunderstanding and I hate that we're . . . whatever this is."

"I'm sorry I didn't listen to you." She steps closer and leans against a bookshelf. "But I thought about what you said and . . . I'm here now."

"Believe me, I have absolutely zero interest in the guy. I mean, he's nice and all and has pretty good taste in superheroes, but that's it."

She doesn't say anything for a while, but then she shakes her head and smiles at me. "You know, I was up all night, thinking about . . . all of this."

"And?"

She lets out a sigh. "I don't know. We come from different worlds, you and I. I mean, you're the daughter of a nawab, and I'm . . . I don't even know if my family can pay all their bills each month. Why would you be interested in someone like me?"

I look at her face, so earnest and sincere, and for a moment I wonder if she's right. Maybe she'll never get over the class difference between us, no matter how much I try to convince her that these things don't matter to me. But I still have to try.

"I've said this to you before and I'll say it again. I wasn't raised as the daughter of a nawab. I only lived in this kind of luxury briefly, and Mom and I have had a pretty basic life for the last twelve years. So please don't think I'm anything like Aleena or Muzaffar because I'm not."

"Okay, I know you're not like Aleena, obviously," she says

with a sudden grin. "How about this? Let's just enjoy each other's company while we can."

I smile at her. "I'd really like that," I say softly. I hold out my hand and she doesn't hesitate even for a moment before reaching out to hold it. We stay like this for a while and browse the bookshelves. I pick up a book of poems by Rabindranath Tagore and flip it open, settling on one called "Unending Love."

I seem to have loved you in numberless forms, numberless times . . .
In life after life, in age after age, forever.
My spellbound heart has made and remade the necklace of songs,
That you take as a gift, wear round your neck in your many forms,
In life after life, in age after age, forever.

Sufiya glances at the page over my shoulder, then looks away into the distance and recites aloud:

"Whenever I hear old chronicles of love, its age-old pain,
Its ancient tale of being apart or together,
As I stare on and on into the past, in the end, you emerge."

"Show-off," I say with a grin, pretending I'm not moved by her eloquence and her clear, melodic voice.

"It's one of the many we had to memorize at school," she says. "This one is one of my favorites."

"It looks like we both have great taste."

She smiles at me and I could drown in her radiant brown eyes.

CHAPTER TWENTY-EIGHT

I didn't think the mahal could get any busier, but the next day it's even more abuzz with frantic activity everywhere I look. Decorators are hurriedly putting the last touches to the stage, and all around the mahal, garlands are strung up everywhere. It looks so festive and gorgeous, I stop to take pictures to send to Norah, but I won't be posting any on social media out of respect for Mom. There are curtains made entirely of flowers in the throne room entrance. Silks and sheer organzas in beautiful gold and maroon are draped along the ceiling and railings, and everything looks magical.

"Mehar beta, there you are." Azra Aunty is coming toward me with a determined look on her face.

"You still haven't picked out your jewelry," she says. "Ammi is having a fit because we couldn't find you."

"I was just on my way to her room," I say. "Will you help me choose? Please?"

"Yes, I narrowed some down for you."

"Thank you, you're the best," I say, giving her a quick hug. "I'd better go find Dadi before she gets mad."

"I think the silver jhumkas will go perfectly with the pale green one," she says, taking off to chase Taimur, who is running around with a kulfi stick melting all over his hands and kurta. "I'll join you as soon as I get this one cleaned up." I decide to bring Dadi some mangoes from our trees and take a detour to the garden. Thankfully there are no mynah birds to fight, so I pluck a few that look mostly ripe. I'm making my way back inside when I hear voices carried over by the wind. At first, I tune it out, but then my ears perk up at the mention of my dad's name. I peek through the foliage and realize that the sound is coming from a window on the second floor of the main house. I know that it's the room Aleena uses for the times she stays over, and I can see her sitting on the windowsill. She obviously doesn't know I'm down here, because she has the other person on speaker. I guess she thinks it's safe because everyone is busy on the other side of the house. I stay perfectly still and listen.

"So, I said to Ammi that she should pretend to be hurt that he even asked her to sign anything," Aleena says. "And at first she said she was fine to sign whatever he wanted, but then I reminded her about Abbu."

"You'd think she'd have learned her lesson," the person on the other side says.

"I mean, when I introduced them, I didn't think she'd actually start to have feelings for him," Aleena says with a snort. "I just wanted her to stop having to deal with the financial mess my father left us in."

"What's he like, your new dad-to-be?" From their tone, it sounds like this person is using air quotes around the term *dad-to-be*.

"He's kind of nice actually," Aleena replies. "But . . . his mother totally controls him, and she thinks she can control me and Ammi too. As if."

"She's probably not going to let him bail you all out, right?"

"I mean, I doubt it. But it's not like she'll be around for much longer anyway. She's, like, ancient." I can see Aleena get up and move away from the window and I can no longer hear her. But I've already heard enough.

I haven't trusted Aleena from the moment I met her and I was right. The way she fawns over Dad when she's around him, it's no wonder she has him fooled. She almost had me fooled. After all her talk about us being sisters and how Dad is so amazing, this is what she really thinks of my family? And poor Dad. He's so concerned for her and what she needs, he probably doesn't even suspect that to her and Naz he's nothing but a lottery ticket to get them out of their financial hole. I knew I should have listened to my gut.

I feel this panic rising in me and I sink to the ground, the mangoes falling from my hands and rolling away from me. What do I do now? The wedding is in eight days, everything is ready, and the out-of-town guests have started to arrive. How will I convince Dad that I was right? He'll probably think that I'm being petty and jealous. I wish I hadn't left my phone in my room, otherwise I could have recorded this entire conversation and let Dad decide what to do about it. But now it's up to me to be the one who ruins my father's happiness.

I find Dadi and the florist in a standoff of some sort when I walk into the foyer. Apparently the gulmohar flowers he brought aren't pink enough and the marigolds aren't bright enough. The florist looks terrified, which is totally understandable because Dadi has a way of yelling without actually raising her voice that is much scarier than if she were shouting. All I can think of right now is that I'm glad I wasn't in charge of the flowers. After a few extremely tense minutes, the florist is dismissed with strict instructions to procure better and brighter flowers. How he will accomplish this remains a mystery. It looked to me like every single flower in the vicinity of Agra is now sitting by the front entrance.

"Mehar." Dadi's eyes fall on me and I can tell she's not happy. "Where have you been? We've been looking for you all morning. There's so much to be done and no one has time to run around looking for you."

"I'm sorry," I say quickly. "I promise I won't leave your sight from now on."

What am I doing? Dad left early this morning for some urgent work meeting and won't be back until late tonight. My entire body is feeling the stress of pretending everything's all right when absolutely nothing is. I take no joy in discovering that I was right about Naz and Aleena. All I feel is a deep sadness for my father, who has been happier than I've seen him before, and for Dadi, who will now have to announce to all her important friends that the wedding is canceled and deal with all the subsequent rumors. None of this is going to be easy.

I wish I didn't feel this compunction to say something to Dad. But I can't in good conscience let him make such a huge mistake. How can I let someone take advantage of my unsuspecting father like this? He's always looked out for me, whether I liked it or not. I'm pretty sure he's not going to be thrilled when I tell him, but in the end he'll understand why I did it. Like I understand now why he was so adamant about Ryan being wrong for me.

So it's settled. I'm going to wait for Dad to get back and then I'll tell him everything. In the meantime, I'm going to pretend that everything's fine. The last thing I want is to give Dadi a big shock. This is definitely going to be a huge blow to her. Even though I know now that she wasn't thrilled about this wedding,

I'm sure she's made her peace with it. And people here seem to worry a great deal about appearances so this news will not go over easily.

I turn my attention back to Dadi. "Come up with me to pick the jewelry," she says, taking my arm so I can help her up the stairs. "Nothing will get done unless I take care of it myself," she grumbles as we make our way up. She pulls out a bunch of keys and unlocks the door to her bedroom. There are velvet boxes of jewelry spread out on her bed, which explains the locked door. With so many people in and out of the palace all day, she probably wanted to be extra careful of someone with sticky fingers.

"There," she says, pointing to the bed. "Pick whichever ones you like but make sure you're not wearing the same ones twice. Everyone will be watching you, so make sure you have something different for each day."

I've never in my life seen so many beautiful earrings, necklaces, and bangles. Each one is more stunning than the next, but now I'm not sure I'll even get a chance to wear them after I tell Dad what I overheard. I have no idea how I'm going to pick so I decide to go with Azra Aunty's suggestion and look for the silver jhumkas she mentioned. There are several to choose from and I finally land on a pair with a matching necklace that will go perfectly with the pink outfit. Then I pick a gold choker and matching earrings for the mehndi ceremony and finally a navratan set with precious, multicolored stones set in gold for the day of the wedding. I'll be wearing a golden gharara on that day and this set will look gorgeous with that. I realize that I'm finally starting to have fun, and I smile at Dadi, who's watching me while she's propped up in her bed for some well-deserved rest.

"Dadi, these are all so beautiful," I say, scooting onto the edge of her bed. "Are they all yours?"

"The newer ones are mine," she replies. "But the older pieces were your great-grandmother's and her mother's before that. They've been handed down for generations. That navratan one you picked belonged to the Begum of Oudh."

"So, I guess I'd better not lose any of them, huh?"

She pretends to smack my arm. "Don't even joke about that."

"Will Aleena get to pick from these ones too?" I don't think she should get to, since she isn't even related by blood. Plus, now I know that she's basically plotting to steal from my family.

"I would hope not, but if Reza insists, I can't do anything about it."

"I'll go and find Sufiya," I say. "She said she wanted to model her finished outfits for the wedding."

"Yes, please go and make sure that they are good," Dadi says. "I told her not to worry about the cost since I'm paying for them. But her taste is a little more modest, so I'm afraid she may have picked something too simple for the occasion."

I know Dadi genuinely likes Sufiya, but I can't help detecting a now-familiar hint of snobbery in what she just said. I leave the room feeling annoyed, but I have bigger things to worry about right now.

Sufiya is sitting by the window, dressed in the prettiest sharara. It's pale pink and silver and she looks divine. Her thick black hair is in a loose braid across one shoulder and she looks up when she hears me coming in.

"Do you like this?" she asks, jumping up and coming toward me, the wide legs of her sharara swishing as she moves.

"I love it," I say. "You look so pretty."

She gives me a dazzling smile and twirls around.

"This one is my favorite too," she says. "I'm glad you like it," she adds softly.

CHAPTER TWENTY-NINE

It's six days before the wedding. Dad has been delayed and is still out of town—worse, he's in some remote area so I can't even reach him on his cell phone. I'm pretty sure I've developed an ulcer overnight from the stress of having to pretend that everything isn't about to blow up.

Meanwhile Dadi has me and Sufiya preparing gift bags for the wedding guests. These are small ones, little gold-and-burgundy organza bags with braided silk tassels that we're filling with whole walnuts, dates, dried apricots, and individually wrapped DeLafée gold chocolate truffles made with edible flakes of real gold. Fancy.

We're making pretty good progress until Sufiya decides to kick things up a notch. Whoever ends up with the smaller pile has to go and give Dadi the news that the fountain in the foyer isn't going to be fixed in time for the wedding. Jameela came and told us because no one is brave enough to deliver such a devastating message to Dadi themselves. Cowards, all of them. But since I don't relish the idea myself, I go into warp speed mode, my fingers flying as I stuff the bags and secure the ties. That is, until my flailing hands knock over a pile of walnuts and they go flying, noisily clacking on the marble tiles. Sufiya and I gasp in unison and dive to the floor, grabbing them as quickly as we can until we collapse on each other, giggling and out of breath.

"I guess no one wins," Sufiya says, laying her head against my shoulder. "I'll come with you to give Dadi the sad news."

She looks up at me, the laughter still in her eyes, and I move closer to kiss her. She kisses me back, softly, her lips sweet and slightly sticky from the dates we've been nibbling on all morning. The door flings open and we jump apart, both frozen with our hands still touching.

"What are you guys doing down there?" It's Aleena. A feeling of dread courses through me. I look at Sufiya, who is petrified and looking at the floor. I have to act fast.

"We dropped all these walnuts and now they're all over the place," I say as calmly as I can. "Can you check under that shelf? I think a few may have rolled down that way."

Aleena throws us a weird look before kneeling to retrieve a couple of walnuts.

"I thought I'd come and help. Dadi said there were, like, a thousand of these to get ready."

"Yes, that would be great," I say. Sufiya is clutching a handful of walnuts and still looks terrified. "We were actually on our way to talk to Dadi about something," I continue. I turn to Sufiya. "Why don't you go help Dadi? Aleena and I can finish up here."

Sufiya carefully puts her walnuts on the table, mumbles something about errands, and runs off.

"She's a weird little thing, isn't she?" Aleena says.

I bite my tongue and point to the different piles of dried fruits. "Dadi wants to make sure the bags are filled to the brim," I say, ignoring her comment. I have no way of knowing if she saw the kiss and I don't care, but I saw how scared Sufiya was and I want to make sure Aleena doesn't suspect anything.

We spend the next hour or so finishing up the gift bags. I'm worried about Sufiya, but it doesn't seem like Aleena saw anything judging by the way she's calmly taking selfies with the four whole bags she's managed to fill while my pile is about to topple over. Whatever. I can't say I'm surprised. I want to ask her outright about the prenup, but I know that's a bad idea. But I have to at least try to get her to admit whatever it is that she's up to.

"So, um, I've been wondering about something," I start, not really sure where I'm going with this.

"What's that?" she says, pouting and clicking away as if the world hasn't seen enough of her duck lips already.

"How does it work . . . you know, after my dad marries your mom, does she get a title? Like Nawab Begum or something?"

She puts the phone down and looks at me, her face devoid of any reaction. How *does* she do that?

"I guess she will." She gives me a somewhat derisive smile. "Why? Does that bug you?"

Of course it does.

"No . . . not really," I reply. I should definitely look up a theater group when I'm back in Kansas. I think I've gotten pretty good at this acting thing.

"I'm sure you'll love being the new Nawabzaadi of Agra." I watch her closely to see if her face will give anything away but I don't see even the slightest hint of discomfort or guilt. She's good, I'll give her that.

She shrugs nonchalantly, as if she hasn't been plotting in her evil mind this whole time. There's not much I can do about it until Dad comes back, so as soon as we're done, I run to find

Sufiya. She's not in Dadi's office or anywhere else that I can see, so I text her to meet me back in the library. Aleena said she was going to a party with her friends so Sufiya and I can talk there without being overheard.

I go there to wait for her, hoping she'll reply soon. I know things aren't exactly easy here for people in same-sex relationships. Members of the LGBTQ+ community are still ostracized and not particularly safe for the most part. Of course, things are a little bit better now than they used to be years ago, but in general it's still very, very difficult to be openly queer. And from what Sufiya has told me about her family, I'm sure it would be seriously bad if they were to find out.

I'm going over possible scenarios in my head when the door opens and Sufiya walks in. I run to her and throw my arms around her.

"Are you okay?"

She steps out of my arms and turns away, shaking her head. "Did she say anything?"

"Aleena? No. I really don't think she saw us kissing."

"Sshhh." She puts a finger to her lips. "Not so loud."

"Here, come and sit down for a minute and we'll figure this out."

I go to sit on our sofa by the window and pat the spot beside me. But she doesn't come closer, leaning on the desk instead.

"It's too risky," she says. "If anyone finds out . . ."

"No one's going to find out." I don't know what to say to reassure her. "I'm telling you . . . she didn't see anything."

"How can you be so sure?"

"Because she would have said something."

"No . . . you don't understand. I know people like her. She'll hold on to this information and then use it when she needs to."

"I won't let anything blow back on you, I promise." I hate seeing her so scared. "Look, I don't think she saw anything. She wouldn't be able to shut up about it otherwise."

Sufiya is silent and I can tell she's not convinced. I take her by the arm and pull her down on the sofa beside me. "Dadi knows you. She knows how much you respect her and she'll believe me when I say it was nothing, that we were just joking around."

We stay and talk for a little while longer and finally Sufiya leaves to go home. My heart is heavy because I know she'll toss and turn all night, worrying about what's going to happen. And there isn't a whole lot I can do about it.

• • •

Dad is finally home. It's late but I've been waiting and if I don't tell him right now, I don't know if I'll have the courage to say anything before the wedding.

I know he'll head straight to his office, and I find him behind his desk, already busy with some paperwork.

I poke my head in. "Hey, Dad, do you have a minute?"

He looks up and smiles when he sees me. "Of course, beta." He steps around the desk and sits on one of the chairs in the corner. "Come, have a seat. I'm sorry I've been MIA for the last few days. It's a passion project of mine in a village up north and I wanted to make sure everything got done in time. But I promise this was my last trip. So, what's up?"

I hesitate. Once I tell him, there's no taking it back. But if I don't tell him, I'll regret it later when things inevitably go wrong. I have to do this for his own good, because despite all the fights and arguments, he's still my father and I love him.

I take a deep breath. Here goes. "Dad . . . I have to tell you something that's going to be difficult for you to hear, but I want you to believe me when I say that you need to know this."

"Oh my, you sound so serious, beta." He gives me an indulgent smile and strokes my hair. "What is it, beta?"

"It's about Aleena."

I tell him everything I overheard and I brace myself for his reaction.

But he smiles.

"Mehar, you can't take everything she says so seriously," he says. "I told you, you don't have to worry about her. I know she likes to put out a certain type of image. You know, being a social influencer and all."

Is he for real?

"Dad, she was talking to some guy about how you're going to pay off their debts. And that she didn't expect Naz to start caring about you!"

He looks a little surprised but not upset.

"Arre, beta, you must have misunderstood her," he says. "She has a strange sense of humor, that Aleena. But she's a good girl and you should give her a chance. After all, you're going to be sisters. Naz and I want you two to be close. It's one of the things we're most excited about."

I stare at him in utter disbelief. How can he be so naive? After all the lecturing when I was going out with Ryan, how is he acting like this now? He cannot possibly buy into all of Aleena's fakeness.

"Dad . . . I think you need to take this seriously. And I don't think you know Naz and Aleena as well as you think you do."

"Mehar, I'm not sure what you think you heard, but Naz and I trust and respect each other. And by the way, since when do you think you can call your elders by their first names?"

I am dumbfounded. This is not the reaction I had expected. At all.

"But, Dad . . . Aleena was saying really mean things about you and Dadi." To my utter embarrassment, angry tears are starting to sting my eyes and I blink quickly to stop them. "Why won't you believe me?"

"Beta, ever since you got here, you've made absolutely no attempt to get to know Naz or Aleena," Dad says. "You told me you didn't like them, and I heard you out, but I've had enough of all this now. I don't want to hear any more about this. Is that clear?"

I can't stop the tears from falling and I hate how I feel right now. Dad's treating me like I'm a petty and jealous kid when all I'm doing is trying to stop him from making a huge mistake. But it doesn't look like I can convince him, so what are my options right now? The wedding is in five days and I don't have a lot of time.

I take a deep, shuddery breath and walk out of Dad's office. There's nothing more to say. I'm sick to my stomach thinking of what life will be like for my father if he goes through with this wedding. He has no idea what Aleena and Naz are actually like and he is so completely blinded by their fake affections that I have no other choice but to involve Dadi, much as I hate to do it.

I find Dadi sitting at her desk in her room, poring over some documents.

"Dadijaan, can I talk to you about something?"

She looks up. "Yes, my jaan, of course. Come in and sit here next to me." She pats the empty chair beside her desk. "Tell me, beta, what is it? You look tense."

"It's Dad. I think he's about to make a huge mistake."

Unlike Dad, Dadi listens carefully to what I tell her about Aleena, and when I'm done, she does not look the least bit surprised.

"I have been afraid of this," she says. "I suggested to Reza early on that he should ask her to sign a prenuptial agreement. But I don't know if he said anything to her about that."

"Can't you ask him?" I say.

"Lately, he gets very upset with me whenever I say anything about Naz. He is very protective of her."

"Yeah, I noticed," I say, still bitter about how he's so worried about her feelings and doesn't seem to be concerned about what I had to say.

"I should have known from the beginning that Aleena was trouble. She attached herself to Reza like a leech. At the time I thought it was sweet that Reza was being so kind and affectionate to her."

"Dad talks about her like she's this innocent little girl, and I don't get it."

"I think he feels sorry for her because her own father left when she was only thirteen. He thinks she sees him as a father figure, but it seems she merely sees him as a passport to a wealthy lifestyle."

"But what about Naz?" I ask.

"Naz makes him happy and that's why I haven't put my foot down all this time. But I'm afraid I'll have to now."

She takes my hand. "Thank you for coming to me with this." I kiss her cheek before I leave the room.

As I walk back to my room, I can't help wondering if Dad regrets inviting me at all. I'm sure to him it seems like all I'm doing is stirring up trouble. And I'm beginning to wonder if he's right. I hate that I had to do this after things had been going so well between us. But I don't think I could have lived with myself if I hadn't said anything.

CHAPTER THIRTY

Breakfast the next morning is awkward. I'm not sure if Dadi has spoken to Dad about the whole Aleena thing yet, but she's asked to be served in her room, so it's just me and Dad at the table. Thankfully Azra Aunty arrives with her children in tow and joins us.

"Everything okay, beta?" Azra Aunty asks after I've been silently chewing on my food for the past few minutes.

"Uh-huh." I help myself to another paratha and a generous amount of sweet, hot mango chutney.

"Someone is certainly used to spicy food now," she says, looking at my plate.

It's true. I've been here for less than a month, and my taste buds have evolved. If only the same could be said for my skills at being a proper nawabzaadi.

I finish my coffee and wander off to the library, but before I can even start moping, the door opens and a head peeks in. It's Muzaffar. Great. He's exactly who I don't need to see right now. But it appears as if I have no choice because he's walking toward me with a hesitant smile on his face.

"Hi, Mehar," he says. "Can we talk?"

I haven't seen him since the day he tried to kiss me, and I assumed he was planning to avoid me until I left. I would have been totally fine with that. But evidently, I was wrong, which seems to be my thing these days.

"Sure." I gesture to the armchair. No way am I inviting him to sit right next to me. Can't risk sending out the wrong signals again.

"Mehar, I'm so embarrassed," Muzaffar says. "I should have apologized much sooner, but I couldn't face you." He's so earnest and I feel a little bit bad for him.

"Look, let's just forget it, okay?" I end up saying. "Let's blame it on the comic books."

"I feel awful," he says. "You were being so nice and friendly, and I got caught up in all the plotting Ammi and Dadima were doing. But that's no excuse for my behavior."

"Nothing happened, so let's put it behind us."

"I just want you to know that I meant no disrespect. Your family means a lot to me, especially Dadima, and I would hate for this to come between us. And I'd really like it if we could be friends. I have no one else who gets my superhero obsession."

I can't help it. I like him; he's dorky and sweet, and I'm equally to blame for what happened, but at least he has the decency to own it. I hold out my hand. "Okay. Friends."

He shakes my hand formally and relief lights up his face

"Do you want to see the latest issue of Ms. Marvel?" he says with a huge smile.

"Are you kidding? Gimme it."

He's brought some more issues as well that I haven't read yet, and for the next hour we pore over our comic books together, and I have to admit that this is way more fun than moping around, waiting for Sufiya to come to her senses.

CHAPTER THIRTY-ONE

The sun is low on the horizon and the shimmering surface of the pond looks like fire. I'm by the window seat in the library and have only taken a few bites of the crispy samosa that Jameela has made when I freeze. There's a peacock strutting about in the garden. It's so beautiful with its iridescent tail fanned out—I have never seen anything so gorgeous in real life. Then another one comes into view and I run out of the library down the hallway to find the exit that leads into the gardens. I have to make it out before they disappear. Mom and Norah are going to die when I send them pictures. I turn a corner and smash right into someone coming from the opposite direction. A scream erupts and papers fly everywhere.

"Oh my god, Sufiya, are you okay?" I say, totally out of breath from running so fast. "I'm so sorry." Her braid has come loose and her dupatta has fallen off her shoulders.

"I'm fine," she says, picking up some of the papers that are scattered all over the floor.

"Here, let me help you," I say, grabbing whatever I can. Our hands reach for the same sheet and our fingers touch. I expect her to pull her hand away immediately, but she lets it linger and I feel a tingle run all the way up and down my arm. Her face looks flushed, but I don't know if it's because she's feeling the same thing I am.

But then she gently disentangles her fingers from mine and the spell is broken. We pick up the remaining pages and stand. The only thing that could make this moment more excruciating is if we bumped heads on our way up, the way it always happens in rom-coms, which I normally adore but which I've been avoiding of late. There's nothing romantic or funny about this tension between us.

"Where were you running to?" she finally says, clutching the papers.

"I saw two peacocks in the garden," I say. "I wanted to get pictures before they run off."

"Oh, they're always around," she says. "You'll see them again."

The papers are starting to slip from her arms. "Here, let me help you," I say, taking the ones that are about to fall. "What are these?"

"Some documents Dadima wants Naz Begum to sign. I'm on my way to make some copies."

My ears perk up at her words. "What kind of documents? Is it a prenup?"

Sufiya nods. "How did you know?"

I pull her down on the sofa beside me. "I have to tell you something."

I repeat everything I overheard Aleena saying and how I talked to Dad and my grandmother. Sufiya's eyes grow bigger and by the time I'm done she's staring at me in disbelief.

"You talked to Dadima and Nawab Saheb about this?" she

says, her eyes huge in her face and lines creasing her forehead. "You can't be serious."

"I had to, Sufiya," I say. "I couldn't let him go through with the wedding after what I heard."

"Even if it means Aleena will probably tell Dadima about us?" Tears spring to her eyes and she balls up her hands. "I can't believe this. How could I have been so stupid?"

"What are you talking about?"

"You don't get it, do you?" I see the frustration in her face, but I'm not sure why it's directed at me. "You have no idea how things work here. This isn't America. The rules are different here."

"So, this is about me being American?"

"No," she says. "It's about you not getting that if Aleena says anything to anyone, nothing is going to happen to you because you are the daughter of this house. But I'm nothing more than an employee."

"I'm pretty sure Dadi doesn't just think of you as an employee." Even as I say the words, I wonder if they're true. Like Sufiya said when we first met, there's a strict hierarchy here that I'm not used to.

"Dadima has been nothing but kind and generous to me," Sufiya says. "But I'm still her employee and she will definitely not approve of us being anything more than friendly toward each other." There's a buzzing and Sufiya checks her phone. "I have to go," she says. "Dadima is looking for me." And with that she turns around and walks away from me.

CHAPTER THIRTY-TWO

"Dadi, did Naz sign the prenup yet?" I ask as we work on yet more gift bags for Naz and Aleena's side of the family.

"I don't know what that woman is doing. I sent Sufiya to deliver the papers yesterday, but she still hasn't called or signed them or anything. I was hoping it would all be done before by now. There are only four days left for the nikaah."

I'm guessing Dadi hasn't said anything to Dad and he doesn't know that I went over his head. He's been acting mostly normal, as if our conversation never happened. In a way I'm relieved, but at the same time I'm also worried because I can't imagine that Naz will take this slight quietly. And when she tells Dad about the prenup that was delivered to her house yesterday, sparks are going to fly. I just have to hope they don't burn Sufiya. What have I done?

"Dad's going to be so mad when he finds out."

"Yes, he will, but I don't care." Dadi juts out her chin in defiance. "Just because he is too blind to see what's going on doesn't mean I will stand by and do nothing. I can't stop the wedding, but I can certainly make sure he is protected. The rest is not up to me."

"What if she won't sign it?" I can't imagine that she'll jump at the chance to sign something that isn't in her best interest. On the other hand, I have to admit that even from the few times I've seen her with Dad, he seems genuinely happy and she seems to really care for him. But I still don't trust her or Aleena.

"In that case, I will have a very frank discussion with my son," Dadi says. "But let's give it another day. We will see."

• • •

The next morning Dadi calls me to her office, quite frantic because Naz has still not signed the papers or called her back. The mehndi is in two days and then the wedding will take place two days after that, so I can understand why she's freaking out.

Sufiya is walking in the door and only gives me a cursory nod as we go down the hallway together to find Dadi pacing on the floor of her office.

"Sufiya, can you please go to Naz's house and find out what's going on?" she says as soon as we walk in. "And take Mehar with you," she adds. "Just in case Naz causes a scene. Who knows with that woman."

"What about Dad? He's not going to be happy about this."

"You let me worry about him. If he had done what I asked, we wouldn't be in this situation now."

I can tell that Dadi is getting agitated, and I don't want her to spiral, so Sufiya and I leave for Naz's place. The whole ride there she doesn't say a single word and by this point I'm too annoyed to care. I don't get why she doesn't understand what a big deal this is. I know she's worried that Aleena may have seen us together, but I'm convinced that she didn't.

Naz lives in a large house surrounded by mango trees and tall date palms. The enormous wrought iron gates swing open as our car approaches and two uniformed security guards salute us as we pass through. I don't know where I pictured her living but it wasn't this. I guess I haven't spent a lot of time trying to get to know her and I wonder if it was because I thought maybe this wedding wasn't actually going to happen. But now that it's so close, I can't fool myself any longer. Whether she ultimately signs the prenup doesn't really matter. Clearly, Dad is determined to start a new life with this woman and there's nothing anyone can do to stop him. Well, except for Dadi, that is. She seems hell-bent on making sure that if she can't stop the wedding, then at least she'll make sure to protect the family fortune.

Sufiya and I step out of the car and another man in uniform opens the massive double doors. He leads us into a large, beautifully furnished living room and asks us to wait before disappearing. He comes back in a few minutes with two tall, frosty glasses of nimbu pani on a tray. The sweet-and-tart lemonade is refreshing and perfect for the sultry day. We wait patiently as a few minutes turn into ten, then twenty. I'm about to go looking for someone to ask where Naz is when I hear voices coming from upstairs. I recognize Aleena's yelling, and the other voice definitely belongs to Naz. I don't see anyone around, so I run up the winding staircase and follow the voices. I know I should go back to Sufiya and wait in the living room with her, but I can't help myself. I have to know what those two are fighting about.

I'm almost at the top when I hear Aleena clearly.

"Ammi, how can you be so naive?" she's saying. "After everything that Abbu did to you, why are you doing this?"

"Aleena, it's different this time." Naz's voice is much softer and I wonder how long they've been arguing.

"How is it different?" Aleena says. "You can't trust him, Ammi. If you sign those papers, you'll be left with nothing."

"Beta, Reza is not like that. He really cares for me. And for you."

"Abbu said he loved us too, remember? Until he didn't."

"Not every man is like your abbu," Naz says. "Reza is a good man. He's not going to do anything to hurt us."

"I can't believe you're actually saying that. You know that family will never really accept us and when things go bad, you'll have no one to blame but yourself."

"Aleena, please try to understand. I care deeply for Reza. He makes me happier than I've been in a long time."

No one says anything for a few minutes and I turn to go back downstairs. But then Aleena starts talking again.

"Ammi, I'm happy for you," she says, sounding a little tired now. "And I want to believe that things will be different for us this time. But I'm worried after I go away to college, I won't be here to make sure that he doesn't hurt you."

The hairs on my arms stand up at hearing her words. What does she mean exactly? I don't know any real details about what happened with her father, but I don't like what she seems to be implying about Dad.

"You said you were happy with Abbu too in the beginning," Aleena continues. "But then he left us and look what you had to go through."

"Aleena, he didn't leave us, beta."

I wish I could get closer to see their faces, but I already feel like a creep eavesdropping on this private conversation.

"What do you mean?" Aleena's voice has lost some of its earlier sharpness.

"I was the one who asked him to leave." Naz's voice has grown even quieter, and I take another step up the stairs.

"But why? You've always told me that he just left one day."

"Aleena, there is so much that I've never told you about your father. One day maybe I'll be able to bring myself to tell you everything. But for now, please trust me when I tell you that I did it so he couldn't hurt either of us anymore. I didn't want you to grow up with a father like that."

My fist tightens around my heart at her words. It sounds like Naz tried to protect Aleena from an abusive man and now she finally has another chance at happiness. And here I am trying to ruin it all for her. Or am I totally getting the wrong picture? I don't have a chance to find out because I hear footsteps, so I turn and run down the stairs back into the living room.

"We need to leave," I say. "Right now."

"Why? What's going on?" Sufiya demands, not budging.

"Just come with me," I say, tugging at her hand. "I'll explain in the car."

She pulls her hand out of mine. "I'm not going anywhere until you tell me what's going on," she says. "What am I supposed to tell Dadima?"

"Fine, whatever." I start to walk out the door and after a second she follows me.

I fall back against my seat. "I overheard Aleena arguing with her mother. But then I thought they were coming down so I knew we had to get out of there."

"What were they arguing about?" Her tone is still cold as ice.

"It sounded like it was about the prenup. Naz wants to sign it but Aleena doesn't want her to."

"Did she say why?"

"I think it has something to do with what her dad did to her mom."

"I've heard lots of different things about him," Sufiya says. "Something about him running off with all her money."

"I guess I kind of get why Aleena is worried," I say. "I mean, if my dad did that to my mom, I'd want to be careful too."

She doesn't respond to that and we ride in silence for a while.

"I think you should tell Dadima exactly what you heard," she says, looking out the window. "Or . . . do whatever you want."

I don't know what to say to her, so I spend the rest of the drive looking out the window as well. But my mind is racing.

Dadi had made her peace with Naz and Aleena being part of this family, until I went and got her all worked up again. And now I'm realizing that I may have totally misjudged the situation. I should have listened to Dad when he said Naz and Aleena have been through a lot. At the very least I should have taken the time to get to know them a little bit better before sticking my nose where it didn't belong and messing everything up. If only I had minded my own business from the beginning and never said anything to Dadi about Aleena's conversation, everything would have been fine. Now it's up to me to make it right again.

CHAPTER THIRTY-THREE

I can feel the tension as soon as I walk in the front door. It's familiar, the same feeling I used to get when Dad would visit me in Kansas and I'd come home from school to find him and Mom fighting with each other. Only this time it's Dadi and not Mom.

We can hear the yelling all the way down here and Sufiya's eyes are huge. I can tell she's not used to this, so I tell her I'll handle it alone, because I'm pretty sure she's going to be very uncomfortable if she finds herself in the middle of Dadi and Dad arguing.

I follow the yelling to Dadi's room and find her and Dad facing off like some mother and son duo from the Indian drama serials Mom and I like to watch and make fun of. From Dad's stance I can tell they've reached Phase Three of the argument. Phase One and Two are Confrontation and Denial. Phase Three is when Dad usually goes into martyr mode, except this time it's Dadi who's playing that part.

"I did everything I could to hold this family together after your father died," Dadi is saying when I walk in. "Do you think it was easy for me as a woman with enough wealth to attract many unscrupulous people who wished to take advantage of me?"

"I came back as soon as I could," Dad says. "I left my job, my friends, and uprooted my family so that I could be by your side." And then comes the big hammer. "Maybe if I had stayed in America, I would still have my family."

"I never asked you to leave your life over there," Dadi says. "I was perfectly capable of doing it all by myself. I'm simply saying it wasn't easy, and if I had been as naive as you are being now, then you might not have a fortune to worry about."

"Ammi, it is not naive to trust someone you care about." Dad has this look on his face, his lips set in a tight, thin line, eyebrows drawn together. "Naz has been through a lot in her life. I did not want to insult her by asking her to sign a document. But you had to go and meddle behind my back."

"Reza, please don't forget who you are speaking to." Dadi raises herself to her full height, her expression stern and her tone hard. "I am not dead yet, so if you think I will let that woman destroy everything your ancestors have built, then you have underestimated me."

"Why do you think everything is about wealth? Have you ever stopped to think that sometimes people can truly love one another and that it could be the only reason they want to be together?"

"Yes, yes, now she loves you, and tomorrow she will realize that she loves someone else and she will take everything and leave. Are you so blind that you can't see what everyone else sees? Even your eighteen-year-old daughter can see through those two, but they have you completely fooled." She shakes her head. "I should never have given you such free rein with our finances. Now you will ruin us all."

A ball of anxiety forms in my stomach at Dadi's words. I

can't stop thinking about how Naz was pleading with her own daughter to trust that Dad could never do anything to hurt them. And I can't deny how happy Dad always seems when she's around. If I hadn't gone running to Dadi after I overheard Aleena on the phone, she would have let this whole prenup thing go.

I step forward and open my mouth to say something, anything to stop this, but I don't get the chance.

Dad turns around and notices me for the first time since I've entered the room. His face is like thunder as he walks right past me, not even sparing me a look of disappointment, and it hurts so much more than if he had yelled at me.

I debate whether I should run after him, but Dadi is waving me over, so I rush to her side.

"Beta, I don't know what more I can do to talk some sense into your father." She is hunched over and suddenly looks old and tired.

"Dadi, I have to tell you something," I say, helping her to her bed. "When Sufiya and I went to Naz's house, I overheard her arguing with Aleena."

"About what?

"The documents you wanted her to sign. But Dadi, that isn't the important part. I think we've both made a big mistake in judging Naz. I think she loves Dad. She said she's willing to sign anything you want."

"Good. Then why hasn't she signed the papers yet? Why is she causing an old woman like me so much stress?"

It doesn't sound like Dadi's is particularly touched by the revelation that Naz really loves her son.

"It's Aleena," I say. "She doesn't think her mother should sign anything."

"Who cares what that child thinks?" Dadi is even more outraged. "Now this spoiled girl is going to dictate what happens to this family? Ya Allah, what has this world come to?" She puts her hands on her head and shakes it slowly. I don't know what I can say or do that would be helpful, and anyway, Dadi seems to be lost in her own thoughts, so I think it's best to leave her alone.

I go to the library and fall onto the sofa by the window, exhausted from the drama of this day. I wish I could call Norah, but a quick look at my phone confirms that it's five in the morning there so I guess I'll have to wait.

I look out the window, where the sun's rays reflect off the shimmering surface of the pond and the mynah birds are at it again, fighting over mangoes and chattering to each other. It's so peaceful and I wish things in my life were as simple as they seem out there. I'm so engrossed in my own pity party that at first I don't notice anything. But then I see Aleena out there, stomping across the garden, heading toward the grove of banana trees. There's a shady spot over there where I go sometimes when it's too hot to sit by the pond. I run out of the library, down the hallway toward the exit to the garden, and fling the door open. The bright sunlight is blinding and I use my hand to shade my eyes as I walk past the mango trees and under the arch of jasmine vines to where Aleena disappeared behind a cluster of banana trees.

She's sitting with her back to me, her knees drawn up to her chest. From where I'm standing several feet away, I can see her shoulders heaving. I'm not sure if I should approach her or let her cry it out in private. It's not like we have the kind of relationship where I can just go and comfort her. But after everything I've learned today, how can I stand here and not do anything?

I take a few slow steps closer, trying to come up with the right words.

"Aleena," I say softly, not wanting to startle her. "Are you okay?"

She turns to look at me, her face wet with tears. Her mascara has left black trails down to her cheeks and a few damp tendrils of hair cling to her face. Her eyes still hold that same scorn that I've become used to, but now I suspect it's part of her armor.

"What do you want?" she says. She sounds defeated, all her usual bravado gone. "My mom's here to drop off the signed papers. You got what you wanted, so if you're here to gloat, just save it."

"That's not why I'm here," I say. "I heard you talking to your mom earlier at your place."

"Why were you at our place?" She turns back and looks out at the rose garden, lush with their vibrant red and pink blooms. "Were you spying on Ammi and me?" She scoffs. "You're so pathetic."

"I wasn't spying. We were there to ask if your mother had signed the papers Dadi is waiting for."

"Of course you were," she says. "You think you're so much better than we are, just because you were born into this family. You have everything and it's still not enough, is it?"

"What're you talking about?" I don't blame her for being angry and I want to make things right between us. But I get the feeling that she's not ready for that yet.

"You're kidding, right?" This time she stands and faces me. "You have a father who would do anything to have you in his life and a grandmother who adores you. And yet you've made it clear that you don't want to be in their lives."

"Look, Aleena, you don't know me. You think you do, but you

have no idea what my life is like. I'm sorry if I haven't been nice enough or whatever, but you haven't exactly made it easy for me either."

She looks at me and I have no idea what's going on in that head of hers.

"I don't care about you being nice," she says. "I just can't stand that you think you're better than everybody. That you don't care enough about your own family to ever visit them or stay in touch with them."

"How I deal with my family isn't any of your business." I'm starting to feel a lot less bad for her and way more annoyed. Who the hell does she think she is?

"It wasn't. But then you had to swoop in here and start sticking your nose into everyone's business. Do you even care that my mom makes your dad happy? When I first met him, he seemed pretty lonely and sad. And now he and Ammi are finally happy and you had to go and ruin it all."

"Me?" I demand. "Aren't you the one who was talking to god knows who on the phone bragging about how you're totally playing my dad?" If she's shocked, she's doing a great job hiding it. "That's right. I heard you. And I heard what you said about Dadi."

"Wow, so you think you understand it all because you overheard one conversation? You know what, you're not as smart as you think you are."

"Trust me, neither are you. You think I'm just going to sit back while you try to take advantage of my dad?"

"You don't even care about your dad. Where were you all these years? You think I've never heard him talk about you to Ammi? You have no idea how much he wants you in his life."

I let out a frustrated sigh, but I have nothing left to say. Then

I look at her and see the tears filling up her eyes, and all the anger leaves me. I keep losing sight of what's important here. She's lashing out because I have the one thing she's always wanted: a dad who cares and will always be there.

"Aleena, I didn't come here to fight with you. I heard what your mom told you about your dad. I came to say I'm sorry that I judged you."

She puts her face in her hands and starts to sob really hard. And despite the resentment and dislike I feel for her, I can't help myself. I reach over and put my arm around her shoulders, and even though she stiffens at first, after a few seconds she stops resisting and leans into me. I let her cry it out, her earlier words echoing in my head. She's not wrong. I may not have the perfect relationship with Dad, but at least he's trying to do better now. He would never abandon Mom and me and leave us in a bad situation, and he would definitely never do anything to hurt us the way Aleena's dad seemed to have done.

Finally it seems like Aleena is all cried out. Her nose is red from wiping and her usually perfect eye makeup is smudged. She just sits there, but she doesn't shake off my arm or pull away. I take this as a good sign.

"Are you okay?" I ask when the silence becomes way too awkward.

She nods but doesn't say anything.

"Do you want to talk about it?"

She doesn't answer, and after a while I figure she won't want to confide in me, but then she blows her nose and takes a deep breath.

"Abbu was always my favorite," she says. "Ammi was the strict one, and he was the one who always convinced her to let me do things."

"You must miss him a lot." My arm is starting to hurt so I remove it from her shoulder and wiggle it a little to get the blood circulating again. She gives me a funny half smile.

"I always thought he left because I got him in trouble with Ammi all the time. I'd hear them arguing whenever he told her to let me get away with stuff sometimes. I spent years being mad at myself and at Ammi for driving him away."

"Did you and your mom ever talk about it?"

She shakes her head. "We were too busy keeping all the vultures at bay."

"You mean like paparazzi?"

"Some. But mostly relatives and friends." She puts air quotes around the word *friends.* "There's nothing juicier than a woman whose husband has run off and left her with a young daughter. They treated us like we were contagious."

"I can't imagine." I really can't. Mom had a hard time when she first moved us back to Kansas, but it was never because she was a single parent. After spending the last few weeks here, watching how carefully Dadi and everyone had to conduct themselves, I kind of get how hard it must have been for Naz and Aleena being under such constant scrutiny and being judged by everyone.

"It was amazing how quickly everyone turned. One day they were our closest family friends and the next they were treating us like a plague. They started seeing Ammi like some sort of threat to their own marriages and me like I was going to corrupt their innocent sons. Because of course, what else would a woman and her daughter do but use their feminine wiles on their unsuspecting husbands and sons?"

I don't say anything because I'm currently in my own shame spiral. Until earlier today, I thought the exact thing as what she's describing, so who am I to judge others for doing the same thing?

"You know, Ammi has an MBA from the London School of Economics. She ran her family's business after my grandfather died. And for years I thought that Abbu had swindled her out of her family fortune and left."

"That's what I've heard too," I say, before realizing how awful that sounds. "I'm sorry," I say quickly. "I shouldn't have listened to gossip."

Aleena gives a mirthless laugh. "Why not? Everyone else does."

"So, what really happened?"

"My father was abusive to my mother. Physically. And she was too ashamed to ask for help, so she paid him to disappear. She sacrificed a lot of her fortune so that I wouldn't have to grow up around him."

"Aleena, I'm so sorry, I had no idea."

"Neither did I. Ammi only told me today. We had a big argument because I said that she was making a huge mistake trusting your father. I've always blamed her for Abbu leaving. I thought it was somehow her fault, and this whole time, she was protecting me."

She looks so distraught and I can't help it: I throw my arms around her and squeeze.

She pushes away and looks at me, her eyes narrowed. "Why are you being so nice to me? I don't need you to feel sorry for me."

I let my arms drop from around her and pin her with a stern look.

"Aleena, could you maybe drop the whole tough act for two minutes? I'm really trying here, okay?"

She tries to hide it, but a smile breaks through.

"It's not an act," she says, but there's a tiny twinkle in her eyes.

"Look, I won't pretend to know what you and your mom have been through," I say. "But I can relate to some of it. Mom and I might live in the States, but it's not always easy there either. People make assumptions about us every day. We're two brown women and we have a great life, but we do have to deal with a lot of things as well. They're just different things. And just so you know, it wasn't easy for me growing up without my dad either."

"But you had a choice," she says. "You chose not to be in his life."

"Aleena, I was six. I didn't exactly have much of a choice. And yes, sometimes I wondered if my mom couldn't have tried harder to stay, but then I'd hear them fighting whenever Dad visited and I realized that they bring out the worst in each other."

"I don't remember ever seeing my parents fight. And now that I know what Ammi was going through, I can't even imagine how hard it must have been for her to shield me from all that."

"You didn't know. And she was trying to protect you."

"What if I've destroyed any chance of her ever being happy again? I'm sure your dad hates me."

"I doubt that. If anything, he hates me. Trust me." I think about the look on his face when he walked out of Dadi's room. I'm sure he'll be very happy when I leave. And I'm also sure that this visit has changed our relationship irrevocably and I don't have a lot of time left to do something about that.

CHAPTER THIRTY-FOUR

I'm about to go back in when Bilquis comes running across the lawn, wildly gesticulating and screaming something at us. Aleena jumps up and joins me as I sprint across the grass to get to Bilquis.

"Nawab Begum ko kuch ho gaya. Jaldi aiyee," Bilquis says as soon as we're within earshot.

"Kya hua?" Dadi was fine when I left a little while ago. That bad feeling in my stomach from earlier gets worse. Way worse. We all run back in and straight to Dadi's room. She's lying in her bed, completely still. As I take in her pale face, my heart begins to pound wildly. This is not good.

"I couldn't find the Nawab Saheb," Bilquis says.

"What happened exactly?" I ask. When I put my hand on Dadi's forehead it feels clammy.

"I came with her tea and found her like this." Bilquis looks distraught. "Will she be okay?"

"We have to call her doctor," I say. "Bilquis, do you know where to find his number?"

"Yes." Bilquis goes to a little desk in the corner of the room and brings me a small address book. "His name is Dr. Kapoor."

I find his number quickly and call. Luckily, he answers immediately and ask me a series of questions to ascertain her condition. He asks me to place an aspirin tablet under her tongue and tells me to call an ambulance. He'll meet us at the hospital.

Aleena has gone to track down Dad and now they're both here.

"Did you call the doctor?" he asks, rushing to his mother's side.

"Yes, he said to call an ambulance." My arms and legs feel cold suddenly and I try hard to get a grip on myself.

Dad is already on his phone and when he hangs up his face is white.

"I put an aspirin under her tongue," I say. "The doctor said I should."

"Good." The lines on Dad's forehead have deepened with worry.

"Dad, is Dadi going to be all right?" Seeing my grandmother lying there, looking so small, is hitting me hard. I don't think I could bear it if anything were to happen to her. Especially because I know I'm to blame for the added stress. What was I thinking?

Dad doesn't get a chance to answer me, because the ambulance is here and seconds later two men are walking in with a stretcher. They transfer her from her bed. She opens her eyes and looks around, totally confused.

"It's okay, Ammijaan," Dad says. "We're taking you to the hospital. You fainted and Dr. Kapoor wants to run some tests."

I run to her and clasp her hand tightly. "We'll be right there with you, Dadi. Don't worry about anything."

We're downstairs now, then Dadi is in the back of the ambulance and Dad jumps in as well.

"Ask the driver to follow us," he calls out to me before the doors slam shut.

Aleena comes running out the door as I'm about to climb into the car. She thrusts a bag into my hands. "I thought she would like some of her things while she's in the hospital."

"Thank you." I give her a grateful smile before getting in. At the last minute, I turn to her. "Are you coming or what?"

She doesn't hesitate and slides into the back seat next to me. I message Sufiya on the way. She says she's still on her way home but that she'll meet us at the hospital instead. Dadi is being taken to a private hospital about twenty minutes away. Unfortunately, due to traffic it takes nearly an hour, during which I sweat buckets while Aleena tries to distract me. She's surprisingly good at it, pointing out places like her favorite coffee shop and local beauty salon, and sharing all the gossip that goes along with them. Finally we pull up by the entrance and Dr. Kapoor greets us before accompanying Dadi to get various tests and scans done. Dad, Aleena, and I are escorted to the waiting room, where Sufiya is already seated. She jumps up when we enter and her face looks gaunt with worry. It's not surprising given that she probably spends more time with Dadi on a daily basis than any of us.

"I've been telling Dadima to take it easy," she says. "But she's been very stressed lately."

I look for Dad and see him talking to Aleena. I lean closer to Sufiya.

"I think the huge fight with Dad really upset her," I whisper to her.

"You think that's why she fainted?"

Sufiya starts to say something but stops and looks past me.

Aleena is walking toward us. "I was going to go and get some chai," she says. "Do you want anything?"

"Actually, why don't Sufiya and I go?" I say quickly. "We'll bring back some snacks as well. It looks like we might be here for a while."

"Are you sure?" Aleena asks, looking at the two of us.

"Yes, of course. We'll be back soon."

I half expect Sufiya not to come with me but she does.

"I couldn't say anything in front of your father," she says when we're out of earshot of Dad and Aleena. "But Dadima has been stressing about the prenup for months. Long before you came here."

"Yes, but I think she was starting to accept that it wasn't going to happen and then I had to go and blab to her about Aleena."

"Yes, that's true."

Okay. I guess she is still mad at me.

"Look, I'm really sorry that I didn't discuss it with you first. But I didn't think I had a lot of time, so I had to tell my dad as soon as I got the chance."

"That's your problem right there," she says. "You're not thinking about the big picture. And there are other people in that picture, so when you just decide stuff on your own, you create problems for everyone."

I don't know what more to say. I already feel pretty awful and this isn't getting us anywhere.

We follow the signs to a cafeteria in silence and order four cups of chai and some samosas. We grab four bottles of cold water as well, pay for everything, and head back to the waiting area. Dr. Kapoor is there and I rush to find out what he's saying about Dadi.

"I have confirmed with an ECG and she did have a very minor heart attack. She will need to have an angioplasty and then possibly surgery to put in a stent, but right now she needs to rest."

"Do you know what may have caused this?" Dad asks.

"Normally it could be a variety of factors, like an unhealthy diet or a sedentary lifestyle," Dr. Kapoor says. "But of course, I don't need to tell you that your mother is one of the most active seventy-five-year-olds I know."

Dad nods and smiles. "So, it is stress, then?"

"I'm afraid so, Nawab Saheb. She needs to be on bed rest for a few days and completely free of any tension."

"When can we take her home?"

"I'd like to keep her here for a few more hours for observation and then if everything looks good, she can go home."

"What about the angioplasty?" Dad asks.

"I want to wait until we have her blood pressure under control before we do that," Dr. Kapoor says. "So she needs complete bed rest and absolutely no stress before the procedure."

"Yes, I will make sure of that," Dad says. He clasps Dr. Kapoor's hands in his own. "Thank you, Ravi. For everything."

"You're most welcome, Reza. I'm going to leave all the instructions with the discharge nurse. It will be just a little while longer and then she'll be ready to go home."

Dr. Kapoor leaves and we sit back in the chairs, relieved that Dadi will be okay

"Dad, can we talk?" I say, handing him a small paper plate with a samosa and some chutney.

He looks at me and I can see the glimmer of unshed tears in his eyes. My own well up immediately. He puts a hand on my shoulder, gives it a squeeze.

"Not here. Maybe later, after we've brought your grandmother home?" he says. "Right now, I have a lot of calls to make." He puts the plate on the small table beside him and walks away.

I guess he's not ready to talk and I can't really say that I blame him. Back when he told me that Ryan was bad news, I hated him for a long time. I know I'll have to give him a little time before he's ready to accept my apology—or even hear it, for that matter.

I look around the waiting area. "Where's Aleena?" I ask Sufiya.

"I think she went to get her mother."

"Hmm. I don't know how Dadi will feel about her being here."

"Annoyed, probably," Sufiya says. "Did you get a chance to tell Dadi what happened today?"

"I did, but not in detail. I only told her that Naz really loves Dad and that she's willing to sign the papers. But I think she was more focused on why it hasn't been done yet."

"So, you weren't even in the room when it happened?" Sufiya's brows are drawn together and she looks worried.

"No, I left and then I saw Aleena in the garden and—"

"How could you leave her alone after she had that big fight with your dad?"

"What was I supposed to do? I tried to explain to her, but then I thought that she wanted to be alone, so I left."

"You know what?" Sufiya says. "Never mind." She sighs deeply and turns away.

"No, tell me . . . what?"

"I can't believe you would just leave her like that. You know she's been stressed and you should have stayed with her and made sure she was okay."

"So, what are you saying exactly?" I can feel my right eye beginning to twitch and that's never good. "You think it's somehow my fault that Dadi had a heart attack?"

"No, I'm saying that if you stopped thinking about yourself

for one second, you may have noticed how bad she was feeling."

Sufiya's hands are at her sides, clenched into fists, and I don't understand why she's being like this.

"What's that supposed to mean? She was upset and needed to rest. And I wanted to go and clear things up with Dad."

"Of course you did," she says, her sarcasm unmistakable. "Don't you ever get tired of thinking you know what's best for everyone?"

"What the hell are you talking about?" I'm so mad right now and the only reason I'm not screaming is that we're in a hospital and Aleena and Dad are on the other side of the waiting room.

"You always think you know better," she says. "But actually you have no idea how things work here. If you did, you wouldn't go around speaking your mind to everyone whenever you want."

"Oh, so I should lie and pretend like you do? And why do you care so much anyway? It's not like it's your grandmother who's lying in there." I know that I've gone too far by the way her face turns white as a sheet, but it's too late now and I'm too angry to care.

She leaves without saying another word. I don't go after her. There's no point. I know I've ruined anything there was between us, the same way I've ruined everything else here.

I walk toward Dad and Aleena, and just as I'm about to ask for any updates, Naz walks in. She's devoid of makeup and her hair is up in a messy bun. Dad runs to her and they embrace, and I don't know what she's saying to him, but I can see that he's visibly relaxing and it makes me happy for him. I know I have a lot of explaining and apologizing to do, but now is not the time and I'm glad that she can provide some comfort for him at this difficult time. To my surprise, she turns and puts her arms around me as well. It takes me a second but I return the embrace even though I still feel awkward.

"Beta, please don't worry, okay?" she says, leaning back and affectionately pushing away my bangs. "I'm going to make sure that your dadi gets the rest and quiet she needs."

"Thank you, Aunty," I say. I'm never going to call her anything else no matter how nice she is. That would be too weird. But I know I need to start showing her some respect if I want to make things right. I'll just have to fake it until it starts to feel real.

"Okay, now both of you, please stop looking so glum," she says in a cheery voice. "We will all make sure that she gets plenty of rest so she'll be in top shape for the angioplasty."

"Chalo, let's go and get her home," Dad says. He seems to be in a much better mood now and I feel a huge sense of relief.

Even though Dadi isn't totally out of the woods, the doctor must not be too worried since he's letting us take her home. I have to focus on all the positives today, otherwise I'm afraid I'll go down a dark path full of guilt and anger. I can't allow myself to think about the awful things Sufiya and I said to each other. I'm going to concentrate on helping Dadi get better, and that's all I can deal with right now.

CHAPTER THIRTY-FIVE

I'm sitting with Dadi, who's sleeping peacefully, finally back at home in her own bed after several hours at the hospital. The doctor has advised her to stay on a very light diet, and apparently patli kichdi, a thin mixture of rice and lentils with a minimum of spices, is the Indian version of chicken soup for when you're sick. I knew she wouldn't be awake so I brought a book with me from the library, but I've been staring at the same page for the last thirty minutes. My fight with Sufiya keeps echoing in my head and I can't believe the things I said to her. And although she said some pretty harsh things as well, what I said was unforgivably cruel, and I'm not sure I can ever forgive myself. Understandably she hasn't shown her face since we left the hospital, but I know she called and checked up on Dadi because Azra Aunty mentioned it. She probably doesn't want to see my face, but I know how deeply she cares for my grandmother, so it must be incredibly hard for her to stay away at a time like this. Naz hasn't left Dadi's side, constantly hovering and making sure that Dadi is comfortable. She only went back to her place a little while ago for a change of clothes and a shower but promised to be back as soon as she could.

I pace the room for a bit, unable to focus on anything else. Then I notice Dadi stirring and rush to her side, grabbing the glass of water on her night table. Her eyelids flutter open and she looks around, squinting against the light.

"Here, Dadi, have some water," I say, holding the straw to her lips. I hold up her head while she takes a few tentative sips.

"Bas, beta, that's enough," she says, laying her head back on her pillow.

"How're you feeling, Dadi?" I adjust her cover, making sure her feet are tucked in. "Do you want to eat a little bit more?"

"Nahi, betiya, I'm fine," she says. "But later on, could you get me some real food?"

I have to smile and it feels like I haven't done that in so long. I bend to plant a big kiss on Dadi's cheek.

"I'll see what I can do. But we have to listen to what Dr. Kapoor said, and he said you have to get well very soon, so they can check out what's really going on."

"I'm an old woman, Mehar," Dadi says. "That's all. Maybe I have been taking on a little bit too much in the last few weeks."

"You need to rest, Dadi." I give her another kiss, beyond relieved that she's going to be fine.

"Beta, will you please find your father and send him up here?" she says, closing her eyes again.

"Yes, of course, I'll get him for you right now."

• • •

I find Dad in his office talking to someone on the phone, but he hangs up when he sees me at the door.

"Is everything okay? I thought you were with Ammi."

"She wants to talk to you."

We start walking back to her room together and he seems to be lost his own thoughts.

"Dad, I have to tell you something."

"Huh?" He looks a little dazed, as if he's just realizing that I'm here. "What, beta?"

"I'm so sorry, Dad. I totally misjudged everything and I made Dadi worry about all the prenup stuff as well. I shouldn't have interfered."

"It doesn't matter anymore, Mehar," he says. "Naz doesn't care about my money. She's already signed the papers, even though I told her she didn't have to."

"But, Dad, I'm really sorry that I caused all this trouble. And now Dadi's having this health issue . . . I didn't mean for any of this to happen."

"Mehar, when you came to talk to me, I told you to give them both a chance. But as usual, you didn't listen, and now here we are."

"I'm so sorry, Dad." Tears are streaming down my face. "Remember when I got so mad at you because you told me to stop dating Ryan?"

He looks at me, his thick eyebrows drawn together. "Yes, I remember."

"Look, I know we talked about that already, but . . . you can yell at me and say awful things to me. Then we'll be even." I know I sound like a child, but I don't know what else to do. I can't stand this coldness between us, especially not after how good things have been lately.

He's still glaring at me, but I can see his mouth twitch a little.

"Tell me what a horrible daughter I am. And how you're glad that I'm leaving soon. And that you'll be totally fine if I never come back." I'm sobbing now, completely overcome with all the drama of today. "You have to say it, Dad."

He's still not moving or saying anything. I tug at his sleeve. My tears fall on his wrist. I look up and realize they're his tears, not mine. He pulls me close and then we're both sobbing together, standing outside my grandmother's door.

"It's going to be okay, beta," he says finally. He buries his face in my hair. "You're not a horrible daughter. You're my pyari betiya."

"I'm so sorry, Dad." I raise my head to look at him. "I'm going to apologize to Naz as well."

We stand in each other's arms for a few more minutes. Then he straightens himself.

"I'm going to talk to your dadi now," he says. "You get some rest." He kisses the top of my head and I walk away, my eyes still watering but my heart a lot lighter now.

• • •

For the next hour or so, I lie sprawled out on my bed, staring at the ceiling and wondering why lately I've been like a tornado destroying everything in its path. At least Dad and I will be okay. Even Aleena and I will. Who would have thought that the only person I wouldn't be able to make things right with would be Sufiya?

Now that Naz has signed the prenup, Dadi won't have to worry anymore, and after the wedding everything will go back to normal. Sufiya will remember me the way someone thinks of a nightmare that they're glad they've woken up from and I will go back to my life in Newton. I doubt if she will ever want me to visit again and I don't think it's a good idea for me to come back anyway. Maybe one day I'll be able to think about her without that gnawing in my stomach and the memory of the look on her face at the hospital. Dadi asked about her earlier and I lied. I told her she's been calling but that she wasn't feeling well and didn't want to risk getting Dadi sick. I don't think I've ever hated myself as much as I do now, and the more I think about all of it, the more I realize I need to leave. To disappear and let things get back to normal. I know it's a cowardly thing to do, especially after the promise I just made to Dadi, but I have this urgent need to get as far away from any chance of seeing Sufiya again as I can. I can still see the cold look in her eyes the last time I spoke to her. I can't face her.

I go to the library to use the computer there to try to get an earlier flight. I don't see anyone on my way there and I'm checking what's available when the door opens. For a brief moment I allow myself to hope that maybe it's Sufiya, but of course it's not. It's Aleena, and she saunters in and drops into the chair beside me.

"What're you doing?" She looks at the screen, not even ashamed of prying, and I quickly close the window.

"Nothing," I say.

"Planning to run away?"

"What? No."

"Seriously? C'mon, Mehar, I'm not blind," she says with an annoying smirk.

"Fine," I say with a big sigh. I'm tired and I don't even care what she thinks of me anymore.

"Wanna talk about it?"

With her? Not really. But it's not like anyone else is talking to me right now.

"I think it's better that I leave," I say.

"Because you stuck your nose in everything and now it's blown up in your face?"

Wow. And I thought I was blunt.

"Yeah, something like that."

"Oh my god, Mehar, will you grow up?"

"What?"

"You think it'll make things better if you just run away from your problems? Have you thought about what it will do to Daddy and Dadi if you leave like this?"

"I'm pretty sure Dad will be relieved if I go." Even though we've sort of hashed things out, I have this nagging feeling that having me around is a source of constant tension for Dad. Not that I blame him after everything that's gone down, but it still kind of hurts,

"Really? Because that's not the impression I got just now. He was talking to Dadi upstairs."

"How do you know? He told me he wanted to talk to her in private."

One side of her mouth curls up in a sneer. "You're not the only one who can eavesdrop. Your dad seemed pretty mad at you, but then Dadi told him you were just trying to protect him." She rolls her eyes. "From me and my evil mom."

I ignore that last part. "So what did Dad say?"

She shrugs. "I don't know. I got bored so I left."

"Seriously?"

"What?" she says, feigning innocence. "Look, don't you get it? Your dad's going to get over it. Ammi's signed all the papers, so Dadi will be happy and everything will be fine. Unless you screw it up even more by leaving."

"I don't get it. I thought you of all people would be glad to see me go."

Even after our conversation in the garden, which was by far the most honest one we've ever had, I can't imagine that she suddenly likes me enough to want me to stay. I mean, I do see her in a totally different light after all the revelations from this day. And I have to admit, I don't hate her as much as I did in the beginning. In fact, I might have even started to like her a little bit. Okay, maybe I shouldn't go that far.

"It's true," she says, twirling a curl between her fingers. "If you leave, I'll get all the attention and everything. But then my mother and your father won't have anyone but me to focus all their expectations on. If you're around, I get a break from all that at least for a little bit. And I guess you're not the worst person to hang out with." She almost smiles as she says this last part. Almost.

"I don't think anyone wants me to stay," I mumble.

"What about Sufiya? You're going to leave things like that?"

"What things?" I think my jaw might have dropped as I stare at her.

"Yeah right, like it wasn't obvious that you two are into each other." She snorts. "Please. Now you're just being insulting."

"You've known? This whole time?"

"Well, it was kind of hard not to notice the two of you mooning over each other." She makes a face at me. "I mean, I don't get what you see in that mousy girl, but who am I to judge?"

"How come you never said anything?"

"Like what? Get a room?"

"Sufiya was terrified that you'd tell someone," I say, feeling annoyed and relieved at the same time.

"Why on earth would I tell anyone?" She looks at me as if I've suddenly sprouted a second head. "I'm not stupid. Although I can't say the same for the two of you. Going at it right here in the library where anyone can walk in. It's a good thing I called the reporters off when I did."

"What reporters?" Obviously I know they've been around, but now that I think about it, lately I haven't noticed them that much. In fact, it must have been after the boat cruise with Sufiya that I noticed them last.

"You're joking, right? You think no one noticed you two sneaking out after dark to go on your little moonlight cruise?"

"I didn't— They noticed—?"

"Oh, they did," she says. "And it wasn't easy to convince them not to post any of the photos they took. It's a good thing I have connections."

"Did you really stop them?" If she isn't lying, then I have one more thing to be ashamed of.

"Yes, of course I did," she says. "If anyone posts embarrassing photos of my sister, it's going to be me." She's avoiding my eyes, almost as if she is embarrassed to show that she cares. "You could have trusted me."

I don't quite know how to respond to that.

"Anyway, what happened between you two?" she asks. "You were being pretty loud at the hospital."

"She thinks it's all my fault that Dadi had a heart attack," I say, pushing my head against the back of the chair, totally exhausted from the events of this day. "She didn't want me to tell Dadi about you and that phone call."

"Well, at least one of you is smart."

"Thanks a lot." I let out a deep, frustrated sigh. "I don't know what to do now."

"First of all, stop being so dramatic," she says. "And stop trying to run away from everything. You're going to have to pull up your big girl panties and deal with all your screwups."

"You're enjoying yourself, aren't you?"

She grins at me. "A little. But hey, listen, seriously, just go and talk to her. If she doesn't come back because of you, Dadi is going to hate you forever."

I stand and stretch and take in a deep breath. "Okay, you're right. I'll go and talk to her." I walk to the door and stop to turn to her. "Thank you."

She gives a little dismissive wave and smiles before I walk out the door.

• • •

I bump into Sufiya the next day while I'm running back and forth between the throne room and Dadi's room. I'm the designated go-between, reporting everything that's happening there to Dadi, who's propped up in bed. Sufiya's carrying a stack of fancy silk napkins that all slide to the floor when I accidentally knock them out of her hands.

"I'm so sorry," I say, bending to pick the napkins off the floor. She goes to grab the same one I reached for and our fingers touch. She yanks her hand back as though it's touched a live wire. I don't need her to tell me that she's still angry. But if I don't try now, I might not get another chance before I leave.

There are too many people milling about the palace. Everyone is lending a hand to pull off this wedding, which starts tomorrow with the mehndi ceremony for Naz. Traditionally, the mehndi is supposed to be at the bride's house, where all the women go and there's basically a big henna party with singing and mostly all women. But because Dadi isn't well enough to go, Naz suggested that it take place at the mahal. I pick up the remaining napkins and hand them to Sufiya.

"So how have you been?" Could I be any more pathetic?

"Okay. I've been pretty busy." She's avoiding my eyes and I hate that she won't even look at me.

"Is this how it's going to be between us from now on?"

"What do you mean?" She's stacking the napkins into a neat pile. It's infuriating how calm she is when I'm so mad right now.

"Can you at least look at me? I'm so sorry . . . about everything."

She doesn't say anything and it takes everything in me to not grab the napkins and throw them on the floor. I'm trying hard to be mature here but she's not making it easy.

"Oh my god, are you even going to answer me?" I'm yelling now and she looks at me in alarm, then throws a panicked glance at the door and then back at me again. But the people who were here before seem to have left. I guess everyone is taking a break for lunch.

"Can you please keep it down?" she hisses. "I don't need everyone to hear."

"Why? Because I'm not the right kind of person for you? Because I'm not Indian enou—"

I don't get to finish because she grabs me by the shoulders and then her lips are on mine and her kiss is angry and sad at the same time and it uncorks all the frustration I've been bottling up over the last few days. I don't care if anyone walks in right now and clearly, she doesn't either. But thankfully, no one does, and when we finally come up for air, she glares at me and punches me hard in the arm.

"You're such an idiot."

"Excuse me? And by the way, OUCH." I rub my arm and she leans in to kiss it better.

"I thought I could stay away from you and just pretend that nothing ever happened." Her eyes get a little misty, but at least she's looking at me now.

"I thought you hated me. And I hate that so much."

"I'm just so scared," she says, taking my hand and lacing her fingers through mine. She looks down at our hands and opens her mouth to say something but closes it again.

"What're you so scared of?" I ask, raising her hand to my lips and kissing it.

"I'm afraid of what I'm starting to feel for you," she says softly, lifting her gaze, and I can see my own uncertainty reflected in her eyes. But I also see the tenderness of her feelings toward me and that makes me happier than I dare to feel in this moment.

"You're not the only one." I pull her closer into my arms and we stand like that for some time, her face pressed against my shoulder. I can feel the tension leave her body slowly and I let out a deep breath, my own worries starting to dissipate.

She leans back eventually to look at me. "What are we going to do?"

"I'm not sure," I say. "You know, when Dad first asked me to come, I wasn't even planning on it. But then Mom told me that I should and that Dadi missed me and I might not get another chance to visit once I start college."

"And?" A smile plays on her lips. "Are you glad you came?"

"I was so focused on all the reasons I didn't want to come, I never thought of what I might miss out on."

"You mean a chance to bond with your grandmother?" she says, fluttering her eyelids.

"I mean the chance to have you in my life," I say before dropping a kiss on her lips. She pulls me back in for a deeper one and this time it's more about passion than confusion.

"So, I'm in your life now?" she asks, twirling a length of my hair between her fingers.

"I hope so." I narrow my eyes. "Why? Do you not want to be?"

"I do want to be," she says. "But I don't know how it'll work out. You're leaving in a few days."

"I'm not leaving the planet. I'll just be a little farther away."

"It's so far. We'll never see each other."

"That's not true," I say. "Dadi said she would like me to come every summer and learn all about the work she does and help her. And now I'll have an even more important reason to come. And you can come visit me in Kansas."

She smiles, but this time there's a sadness in her eyes.

"It's not that easy, Mehar, you know that. I have obligations."

I take her hand and bring it to my lips. "We'll figure it out, I promise."

She takes a deep breath and lets it out slowly but doesn't say anything.

"Why don't you go and put away those napkins and I'll wait for you in the garden," I say. "We can have a picnic and hopefully I'll get some pics of the peacocks."

She gives me one last kiss before leaving and I collapse on the throne where Naz will be sitting tomorrow. Despite all my big declarations of positivity, I'm not so sure this long-distance thing will work. But I do know that I want her in my life and that I want to try as hard as I can. For now, this is the best I can do.

CHAPTER THIRTY-SIX

The time for the first of the wedding festivities has arrived. Thankfully Dadi is much better and is able to get out of bed and come downstairs. It's been amazing to see the transformation in Dadi since Naz and Dad have been overseeing all the arrangements for their own wedding. Dadi looks well rested as Jameela walks her to a comfortable chair on the stage right next to Naz.

We get ready in a receiving line with flower petals and garlands of marigold to greet the guests with. I'm wearing a yellow sari with tiny golden flowers and a gold border and a garland of jasmine flowers braided into my hair. Sufiya helped me put on my golden glass bangles when we got ready together. She looks like sunshine and flowers in her yellow-and-red sari, with matching red and gold bangles on both wrists. As the bridal party starts to arrive with great fanfare, we shower the guests with rose petals and hand each one a garland of marigolds. Once they're all seated, chai and coffee are served. On the tables, at each place setting are the little gift bags we've been preparing, which the guests will take with them as they leave. That is of course not the only gift they will receive. Dadi and Naz have handpicked expensive, heavily embroidered saris for each of the ladies attending the function as well as delicate perfumes flown in from France. Soon dinner is served, an elaborate affair with a variety of kebabs, flatbreads, vegetables sautéed in fragrant spices, and a large assortment of sweets. A band plays classical music and after everyone has eaten the festivities begin. The women sit together in circles and sing traditional wedding songs. Since this is a women-only event, the songs are of a somewhat suggestive nature meant to tease the bride-to-be about her upcoming life with her husband. It's all good-natured and even Dadi gets in the center of a circle and plays the dholak, a traditional Indian drum. Some of the younger girls begin a choreographed dance and pull me to my feet to join in. Since I don't want to cause any of the guests bodily harm as a result of my uncoordinated feet, I politely decline. Sufiya, on the other hand, enthusiastically joins in and I watch her sway in perfect rhythm with the other girls as they hold hands and dance, all somehow knowing the steps to each new song. Weird, must be some sort of inherent flash-mob gene that bypassed me.

After all that, Naz sits on one of the thrones, looking radiant in a deep yellow sari with marigolds braided into her hair and a huge nath wrapped in flowers hanging from her right nostril. She's wearing earrings that are also adorned with flowers, and there are more on her wrists and around her neck. She rises to greet Dadi in the traditional manner by bending to touch her feet. Then Dadi pulls her up into an embrace. I'm standing really close, so I see the tears falling from Naz's eyes and I watch as she slowly walks away to a private room on the side of the large staircase. I don't know exactly why, but after a moment, I find myself following her and knocking on the door. I haven't had a chance to talk to her privately since all the drama went down and now I don't want to miss the chance to clear the air before the wedding.

"Come in," she says, and I open the door, not quite knowing what I'm going to say. But she's looking at me with her eyes still swimming in tears and the words come pouring out of me.

"I'm so sorry, Aunty," I say, going to her and taking her hand. She looks at me in surprise. "It was all my fault. I thought I knew what was happening, but I was wrong, and I'm never going to forgive myself."

"My sweet child, what are you talking about?" Naz looks perplexed, which confuses me even more.

"I saw you crying after you spoke to Dadi and I wanted to apologize for making everything harder for you."

"What? No, of course not, you silly girl." Naz takes a tissue and dabs delicately at her eyes. "Your grandmother thanked me for making her son smile again and I got a little emotional, that's all."

"Oh." Now I feel stupid but happy at the same time.

"I love your father, Mehar. He is a good man and we've both been through some tough times in our lives, but now we'll be there for each other."

"I hope you can forgive me for the way I behaved."

"It's all forgiven and forgotten," she says with a smile. "How can I be angry at you for trying to protect your father? You're a good daughter, Mehar."

I haven't felt like a good daughter or even a good person these days. But it helps to know that Naz thinks so.

"Shall we go back before everyone starts to wonder where the bride has disappeared to?"

We walk back out together and Naz returns to her seat and a mehndi artist sits on a stool in front of her. For the next hour or so, this incredibly talented woman creates the most beautifully intricate pattern on Naz's palms, going all the way up to her elbows in henna paste. As is tradition, she hides Dad's initials in the pattern, which he will then have to find during the actual wedding ceremony in two days.

Other henna artists are circulating among the guests, offering their services to anyone who would like to get mehndi done on their hands or feet. Azra Aunty and the kids are already there getting theirs done. Dadi is mostly watching but agrees to get a small pattern on both her palms. There are platters of sweets and savory snacks everywhere, along with copious amounts of chai and lassi. Other women I don't know are congregated around another table with their kids, watching the henna artists do their magic.

Once the guests begin to leave, it's our turn, and I'm awestruck at the ease and speed with which the artist draws the intricate patterns on both my arms, from my hands all the way up to my elbows. I've never had this done before, so I go all out. Of course Bilquis is right next to me, making sure I'm eating something and staying hydrated because I can't use my hands anymore. Sufiya only gets a small design on her left palm because she has a lot of stuff to do before the actual wedding ceremony in two days. With Dadi out of commission, Naz has been leaning on Sufiya a great deal.

After it's all done, I can barely keep my eyes open, and once the henna is mostly dry, I'm allowed to go to bed with little baggies tied over each hand.

CHAPTER THIRTY-SEVEN

It's the wedding tonight, and the excitement of the past two days has left me exhausted. I'm not used to such a busy social life. The mahal is buzzing with people, some of them guests who are staying in rooms in the hotel wings, as well as workmen finishing up the last of the preparations. The wedding planners are running around barking orders, Azra Aunty's kids are getting in everyone's way, and I'm on my way to get my hair done. The hairdresser and aestheticians have been busy since yesterday, giving facials and mani-pedis to all the ladies in the house.

Ever since the hospital, Dadi and Naz have been spending a lot of time together. I think Dadi's seeing a side to Naz she has never cared to get to know before, and it looks like they have started a new chapter in their relationship with each other. They bond over Dad's quirks, making fun of him at the breakfast table, and I can tell Dad is questioning his decision to get them to like one another. In any case, Dadi and Naz have been getting along famously. In fact, Aleena told me that Dadi ripped up the prenup as a sign of good faith. I wasn't there to witness that, so I guess I'll have to take Aleena at her word. She's been really decent to me these last few days and she's even been a lot nicer to Sufiya, who is still very much intimidated by her. I've told her what Aleena said about getting the reporters off our backs once she realized that we were into each other a lot. But Aleena being Aleena, she doesn't even realize she's being rude when she suggests that Sufiya get a makeover or that she go on a shopping spree with her. I guess you can only expect a person to change so much.

Sufiya and I are getting dressed together again. Once we lock the door to my room, we get busy, stealing kisses as we change. I put on my gold gharara and the navratan necklace and matching earrings I had picked out before. I strap on my heels and slide sets of twelve multicolored glass bangles onto each of my wrists while I wait for Sufiya.

I look at myself in the mirror, admiring the way my thick braid falls over my right shoulder, with little flowers adorning my hair. My eyelids are a smoky gray and I love how the silk of my gharara skims my curves. The gold thread and sequins embroidered on the bodice catch the light and I'm thrilled with how everything has come together. I promised Mom that I would send pictures, so I look around for my phone. I go to the bathroom to check if I've left it there. I find it sitting on the counter and walk back out to take a mirror selfie. When I look up, I almost scream and drop the phone because Sufiya is standing next to me in the reflection.

She bursts out laughing. "I'm sorry. I didn't mean to scare you," she says. She looks positively radiant in her pale green sharara and pearl jewelry. I can't believe how gorgeous she looks and I seem to have lost the ability to speak.

"You look so beautiful," I say softly, my breath catching in my throat.

"You're not so bad yourself." She looks at me, and I can still see a little hurt lingering in her eyes. I want nothing more than to make it all go away and suddenly the words come out in a rush and there's nothing I can do to stop myself.

"Sufiya, have you really, truly forgiven me for what I said?" I grab her hands and hold them to my heart. "I didn't mean any of it. You have to believe me. I was feeling so guilty about Dadi, and then when you said I should have stayed with her, I lashed out at you."

"I shouldn't have said those things either," she says. "I was so worried about anyone finding out about us, and then when Dadima was in the hospital I got scared and I took it all out on you."

"No, you were absolutely right," I say. "I wasn't thinking about how it was all going to affect you and I just had to meddle and I made everything worse. I said such awful things to you."

My eyes start to fill with tears and Sufiya quickly grabs a tissue and starts to dab at my eyes gently. "You don't have time to redo your makeup. Besides, all that is behind us now. I'm so glad we made up before the wedding," she adds with a smile.

"Why are you so glad?" I whisper.

"So I can do this." She lowers her face to mine and our lips meet in a soft kiss. I put my arms around her and draw her close and our kiss deepens. I lose track of time, but luckily, she's still in her senses.

"We should go down," she says. "Otherwise they'll send someone to get us."

"I think we should freshen our lipstick, don't you?" I say, smiling at her in the mirror.

We do a quick check to make sure we're good to go and then we make our way downstairs.

The whole mahal is decked out like a bride. There are strings of twinkling yellow lights everywhere and garlands of bright marigolds strung up on every pillar and canopy. The throne room is already full of guests, the women wearing gorgeous ghararas, saris, and shararas and the men in their stylish sherwanis and suits. The men and women are seated in separate sections, as per tradition, but Muzaffar sneaks into the ladies' section shortly after we enter.

"Let's take some pictures before I get booted out of here." He grins at us and holds out his phone. We all smile and then take some goofy pictures, and just in time too because a nosy aunty descends upon us and shoos him away. He promises to send me the pictures before he disappears behind the partition that's been put up to divide this huge hall into two separate areas.

Sufiya and I go to look for Dadi and we find her at the center of a group of women, mostly aunts and female cousins whose names I don't remember even though I recently met them at the party Dadi had for me.

"Sufiya, beta, you came." Dadi reaches out to Sufiya, who bends to embrace her. "Let me look at you," Dadi says. "Masha Allah, you look beautiful."

"Thank you, Dadima," Sufiya says. "How are you feeling now?"

"I am perfectly fine," Dadi replies dismissively. "Everyone is simply making a fuss over nothing."

She looks at the two of us.

"Go and enjoy yourselves. You both look so beautiful, I'm sure there will be many marriage proposals for you both after tonight."

We promise to come back and check on her and walk away to find a spot with fewer aunties, but that's virtually impossible.

"I wonder how many proposals you'll get," I say to Sufiya.

"Not as many as you will, that's for sure."

"Is it weird that I'm not even bothered by what Dadi said?"

Sufiya shrugs. "Not really. I mean, she has no idea, and weddings are always like that."

"I guess you're right." I don't want to talk about the many ways it sucks that Sufiya and I can't be honest about who we really are. But this is not the time or place for that conversation. I'm realistic enough to know that I can't decide for her and that how she chooses to live her life is up to her. I can only hope that one day we can be together in the way we want.

It's finally time for the nikaah ceremony, and I let out an audible gasp when I see Naz dressed in a dark-burgundy-and-gold gharara, gold jewelry covering most of her bodice, a matching veil covering her hair. Next to her is Aleena, radiant in a blue-and-gold sharara. Our eyes meet and she smiles at me, a genuine one, and for the first time I truly realize that I am gaining a sister. I return her smile as I walk up to the stage to stand between my father, who looks regal in a dark gray sherwani and cream-and-gold turban, and Dadi, seated in a chair.

As the nikaah ceremony begins, I feel a fullness in my heart. This is my family, just as much as Mom is. I know now that I want to be part of it, with all the drama and messiness, because that's what families are. I realize I'm lucky enough to get a second chance with mine, and I'll never give that up.

ACKNOWLEDGMENTS

This book was the hardest one I've written so far, not because of the story, which brings me joy, but because of how the world was while I was writing it. It was as if suddenly I could see people more clearly than I ever had before. I'm no stranger to racism and microaggressions, but these cuts went deep and it changed the way I look at the people around me. So, as I was writing this book, I was also dealing with loss. The loss of old friendships, the loss of trust in people I have known for years, and most of all the loss of joy. I'm slowly reclaiming my joy through meaningful, thoughtful conversations with individuals I care for deeply.

Throughout this journey, I've been incredibly grateful for the unwavering support of my agent, Hillary Jacobson. To Jeffrey West and David Levithan, I would like to say thank you for your wisdom and your trust in my stories. Thank you for your feedback and guidance when I started out with this story. Change is always a little scary, so when I heard I was going to be working with a new editor I was a little nervous. Turns out, I didn't need to worry one bit. Thank you, Emily Seife, for making this such a joyful experience and for your invaluable guidance in shaping this book. To everyone at Scholastic, I am so grateful for all you do to make my books the best they can be. Janell Harris, Jessica White, Priscilla Eakeley, Esther Reisberg, and Madeline Newquist, thank you for your eagle eyes and your endless patience. To everyone in marketing and publicity, including Rachel Feld, and of course my amazing publicist, Elisabeth Ferrari, thank you for everything you do to support my books. A giant thank-you to Maeve Norton and Param Sahib for creating the most gorgeous cover; I am obsessed.

This journey would be so much harder without writer friends Nafiza Azad, Meredith Ireland, Mason Deaver, and Julian Winters, whose support and general awesomeness have helped tremendously and is greatly appreciated.

To my readers, for whom I write these stories, thank you for your kind and thoughtful messages, which bring me light in the darkest moments. I write for you.

Last but definitely not least, thank you to my husband and my girls, my most ardent cheerleaders, without whom I would have given up so many times. I love you beyond measure.

ABOUT THE AUTHOR

Sabina Khan writes about Muslim teens who straddle cultures. She was born in Germany, spent her teens in Bangladesh, and lived in Macao, Illinois, and Texas before settling down in British Columbia with her husband, two daughters, and the best puppy in the world. She is also the author of *The Love and Lies of Rukhsana Ali*, *Zara Hossain Is Here*, and *Meet Me in Mumbai*. Visit her online at sabina-khan.com.